The Blackney Swans

and other troublesome creatures

The Blackney Swans

Copyright

This work of fiction is a collaborative work and as such, copyright is equally shared between all who contributed to its content as members of the Martock U3A Writers' Group:

Amanda Bayley

Christine O'Brien

Elizabeth Kirtley

Helen Ibbotson

Jenny Chapman

Larry Jeram-Croft

Simon Hodgson

Su Seeley

Published by Larry Jeram-Croft

Cover art: Su Seeley

Blackney Map and all the feathers: Elizabeth Kirtley

U3A, short for University of the Third Age, is a UK-wide movement of locally-run interest groups for people who are no longer in full-time work.

Martock is a medium sized village in Somerset on the edge of the Somerset Levels.

All proceeds from this book will be donated to charity.

We hope you have as much fun reading it as we did writing it.

The Blackney Swans

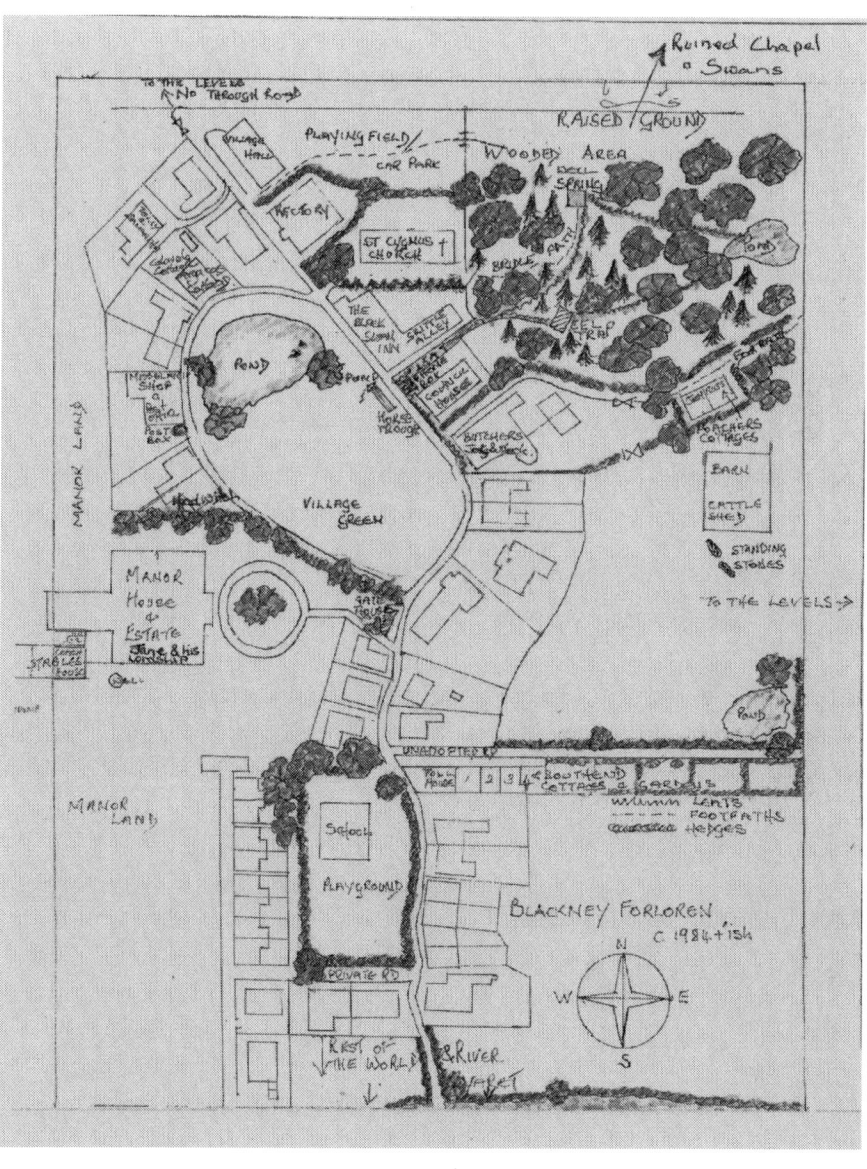

The Blackney Swans

Dramatis Personae

Russell Cooper: mid 30s, balding, ex-navy, lives in deceased father's cottage where he earns a living from distilling moonshine.

Josh Summers: mid 30s, deserted by his wife, wears specs, has known Russ since childhood, introduced flavours to the moonshine.

PC Charles Cridge: early 30s, neighbourhood policeman and busybody, lives with his younger scheming wife **Carrie**.

Daisy and Violet Coombes: twins, who run the shop, Daisy outgoing and Violet timid, owners of spoiled cat **Georgiana**.

Janet Grinter: landlady of the Black Swan.

Jane: from the big estate.

Morgana Crowe: goat-keeper and supplier of various goods and 'special herbs' to the shop.

Sally Fairweather: the Vicar's wife.

The Vicar himself.

Mrs Thingleton (Mrs Thing): cleaner.

Lesley: leader of the local witches.

Gilbert: Lesley's relative and a very short lived leader of the witches.

Tollemina Clarke (Tolly): a local teenage girl.

Samantha Clarke: Tolly's mum

Constance Grey-Williamson: another local teenage girl.

Penelope Jones: local lady of leisure.

Tom and Jonty Bullock: the butcher and his wife.

Pete Sturrock: President of the local Young Farmers association.

Dirk Thrust: (yes really). Aged Rock God and leader singer of the world famous 'Pistons' Cousin to Janet not that he knows it when he arrives.

Zack : Daisy and Violet's occasional helper with a past (read the stories to find out).

Dramatis Animalium

Lucifer: the pub's rather old and decrepit male pussycat.

Georgiana: the village shop's spoiled female pussycat and latterly mother to five kittens.

Sybil and Gertie: Morgana's single minded feral goats.

Dinsdale: a swan of singular character and variable colour.

The Black Swan

A black swan is an unpredictable event that is beyond what is normally expected of a situation and has potentially severe consequences. Black swan events are characterised by their extreme rarity, severe impact, and the widespread insistence they were obvious in hindsight.

Chapter 1

The sun shone down on the village of Blackney Forloren as it had always done over the millennia.

The village was ancient. It was also remote. But only in relation to the rest of the country. To those living there it was, of course, the centre of the universe. In many ways, it was a typical English village. It had a church and a small school and a pub and a village shop and lots of cottages and a village green (with ducks) and a telephone box and some reasonably content villagers. It had been there a long time but more unusually had been ignored for nearly all that time. Being on the Somerset Levels, it was hard to access as there was only one road going in. In the distant past this road had been a wooden platform above the semi flooded fens. With the draining of the area, the road had turned into a tarmac strip but as it was laid on dodgy, soggy foundations, it was rippled. Driving down it at any speed was akin to a fairground ride and one that could remove the bottom of your car in the process.

The Romans had ignored it, the Vikings never found it even though Alfred the Great had hidden in the fens not far away. The

The Blackney Swans

Black Death gave it a miss as did James Scott the First Duke of Monmouth who fought his last revolutionary battle only a few miles away at Sedgemoor. The fact that there had been a civil war and a republic for many years before a King was brought back was totally ignored by the villagers as no one came to tell them. Even the industrial revolution passed it by. The two World wars of the twentieth century did have a minor effect in that some of the young men went away and never came back. Even the current Prime Minister, Margaret Thatcher had never heard of it but that was alright as most of the villagers didn't have a clue who she was either.

This isolation was never really felt to be a problem by the locals. They were content with their lot, living off the land, although technology was slowly bringing it into the modern world, at least a little. However, it did do one thing. It bred a strong tradition of self reliance in its small population. Ignoring the world at large also led to a strong tradition of not worrying about stupid, irrelevant rules and laws imposed by strangers from far away.

At the north east end of the village was a cottage. Like its neighbours, it was old and had been home to the same family for many years. Set back from the other houses up a little lane it had a large garden which overlooked the Levels and a shed. The shed was a more modern addition to the property, although that would not be obvious if you studied it, which was how it was meant to look. This was because the shed was an example of the entrepreneurial skills of the locals. The shed contained a still. And sitting in two old deck chairs at the back of the shed were two men conducting some quality control.

Russell Cooper was a tall thin man. Although only in his mid thirties he was already losing much of his hair. This didn't worry him too much and nor did it seem to worry the local womenfolk with whom he had a bit of a 'reputation'. Russ was also an escapee. Unlike most of his contemporaries, as soon as he had finished school, he left to explore the wide world. He had believed the propaganda and joined the Royal Navy and had seen some of the world, mainly naval dockyards and one trip to Australia. Then his father had died so he came home to his cottage and hung up his hat. He had inherited his father's house, his thinning hair and the still.

Sitting next to him, sipping at his glass was his best friend, Josh Summers. Josh and Russell grew up together, they lived next to each other, went to the same school, played the same games and chased the same girls. But where Russ was outgoing and wanted to see the world, all Josh wanted to do was stay at home and live quietly. He was a small, round man with rather thick glasses and dark hair. He had even been happily married to Jane, one of the girls he and Russ had pursued in their teens. Then a travelling salesman had tempted her away to the dizzy lights of Bridgwater and suddenly he was alone again, divorced and a little lonely. When Russ had returned to the fold, it was the lifeline he needed. The two rekindled their friendship and combined their intellects to make ends meet.

Russ took another sip of his drink. 'That,' he said. 'Is the nectar of the Gods. What was it this time?'

'Oh, Strawberry from last summer.' Josh said. 'Just about ready for market I would say.'

The product of the still had been pure rotgut when Russ's father operated it. Josh had suggested that flavouring was the answer and so every batch was taken from the still and watered down before being infused with whatever was to hand at the time. There was plenty to take from the countryside, Elderflowers or berries, Sloes, Blackberries and in this case, Strawberries. The results were always different but that was part of the charm and their customers rarely complained.

'Did we water it down properly this time,' Russ asked. 'Seems to be rather stronger than usual.'

'Yes, we did and that's your third glass old chap. Remember what happened to the Vicar when he managed three glasses at last year's Harvest Festival?' Josh replied.

'Oh yes,' Russ said. 'He tripped over Mrs Fothergill's little dog and ended up having to be removed from that rather good display of harvest vegetables. He hasn't spoken to me since.'

Both men sat for a few moments, remembering the tableau of scattered sheaves of corn and root vegetables with the Vicar's legs sticking almost vertically out of them.

'Anyway,' Russ said. 'I'm a qualified sailor. I can take my booze.'

'If you say so old chap,' Josh replied. 'Just remember that once that big ball of orange in the sky over there goes down, we have some provisions to lay in.'

'Good point. Let's have another one.'

The Blackney Swans

An hour later, two well oiled men stood and contemplated the approaching darkness. Russ had a hunting rifle in his hand and Josh had the binoculars. They were going to hunt deer. Something they had done many times. It was probably illegal but neither of them had ever bothered to find out and anyway it was something the village locals had done since time immemorial. Josh had identified a good hide for them and would act as spotter and Russ would do the business with the gun. Although mainly surrounded by the flat and damp terrain of the Levels, the village itself was on a slight rise in the ground which is why it never actually flooded and why sensible people had built there in the first place. The higher ground extended a fair way beyond the village boundaries to the north which was how the original settlers had been able to dabble in a little farming. There was also a wood which was where the two men were making their slightly erratic way. As it was late spring, there was a freshness to the air and it was quite warm but now that things were growing in profusion they needed to watch their step. Falling flat on your face in the dark was not a good idea.

'You just be careful with that bloody gun.' Josh said to Russ.

'Of course,' Russ said. 'Always am, you know that.'

Josh didn't say anything but knew that Russ could be careless with guns on occasions and so despite the moonshine circulating in his bloodstream, he made sure to keep behind his friend just in case.

The bloody gun in question was older than both of them. Russ had inherited it from his father and by the looks of it, father had inherited it from his father. There was a large box of ammunition that went with it and they had no idea where to get bullets from when they ran out but that was tomorrow's problem. At least it was reasonably accurate and could stop a deer in its tracks.

'Now where exactly are we going?' Russ asked as they approached the edge of the woods.

'Round the edge a bit,' Josh said. 'To the pond. Now that water levels have dropped the deer seem to go there and drink most evenings. The wind is in our faces so if we are careful, they won't smell or hear us. If there are none there, then there's a fallen tree, we can use as a hide until they do turn up.'

The going got harder as they approached the woods. Tussock grass was just waiting to trip the unwary and was getting bigger the closer they got to higher ground. In between, the ground was soft

The Blackney Swans

and boggy which also was very good at catching feet. Imbibing large quantities of hooch wasn't helping either. They had chosen this particular evening because there was an early and almost full moon so at least they had some light. But their progress was slowing, although once at the treeline, the going should get easier.

They didn't reach it. Just at the wrong moment, the moon decided to hide behind a cloud and everything suddenly went dark. At the same moment, Josh was lifting his foot to clear a particularly large tussock and having completely lost sight of it, he caught his foot and tripped. He sprawled forward and put out both his hands to cushion his fall. Unfortunately, Russ was in the way. With a grunt, he slammed into Russ's back and both men started to fall.

There was an eerie, angry, undulating scream, accompanied by a strange otherworldly noise, a sort of flapping rushing sound. As Russ hit the ground the night was broken by the very loud crack and muzzle flash of the rifle going off. Then, just as suddenly, silence came back.

Russ lay on his front with his face in the mud, wondering what the hell had just happened. 'Get the sodding hell off me you fat idiot,' said a muffled voice.

Josh realised he was lying half on Russ's back and managed to roll clear and then get onto his knees to look around. There was something on the ground to their right but he couldn't make out what it was.

'You silly bastard,' he said to Russ. 'I asked you if you'd made sure that bloody gun was safe.'

'It was, the safety catch was on,'

'With a bullet up the spout? You're a bloody idiot Russ and you've shot something. Look over there.' Josh fumbled in his pocket for his torch and turned it on. He shone it on the ground where he had seen the outline of something, praying they hadn't shot anyone. There would be hell to pay. It only took seconds to realise what their victim was.

Both men stopped and stared.

'Oh, bloody hell,' Russ said in a quavering voice. 'We're in serious trouble now.'

'Not me sunshine, you fired the rifle.'

'But you pushed me over, anyway now's not the time to be blaming each other. What the hell are we going to do? You know what the village think of these things. All those ancient legends and stuff. They'll never forgive us.'

Russ and Josh looked down at the corpse. Both now realised what had made the odd noise. At their feet was the body of a very dead, large, white, Swan.

Chapter 2

Charles Timothy Cridge was born in the autumn of 1953. His parents were farmers and had inherited a once prosperous sheep farm but times had moved on and their farm was very much a case of former glory. Charles had an elder brother, Paul, who could do no wrong in his parents' eyes. He had been sent off to a private school and then on to grammar school and now he was a successful vet. There was also a younger sister, Vivian, who was the apple of her father's eye. She too had had an expensive education and was now a deputy head teacher at the local school.

One way or another Charles was quite different. He was a chubby baby; in fact he was very much a porker. Growing up his brother and sister were treated like royalty by their parents and he was treated as an also ran. In fairness, he was a lightweight in the brains department. His parents saved money on his education and sent him to the local state schools where he had managed to perform below par in all areas. He felt that he had been treated very unjustly and this led to huge resentment on his part. The rest of the family hardly noticed. They were after all, far too busy with their own very important lives. It didn't take too much for Charles to decide that he would show the whole world just how important he could be and after considerable thought, he decided that being a policeman would make him important in the local community. It might also give him an opportunity to pick his siblings up on some breach of the law. Oh, he had dreams about stopping them for speeding or failing to come to a halt at a stop sign or failing to keep records of animal movements. Yes, there were a lot of things on the farm he could pick up on. As soon as he was a fully trained Police Constable, he was posted back to his home village of Curry Episcopi. Now he could plod the streets of his own village and several surrounding hamlets and check out local farms.

Coming from a farming family, he was now a bit of a poacher turned game keeper and it wasn't too long before he started to poke his nose into every nook and cranny of local life. Most people had little time for this intrusion, after all, this was rural Somerset and there were still long established local customs, some of which were frowned on by the outside world. Charles knew this only too well and he had made up his mind to find all of those little old matters which in his mind at least didn't quite conform to modern legislation. Yes, his family and all of their friends and neighbours would learn to rue the years they had treated him so badly.

However, he made a few mistakes along the way. The first of these was really quite simple. He got involved with a scheming young widow. She lived on a small farm with a tumble-down two up two down cottage and a rudimentary bathroom and toilet in an attached outhouse. The place was always filthy, not the sort of place you would have a cuppa if offered. There were rickety ancient barns full of old machinery and equipment. Hidden at the back of one of them was an old showman's steam engine. There was also a collection of motorcycles of all ages up to the modern day. The farm pond was huge and full of fish and they had a collection of rare breeds of chicken. There was also a sideline of peat extraction and a very useful cider orchard, which to the less well informed appeared to be very ancient and of little value. The widow had a habit of not paying taxes and any authority that turned up to seize goods failed to see the value, indeed riches all hidden in plain sight.

Life was perfect at the old farm. Charles thought that he was in control of his life and everyone could now see what a big man he was.

The scheming widow was also very well pleased with the progress she had made with her plan.

In the heart of the village overlooking the green, there was a shop with the name 'Misselania' in curly letters on the door, a name chosen by Miss Daisy and Miss Violet Coombes, who looked after the shop. However, to most of the locals, it was known as 'The Inconvenience Store,' because of its erratic opening hours and even more erratic stock. The shop sold (or at least contained) some useful items such as milk and eggs, but on the shelves and stacked on the floor there was usually an eccentric range of objects and foods of uncertain provenance, often with illegible or non-existent use-by dates.

The Coombes twins, also of uncertain provenance and age, had run the shop for many years and lived above it, but no one knew who actually owned it, or where most of the stock was obtained. Daisy, the older by 30 minutes, conversed confidently with customers, but Violet spoke inaudibly and rarely to anyone other than her sister. Daisy enjoyed being 'front of house' as she liked to rather grandly refer to it, but Violet, true to her name, tended to shrink from contact with people and usually lurked in the back room. The other resident of Misselania was Georgiana, a large, sleek tabby cat with green eyes and an unpredictable disposition.

On a rather damp grey day, Violet and Daisy were in the shop arranging some new stock: cat food, gardening gloves, eggs, children's toys, orange woolly hats (reduced) and some rather tired looking vegetables. When the door opened with a loud jangle of the bell above it, Violet squeaked, jumped and nearly dropped a box of eggs.

'For goodness sake Violet, how long have we had that bell? You really should be used to it by now,' Daisy glared at her sister, who scurried into the store room.

Morgana Crowe, a frumpy, slightly plump woman entered in a flurry of black and purple garments, unruly blonde hair with magenta streaks and only slightly muted swearing. She was wrestling with a large basket. She dumped the basket on the floor with a sigh of relief.

'I swear that grew heavier as I carried it here.'

'Well, we certainly heard the swearing,' muttered Daisy. 'What can we do for you today?'

'I've brought you some duck eggs, goat's milk and some special herbs.'

There was a meaningful silence. Daisy frowned. 'I'm not sure about the herbs....you know, after what happened with the last lot. It was quite funny at first, people wandering around talking nonsense, but when Fred Winter tried to fly off the top of his hay stack it wasn't so amusing. Especially for him. I know falling in the muck heap was a soft landing but even so... And as for the stomach problems,' she paused.

Morgana smiled winningly, 'Oh don't worry, I've kept back the um... medicinal ones, so they should be OK. And anyway, you owe me, remember?' The smile vanished. Georgiana stopped washing an elegant paw and stood up, tail bristling, eyes fixed on Morgana.

'Oh, we don't need to go into that,' said Daisy hastily. Violet came back in and whispered in Daisy's ear. 'It's all right Violet, I know, don't worry,' she turned to Morgana. 'Very well, we'll take your produce, including the herbs. I suppose you want money, not a swap, do you?'

'Of course,' Morgana always wanted money.

Violet opened the ancient till and withdrew some notes and a few coins, handing them over silently, at arm's length. Morgana tossed her hair over her shoulder dramatically, picked up her basket and left, closing the door with exaggerated care.

Daisy and Violet exchanged looks. 'I still don't know how she found out,' said Violet.

Chapter 3

'Oh shit,' Josh said. 'What the hell do we do now? You know how obsessed the village is with bloody swans. And where's the other one?' he asked looking around. 'There's always two.'

'Calm down Josh,' Russ said. He knelt down and looked at the big bird. 'This is the mum, if the dad was anywhere around, we would know by now, they do tend to get very protective.'

'How the hell do you know that?'

'What? How to tell what their sex is or where the dad is?'

'Both.'

'Easy, swans have a black lump above the beak but the female one is small, the male one quite pronounced,' Russ said. 'And when there are eggs, they take it in turns to stay on the nest, so they never go far. The males are pretty aggressive and despite the noise if he was around then we would know it by now. I expect a fox has had a good dinner recently.'

'Eggs? Where's the nest,' Josh asked as he shone his torch around.

They soon spotted it between two large tussocks on the edge of a pond. Inside were seven large eggs.

'What are we going to do about those?' Josh asked.

'Well, there's not a lot we can do is there,' Russ said. 'I suppose we could make a very large omelette.'

'Oh shut up Russ,' Josh replied in an annoyed voice. 'You shot the mother, the least we can do is try to save her offspring. I keep some Geese and chickens. Maybe we can get them to surrogate for the mother.'

'And then have seven cygnets in your yard. What the hell would people say?'

'Well, we have to do something, they do belong to the Queen.'

'Actually, that's not quite true,' Russ said. 'Only the ones on certain parts of the Thames belong to the Crown. Everywhere else they only have the same protection as any other wild bird.'

'Look, I don't care, we can't leave them here, it's bad enough that we've killed their mother, we have to try. And we need to take the mother's carcass as well, if it's found with a bullet in it, there will be hell to pay.'

Russ could hear the determination in his friend's voice and realised it was an argument he wasn't going to win. 'Ok, Josh, I get it. But you're going to have to take the eggs because that's a bloody big bird.'

They were soon heading home. Russ with the bird over his shoulder and Josh with the eggs wrapped up in some of the straw of the nest in his jacket. It took almost half an hour to get back to the shed. They left the bird there and then took the eggs to Josh's house. At the rear, he had a large hen house for his chickens and geese. They laid the eggs which had all miraculously survived in a couple of the roosts the geese had been sleeping in. The geese were not too happy but in the end settled down.

'Well, there's not a lot more we can do,' Russ said. 'It's in the lap of the geese gods now.'

The next morning Josh went in to see what had happened overnight. Three of the eggs were cold but the other four were broken and one of the female geese seemed to have got itself a new family.

'What on earth am I going to do with you?' he asked himself as he looked at the tiny cygnets. Suddenly, he had an idea. The more he thought about it, the more he thought it would probably work. He closed the door behind him and went to get the local ordnance survey map he kept in the house. After studying it he went for a walk.

That evening he went over to see Russ.

Russ was in the shed as usual. 'Ah hello there,' Russ said as his friend appeared around the door. 'Did any of those eggs hatch then?' he asked, fully expecting the answer to be no.

'Four,' Josh replied. 'Bet you didn't expect that. The geese seem to have adopted them. Though quite what I'm going to do with them has been taxing the old brain cells. You know what the village is like about swans and I don't think it would go down too well if they discovered I was raising four cygnets.'

The Blackney Swans

'No there would be all sorts of questions, none of which we would want to answer, especially if that damned policeman got wind of anything. So, any ideas about what you are going to do?'

'I think you mean 'we' Russ. It was your cock up that caused all this.' Josh said. 'But yes, we will need to keep them for quite some time. If we let them loose, the foxes will have them in minutes. They need to be big enough to look after themselves and to be able to fly.'

'Jesus Josh, that's over a year. How on earth are we going to do that and more importantly, why should we? They're only birds and they could get us into all sorts of trouble.'

Josh looked pained. 'You may be right but just in case, I went and looked at somewhere that might be a suitable place to rear them where no one would look.'

'I can't imagine where that could be, it would have to be fairly close but also somewhere where nobody goes.'

'Exactly old chap. I checked a map today and went out to the back of the woods. The Old Chapel.'

Russ looked startled for a second. 'What? No one goes there, in fact most people don't really believe it exists, not sure I do for that matter.'

'Exactly but it does exist and it's actually not too far away. As I understand it, there was some sort of local plague many hundreds of years ago and they dug a mass grave next to the chapel. But then there were stories of hauntings and they built the new church in the village. And it all became a local myth. But the walls are still standing and it would be perfect for keeping birds in with just a little work.'

'Alright,' Russ said. 'We can think about it. There's no rush. Now I've got a little surprise for you. Come on up to the house. You haven't eaten yet, have you?'

'No, I was going to go down to the pub.'

'Right, well follow me.'

The two men went into the kitchen. There was the smell of something roasting in the oven. Russ got two beers out of the fridge.

'What is that you're cooking?' Josh asked, although there was the glimmer of suspicion in his mind.

'Ahah, well I've always wanted to try one and as I had one hanging in the shed, I thought now would be a good time to try and also get rid of the evidence.'

The Blackney Swans

'Bloody hell Russ, you mean that's the swan in the Aga?'

'Yes, any issues with that? It wasn't going anywhere and I won't tell if you don't.'

Josh thought for a moment. 'Actually, why not? As you say, we've got to get rid of the body.'

Fifteen minutes later, the bird was on the table along with some vegetables and Russ carved them some large slices of the breast.

The two men ate for a few minutes in silence and then Russ put down his knife and fork and looked at his friend. 'Are you thinking what I'm thinking?' He asked.

'What, that this is the tastiest bird I've ever eaten?'

'Yup and other people might think the same. And we've got four more and you've already found somewhere to rear them.'

Chapter 4

Behind the Skittle Alley, of the pub universally known as the 'Mucky Duck' even though its real name was unsurprisingly 'The Black Swan,' Janet was enjoying a Rothman's and a tequila sunrise. There was a chill in the air, but better to sit out here than watch Charlie Cridge emptying the bar. He'd be off home to Curry soon, thank the Lord. Maybe some of the regulars would come back when he went, maybe not. But at least he and his little piggy eyes would be gone.

Had he always been like that? She couldn't remember. A fat kid, yes, but not nosey and sneaky with it. And not particularly interested in anyone who wasn't posh. But since he'd been made local constable, he started turning up on that bike of his, locking it to the railings, as if anyone round here would nick it and marching straight up to the bar.

'Half a pint of your best lemonade, Mrs G,' he'd say. 'Don't want to be found drunk in charge of a vehicle, eh? How's things in Blackney?' And all the time his eyes swivelling round the room, clocking who's in and whether there's any sign of what he called 'illicit activity' and what ordinary folk called keeping down vermin and giving the hounds a run of a Saturday morning.

So far, she didn't think he'd got even a whiff of the annual mouse-racing, but she'd have to tell everyone to be extra careful in future.

She got up and peeked cautiously round the side of the building to see if the bike was still there. No, gone. Good. But there was a kerfuffle going on over by the shop. Women with candles, and feathers and whatnot, having some kind of meeting.

Then Janet recognised one of them. Jane, from the big estate, done up like something out of the Christmas panto, called herself a witch these days. You'd laugh if it wasn't so sad. All the old Somerset ways being got at by people who didn't understand them,

The Blackney Swans

incomers often as not. And not just the hunting and pest-control, the stuff Charlie Cridge was after but ducking the snollygosters in the village pond and drinking the weight of the mayor in cider.

At least there were a few people left, keeping up the things that mattered. The pair at the shop wouldn't say boo to a goose, but they'd kept that place going through thick and thin, always something unusual on the shelves. And now there were rumours……..

Lesley 'the witch' was adorned in white crepe. Her ample bosom bounced as she waddled into a Blackney Forloren twilight even though the material clenched her breasts into a v-shape. She wore a swan feather in her hair and salmon pink leggings showed beneath the hem of her dress.

'Twilight is the best hour for our ritual,' Lesley proclaimed. 'We shall see the full moon as it rises.'

Behind her were a small clutch of would-be witches. Some had earned their coloured ribbon and wore amulets or carried a talisman. All were dressed in a shade of white; pearl, snow, ivory, cream or porcelain.

Jane from the big estate stood out amongst them. Her outfit was glorious. A mohair jumper in off-white covered a ruffed, sleeping queen classic coconut-white shirt and a salt coloured chiffon skirt. Her leggings were black and two webbed slippers made from orange felt poked out beneath her hemline. Noreen came in a close second with her feathered headdress. Each swan feather had been carefully hand sewn onto a sequined Alice band and stood up boldly on her head. They moved in unison like a row of antennae.

Each of the women carried a candle. Two of them carried a basket of coloured paper and inks for written spell work. In one hand they carried their candle and in the other hand was a wicker handle.

'Who has the mushrooms?' exclaimed Lesley.

A rotund man with a bulbous black circle of felt attached to his forehead replied. 'Today, I have some dried mushrooms from last year; chicken in the woods, chanterelle, shaggy parasol, glistening inkcap, giant puffball and oyster mushrooms. They will be delicious.'

'What, nothing medicinal to help our ceremony?' asked Lesley, the coven leader. 'We will have to smoke a little mugwort.'

As the gloom deepened, the little group passed the great yew tree that stood inside the gate of Saint Cygnus church. In the porch they could just see the feathered edges of a ghostly alabaster model.

'Stay close to me in the cemetery,' Lesley said whilst holding a long white feather in her hand. As she walked there was a deliberate touching of headstones and she muttered incantations.

'It will soon be a very special night,' Lesley exclaimed. Then, led them out of the church yard and past the pub where PC Charles Cridge stood at the bar and towards the Coombes twins' shop.

'We are going to make a powerful spell. For this, I insist two of us enter the swan shapeshift and fly free. Those glorious witches will stand sky clad in the middle of us.'

Jane was delighted whilst Noreen's white feathered headband seemed to droop to one side and the portly man's felt, basal knob shrank visibly.

After her pronouncement, Lesley declared. 'Our work will take place at the pond in the woods at Beltane. There we will hold the Blackney Forloren annual Cygnus ceremony.

Chapter 5

Russ and Josh weren't looking. They were sitting outside the pub with a pint and deep in discussion.

'How much trouble will we be in if we do this?' Josh asked. 'I'm sure that nosy policeman would have a field day.'

'Actually, I've been doing some research in the library in Bridgwater,' Russ replied. 'You see, swans are wild birds and as such they are protected by an act of parliament. But and here's the big but. What if they're not wild birds at all?'

'Not with you old chap.'

'Well, if they're domestic birds then they're not wild, are they? If we farm them, then arguably they're not wild either. When I was in the Navy, I visited Australia. Over there, if you find a wild crocodile, it has to be protected but once they have laid eggs in captivity, you can rear the baby crocs and do what you want. Apparently, most end up as hand bags.

'Yes but we're not in Australia, we're in England on the Somerset levels,' Josh said.

'True but I can't find anything in British law that says we can't do exactly that.'

'Right, assuming you're correct, we have four cygnets and that's all. They will take at least a year until they're oven ready and then we have no breeding stock.'

'Good point. But there are hundreds of them out there, quite a lot will be young males and very few will have been ringed so no one will know where they came from or that they've even gone missing. We avail ourselves of a free resource but if anyone stumbles upon our operation, we simply claim that we have been rearing them for some time. We explain that we recover eggs and cygnets who have lost their parents due to predators, which let's face it, that is almost what we have done. If anything, we are being very conservation minded.'

The Blackney Swans

Josh laughed. 'If by predators you mean idiots with guns then I would have to agree. But I see your point. We would have to do quite a lot of work at the chapel to make it look like it's been an ongoing operation for some time, but I could see that working.'

'Glad you agree. I suggest we go out tomorrow and start work. Of course, there is still a bigger issue.'

'Oh, what?'

'Well, we will need a market. Maybe we can have a word with the butcher, he's always happy to pass on any venison we accidentally acquire. But you know how obsessed some of the locals are about swans, the bloody church is even dedicated to a saint who is named after them. Then there are those loony women and their so called ceremonies that they think no one knows about, that's all 'swannery' stuff as well.

'Hmm we will have to think this one through,' Josh said. 'But funnily enough, I've been thinking of that problem as well and might have the glimmering of an idea that might literally kill two birds with one stone. Tell you what, let's go and see what we can actually achieve out in the woods first. One step at a time. Oh and it's your round.'

The old chapel was barely visible. Four stone walls were about all that could be seen and they were almost totally covered in ivy but they were well over head height and the space inside was clearly big enough for what they had planned.

'Is this place spooky or what?' Russ asked as he looked around. They were surrounded by trees, although some sun was getting through. Finding the place hadn't been easy either. It was set right at the back of the woods, which terminated in a steep hill, blocking any further progress. The whole area was overgrown with brambles where there weren't trees.

'I'm amazed you even found the place,' he continued.

'Yes, it was on an old map I had, it's not even shown on the newer ones,' Josh said. 'I've no idea quite why they built it so far away from the village in the first place.'

'Maybe it was the village that moved, once the levels were drained,' Russ said. 'The land is much better where it is now.'

'Good point, I hadn't thought of that,' Josh replied. 'Now come and have a look around. There's a bit of a clearing on the other side.

The Blackney Swans

We will have to fence it in and do some repair work on the walls but it's pretty solid. I reckon we could have it ready for the geese and cygnets within a week or so. There's even room for chickens.'

'So then we can go and get extra stock.' Russ said. 'Mind you how are we going to stop the swans just flying away?'

Have you ever watched a swan take off?' Josh asked. 'They need a load of room to get up speed and there's just not enough here, with the trees and undergrowth. And if they're anything like geese and chickens, once they know that they will get fed here, they'll stay anyway.'

'Well, you're the poultry expert,' Russ said.

They walked around to what was clearly the main entrance. 'Must have been quite big doors,' Russ remarked. 'We'll have to put something here and also make some sort of roof. There's a load of corrugated iron I know I can get my hands on which should do the job.'

Inside the chapel, it was quiet. The sounds of the wood seemed muted. There was little growth inside as the floor was stone flagged. A few enterprising saplings had attempted to grow in the cracks but had not made much progress.

'That must have been the altar,' Russ said, pointing to a large square stone at the far end. 'Can't see us being able to move that.'

'No need, there's plenty of room,' Josh replied.

The two men used the altar as a seat and Russ opened his rucksack which contained their sandwiches and a bottle of their home made hooch. The two men ate in companionable silence for a while.

'So, this new idea of yours, will it work?' Josh finally asked. 'I only ask as it's going to take quite a deal of effort and we've no real idea whether it will be worthwhile.'

'Hopefully and we've got to start somewhere, our first thoughts are just not going to work and you have the geese and chickens.' Russ said. 'We can test the waters carefully and see what sort of market we might have. The May Day celebration is coming up soon. That's when we can test things out.'

'Ah, I'm ahead of you there Russ,' Josh said. 'As I mentioned earlier, I had an idea. An old mate of mine has a burger van we can borrow. I was going to suggest we use it anyway on the day. So we can offer some of our new product then and see how it goes down.'

The Blackney Swans

'Now that's a good idea and talking of May Day don't forget we need to go and catch some mice.'

Chapter 6

Violet looked out of the shop window at the apparently endless rain and sighed deeply. She hated being in the shop alone and hoped anxiously that no one would come in. Daisy had, as always, given her strict instructions not to close, but the temptation was huge. She sighed again. It was the lesser evil she supposed, as Daisy had gone off to pick up some stock from their supplier and Violet certainly didn't want to be the one who did that. With the May Day Festival coming up they needed to have some new stuff in the shop; Violet wondered what interesting things Daisy would bring back. So here she had sat all afternoon, perched on her stool behind the counter, constantly checking the door, rather like an anxious dog left at home by its owners.

'It's all right for you,' she whispered to Georgiana, who was curled up cosily, if rather un-hygienically, on a pile of tea towels which were priced very reasonably, as they commemorated an event which had been cancelled. Violet often wished she were a cat, but admitted that actually she was more of a mouse really. That reminded her of the horrible Mouse Racing they ran at the pub. She shuddered.

At that moment, the shop door opened, with a clang of the bell and two local teenagers, Tollemina and Constance, came in dripping water all over the clean floor and not even wiping their feet on the mat. They wandered around the shop, whispering and giggling. Tollemina reached out to stroke Georgiana, who hissed and swiped at Tollemina's hand, just missing it.

'Steady on Georgiana,' she said indignantly. 'We were friends the other day!'

'That's because you gave her a piece of your tuna sandwich,' Constance pointed out, a bit smugly, Violet thought. She also thought, 'Oh why don't they just go!'

The Blackney Swans

Constance picked up a bar of chocolate, walked up to the counter, giving the cat a wide berth, and held it out to Violet.

'I'll have this please,' adding casually. 'And do you have any of that local cider you had a while back?'

Violet shook her head, took Constance's money without making eye contact and rather pointedly, stroked the cat, who began purring loudly. She thought that might be their real reason for coming in. The cider had been quite popular, Violet had noticed, especially with the younger customers. She wondered if perhaps some of them had been a bit too young, but it seemed rude to ask their age, so they never did.

Constance shrugged, turned to Tollemina and said, 'Come on, we should go. Thank you so much Miss Coombes, lovely chatting with you,' and with a final giggle the girls left.

'Well at least you can tell which one's which from the sparkling conversation,' laughed Tollemina as they splashed their way down the street.

Violet glared at the door as if daring anyone else to come in. She felt exhausted after having to deal with two customers at the same time. A loud bang came from the rear of the shop, made her gasp and start breathing quickly.

'Come on Violet, don't just sit there, lock the door and get back here and give me a hand, I've got lots to unload,' Daisy sounded reassuringly loud and cheerful.

'Oh, thank goodness you're back safe,' Violet hugged her sister. Gently detaching herself, Daisy pointed out that she'd only been to Bridgwater.

'Now, I've got boxes of things that might sell for the Festival: picnic sets, flowery T-shirts, umbrellas, fizzy drinks, flip-flops, crisps, welly boots, tins of soup.... You never know what the weather might do......Oh and hair dryers, Zack said they were a special bargain.'

'Did you say flip-flops?' interrupted Violet.

'Yes, and no, you aren't having a pair. You know what happened when you tried them before. You got blisters and wearing them with socks was never going to work. Don't look so disappointed, it will probably rain, again , so have a pair of wellies instead,'

The Blackney Swans

The sisters finished unloading Daisy's scruffy van, a former post office vehicle with the insignia painted over, badly. Daisy liked it because no one could see inside, which was useful when Zack wanted to borrow it for his 'undercover' work. She smiled to herself and thought, as she often did, if the villagers knew about him and their relationship how surprised they would be. She loved having secrets and provided that nosey Morgana Crowe kept her beak out of their business, all would be well.

Morgana had somehow found out about them selling cider to some especially young customers and made a bit of a fuss about it. So hypocritical when you think of some of the 'produce' she made available but she agreed to keep quiet about it and not tell PC Cridge, provided they gave her a good price for whatever she brought to the shop. What goes around comes around, or whatever the saying is, Daisy thought to herself, finally sitting down with a cup of tea. Yes, all will be well and Violet, well she can be managed just as she always has been.

Morgana had been Maureen Grey.

When she was Maureen, she had worked in the sales accounts office of a large company in a city in Middle England. She was not very happy with her life and spent a lot of time day-dreaming and making up stories in her head about other lives she could be leading. All she needed was to meet the right man, who would be strong and romantic and handsome, and her true self would be freed, like a butterfly from its chrysalis.

Then a new salesman joined the team. Julian was tall, good looking, in a shiny suit, too much after-shave kind of way and Maureen felt the flutter of that butterfly seeking its mate. She bought new, more flattering clothes, had her hair cut differently and made a point of being the one who dealt with Julian's admin. He responded by flirting with her and asking her to do all kinds of little extra accounting jobs for him, stressing that she was the only one he could trust to get it right for his special customers. He said he knew she would be discreet about a lot of his work because he didn't want the

The Blackney Swans

other sales staff to steal his selling techniques and poach his customers. He used his charm and humour on everyone at the company, as well as his customers and was generous at after-work drinks and with donations to birthday collections, always ensuring, coincidentally of course, that he was seen doing so. As for Maureen, he took her out for romantic meals and told her how strong his feelings were for her but that as work colleagues, he felt that they really shouldn't take the relationship any further. He even became friendly with her brother, offering him all sorts of contacts, advice and good deals.

Predictably, trouble eventually arrived. After his first year at the company, when year end accounts were audited, a number of discrepancies were found. These all indicated that Julian was receiving considerably more commission on his sales than he should. Also, some of his customers had been impossible to locate. Very awkward questions were asked, to which Julian's answers indicated that he really had very little expertise in accounting at that level. He had left all of that to Maureen and completely trusted her calculations and the commission he received based on them. He also implied that he hardly knew her at all but that she did seem to be very keen to deal with his accounts and even tried to flirt with him, so perhaps she was the one they should be questioning.

When Maureen was duly questioned and her financial affairs examined, it was explained to her that a certain member of staff had made suggestions about her honesty. She soon realised, from the questions asked, who else they were investigating and therefore who was accusing her. Too late, she understood that she had been taken for a fool and when Julian disappeared rather suddenly and the police were called in, Maureen's world fell apart. The police discovered that Julian wasn't Julian, that the qualifications he had shown were false and that he was wanted for similar fraudulent activities in other parts of the country. They accepted that Maureen had acted out of naivety rather than deliberate dishonesty on his behalf and she had not, in fact taken anything from the company for herself. The company decided not to press charges, but she was sacked from her job. This left her feeling humiliated, resentful and furiously angry.

Meanwhile, her brother had also got into trouble. Under Julian's influence, he made some very unwise transactions and was about to be charged with Insider Dealing. He also got on the wrong side of some very dangerous friends of Julian's, who had become very threatening with regard to money they had lost.

Once she had calmed down a little Maureen did some very serious thinking. She made several decisions. She would never trust a man again, especially a good looking, romantic one. She would change her lifestyle, no more boring admin work or being told what to do. She would live in a different part of the country where nobody knew her. She would completely reinvent herself, new name, new appearance, new everything.

All she needed to do next was to decide where to go, who to become, and what she was going to live on. She did a lot of research. By this time, her brother had been charged, and his wife, Samantha was terrified, also receiving threats about the missing money. They talked and decided to help each other to disappear; they would go to the same place but would protect each other by concealing their relationship. Maureen would change her name to Crowe, and Sam and her daughter Tolly would change their surname to Clarke.

With her sister-in-law, she decided to head a long way West, somewhere rural and a long way from anyone who knew her and to cut herself off completely from former friends and even family, who all despised her now anyway, apart from Samantha and her daughter. She would become a woman who wore informal, colourful clothes and had untidy hair. She had some savings. Legal, as she hadn't actually stolen anything from the company and would use those to set herself up when she found the right place. She would rent a cottage with a garden, maybe grow her own food, live close to nature. Something like that. She would always make sure that she knew more about the people around her than they knew about her. Because knowledge is power; this she had learned and she would never be made a fool of again. After much research and not a little luck she discovered Blackney Foloren.

Cobweb Cottage, a name chosen by Morgana, wanting it to sound Olde Worlde and mysterious, was just off the Village Green. She liked its position as the windows gave a good view of what was going on, people passing by, who was with whom and how they behaved. Sometimes, with the windows open, she could even overhear conversations. But on a wet and windy day in April, the windows were closed and the few people around hurried along to get out of the rain.

Morgana wanted to get out of the rain too but she was seeing to her goats; they needed feeding and milking twice every day and there were times when she rather regretted acquiring them. They lived in a currently very muddy little paddock behind the cottages and Morgana was squelching through the mud carrying a bucket of water and a net of hay. Both goats of course were tucked up in their stable; they hated getting wet and ran inside, bleating pitifully at the first drops of rain. As Morgana staggered in, they glared at her as if the weather was her fault.

'No need to look at me like that,' Morgana glared back. 'Oh God, now I'm talking to them as if they can understand me.' She caught Sybil and tethered her on the milking platform. Perching on the edge and leaning against the goat's warm side as she milked her, Morgana's thoughts wandered and she allowed some memories to surface. Everything was so different now. In her previous life, in a large city, there were few encounters with mud and she had never even been near a goat, never mind leaned her head against one. Well, she had made the decision, changed her name and her appearance and had disappeared. She hoped no one would track her down now that she lived in this remote backwater. A flicker of anxiety passed through her and she gave a shiver.

She stood up briskly. That was all behind her now and she had new interests and although the goats were a pain at times. Especially when they escaped. They had their attractions too, a source of income being one of them. She released Sybil and grabbed Gertie, tying her rather more thoroughly on the milking stand. Gertie was especially mischievous and loved turning round and snatching mouthfuls of Morgana's abundant hair while being milked. Morgana went back to her thoughts but this time began making plans.

The May Day Festival was a useful opportunity to make a few pounds. She would have a little stall selling some of her herbs and plants, not milk or eggs, the Weird Sisters (as she liked to think of them) at the shop could sell those for her. Maybe some of the swan related items she had made would sell too. This was a new enterprise and although some of what she made didn't turn out quite as planned, she hoped the witchy women would be naïve enough and obsessed enough with all things swanny to buy them.

Morgana wondered if they realised how ridiculous they were. 'Sky-clad,' really? She still felt humiliated by the way they had made it clear that she was not welcome to join their group. They said it was only for those who had lived in the village for long enough. Not that she had really wanted to get involved, but it might have been amusing or even useful. She liked learning, finding out about people. With secrets of her own to hide, she assumed that others had them too and felt it was almost her duty to be observant, to gain knowledge. For, as she knew from her former life, knowledge was power. She smiled to herself, recalling the little exchange in the village shop and how anxious Violet had looked. Serve them right, they shouldn't be selling that awful locally made cider to anyone in her view, never mind kids. Also, Morgana had another line of enquiry she wanted to follow up regarding the twins. By chance, she had seen something that definitely looked suspicious and now she was determined to find out more.

Chapter 7

With the May Day holiday approaching, Janet was beginning to fret about the mouse-racing. She'd been discreetly putting the word out that there'd be the usual 'special event' this year for any interested locals, and so far, the response had been encouraging. Charlie Cridge had been getting a tad too interested in the village lately but nobody liked him and she doubted anyone would spill the beans. The problem was that for some reason she was finding it difficult to get hold of Russ and Josh.

Usually, it was them who approached her. Towards the middle of April, one of them would drop in to make sure she was planning to hold it again and they'd negotiate a price for the extra runners, with a promise to provide only fully grown field mice so they put on a good turn of speed. But this year nothing. And though she'd left a few messages on their phone, they still hadn't got back to her. In fact, come to think of it, she hadn't seen them around the place for a while. Perhaps she should walk around there herself and speak to them face to face. If they were going to let her down, she'd need to set about organising a supply from somewhere else sharpish. Some of the kids in the neighbourhood might be interested in earning extra pocket money.

There was also the cat to think about. Up to now, Lucifer had done very well. She'd started training him when he was little more than a kitten and he'd soon got the hang of it. He kept a fairly constant speed once you let him out, so you could gauge the right moment to lift the gate and guarantee there'd be a decent delay before he caught up with the first of the stragglers. But over the last year, he'd begun to slow up in general. It was almost as if he'd lost interest in chasing things. Once, she'd been able to guarantee that if the Coombe twins' spoiled moggy strayed across the green from the shop – what was its name? Michaela? Thomasina? something unsuitable like that - Lucifer would see her off in no time. Now he was just as inclined to take not a blind bit of notice of her. There was no getting away from it, he might just be past his prime. She'd have to hope that this year he'd rise to the occasion once she'd set up the course and the punters were cheering him on. And then she'd need to consider putting him out to grass and training up another kitten.

On the other hand, perhaps the time had come to stop holding the specials? So much in the village was changing these days, all sorts of people with more money than sense moving in, buying up the old cottages and spending a fortune on them. Gentrification was what some folks called it, but they weren't Janet's idea of gentry. And they were inclined to interfere in country ways if they disagreed with them. Some busybody had even started a petition to ban otter-hunting. It hadn't got many signatures so far, but it was a sign of the times. The old squire would never have done such a thing. He enjoyed a morning out with the beagles himself. And he'd never reported her for holding the specials. In fact, he'd occasionally had a flutter on an outsider himself and brought his house guests to join in.

In the meantime, she'd better get on with polishing up the trophy and the silver plaques, and checking over the exhibits, a job she never trusted to anyone else. Most people had got so used to them sitting there on the shelf in the skittle alley they didn't look twice at them. But she'd spotted the other day that the whiskers had dropped off Speedy Gonzales, proud winner in 1966, and the moth seemed to have been feasting on the fur of a couple of the others. She could probably patch them up enough to escape notice. But it made you think. Perhaps the whole business was getting to be more trouble than it was worth and she should just abandon it. No, perish the thought. The village might be changing but some things were worth taking a little trouble over. And when it came to seasonal pursuits in Blackney Forloren, the Mayday specials at the Black Swan were every bit as traditional as maypole dancing, Morris Men and well-dressing, thank you very much.

It was a nuisance to discover she'd run out of silver polish. If she had, that is. She wouldn't put it past Shirley to help herself to it. That woman did seem to get through supplies a lot more quickly these days. It wouldn't be easy to replace her, though, especially not at the hourly rate she was prepared to accept, so Janet would just have to buy some more. But she wasn't inclined to wait until her next visit to the cash and carry. Better to get on with the job while she was in the mood. And while the weather was so awful, she didn't feel like sitting in the garden. Perhaps they stocked something in the shop. It was a good few weeks since she'd been over there, and they never did seem to have anything she wanted, but rain or no rain, it was worth a try.

On the way across the green, she noticed two of the posh girls coming out of the door, but by the time she got there herself the place seemed to be locked. Odd. Perhaps they were taking one of their deliveries of 'unusual herbs' from Morgana. They thought nobody else knew about them, but it was pretty much an open secret. Perhaps that was what the teenage girls had been after. They'd been giggling enough as they left.

Taking care to avoid being seen, Janet sneaked round towards the back of the shop. Yes, there they were, the pair of them, unloading boxes from that beaten-up old van of theirs and far too busy to notice anyone watching them. Now she knew they were here, perhaps she'd go back to the front and bang on the door till one of them answered. Or perhaps she'd wait until tomorrow and see if she could catch shrinking Violet on her own, then threaten to expose them to the authorities. It was always good to be one up on your neighbours.

PC Cridge pedalled his police bicycle along the dreadfully bumpy road that was the only access to that damned village. It was unlike any others in his area and in some ways it scared him. The locals all seemed to be up to no good, yet they always closed ranks when he was around. But it was also an enormous opportunity. If he could only catch some of them, it would be a great feather in his cap and an almost certain path to promotion. In his dreams, he saw himself dressed as an Inspector rather like Morse in Oxford with all his subordinates calling him Sir and running around at his slightest whim.

Last year's May festival had been exciting, as a load of Mods had turned up on fancy scooters, probably lured by stories of plentiful and cheap cider and almost immediately started a fight.

Luckily for him, he was too far away to get caught up in it and some of the local lads had put them to flight. He was then able to make an appearance and claim the credit back at headquarters.

However, he just knew there were other nefarious things going on. He knew what the smell of burning hay and people with glazed looks meant, though he had never once been able to catch anyone with the stuff on them. Then there was almost certainly an illegal still somewhere. He had caught hints from overheard conversations but had never been able to track it down. And what really went on at the pub? In the skittle alley, there were a number of stuffed mice that looked like trophies of some sort but he'd never been able to get a straight answer from anyone as to what they meant. He realised he was grinding his teeth in frustration.

Then there was all the dodgy farm machinery, much of it totally non compliant with health and safety regulations. He had even heard of youngsters using tractors to race each other. No, this year he was going to get results. He would get hold of a police car and park it prominently, making sure that everyone, including his family, who would also be there, understood that a man of importance was overseeing the event. This was his chance and he was going to make the best of it.

Chapter 8

It was a pleasant spring evening as Tollemina Clarke walked along to call for Constance Grey-Williamson.

'What are you wearing that for?' asked Constance as she surveyed the large lilac coloured straw hat which Tollemina was wearing.

'It was Mum's creation, she wore it to my last School garden party,' replied Tolly as she tilted it this way and that.

'Very posh,' observed Constance. The girls chatted as they made their way to the Vicarage. They had been asked to help carry the Well Dressing donations for the Vicar's wife, Sally Fairweather. As the Vicarage door opened, Sally was with old Mrs Thingleton, known in the village as Mrs Thing, who used to clean for the previous Vicar and still pottered about the Vicarage with a duster now and again, though you couldn't actually see where she had been.

Sally and Mrs Thing were the sort of people who seem to know everything that goes on in the village, both being adept at extracting information which people didn't intend to share, quite a double act.

'You and your Mum went to tea at the Manor then Tollemina?'

'Yes, we did, Mrs Thing.'

'Did you have a nice tea, good cake?'

'Yes, we did thank you, posh finger sandwiches, lovely lemon drizzle cake and some of those little meringues.'

'Mrs Thing makes a mean lemon drizzle,' smiled Sally.

'Did you make the tea Mrs Thing?'

'Just the cake dear, pleased you liked it.'

'Did Jane ask you a lot of questions,' enquired Sally.

'Yes, wanted to know about my Dad, what he did, where he was, where we used to live, which school I went to, all that sort of thing, of course Mum is always very cagey because of my Dad, so Jane didn't find out as much as she expected to.'

The Blackney Swans

'So, she didn't let on about your Dad then?'

'No, that's just between us, in fact Mum would have a fit if she knew I had told anyone.'

'Your secret is safe with us, isn't it Mrs Thing?' assured Sally. Mrs Thing nodded, crossing her fingers behind her back.

'I thought we only put extra ribbons and flowers near the Well usually,' said Constance.

'Usually dear,' sighed Sally. 'But this year we seem to have all sorts, which is why I needed your help.'

'I think Mum has misunderstood, she has had a good clear out of her town wardrobe,' groaned Tollemina, pointing to the hat.

'Not to worry dear, we can find a use for anything,' said Mrs Thing as she patted Tolly's arm. Sally discreetly pulled a face.

'So do you think you passed muster with Jane?' asked Sally.

'Not sure, she knew Mum was being evasive and she didn't seem impressed about my school. On the other hand, when we had 'The Conducted Tour'. Mum was shocked that it wasn't wall to wall cream deep pile carpet and five foot chandeliers. Only 'old rugs' and sisal runners on bare wood and tiles.'

'Ahh,' said Sally. 'That goes back centuries, when people packed up all of their earthly possessions to take with them when they moved from town to country, the gentry were never as rich as they liked you to think they were.'

'They lived on credit most of the time,' winked Mrs Thing.

'Really?' gasped Tollemina.

'Oh, like the Tudors,' said Constance, 'I remember learning about that on a TV programme.'

'Mum doesn't watch educational programmes, she always has her nose in Harper's Bazaar or Paris Match.' They arrived at the village hall.

'I didn't know your mother was fluent in French,' said Sally.

'She isn't, she just looks at the pictures and asks me to translate,' said Tolly. 'Still, it has helped my French marks no end.'

The other three digested this information without further comment as they took their places by the bags of donations and the table.

'Good evening, everyone,' Sally greeted the committee. In addition to Mrs Thing and the girls, there was Penelope Jones and Jonty Bullock, the butcher's wife. 'Jane has sent her apologies and asked me to stand in,' announced Sally. 'So shall we dive straight in?'

The committee looked through all the clothes with astonishment.

Old Mrs Thing held up a used peach satin John Paul Gaultier corset.

'I suppose we could use the suspenders to hang flowers and offerings from. That was Mum's when she was going through her Rock Chick stage,' said Tollemina. 'Before we moved to the village.'

'There are a few old lady satin cotton corsets with steadfast suspenders left over from the last jumble sale,' said Sally the Vicar's wife.

'We could do with more variety,' announced Constance. 'Maybe some black,' she added.

'I may be able to find some,' mumbled Sally.

Everyone looked at her, she blushed and fluttered her hands ineffectually. 'Well, we were all young once and besides it's surprising what turns up at jumble sales.'

Old Mrs Thing, who cleaned for the previous Vicar said, 'I found some patent leather boots in his wardrobe.'

'Perhaps he played a horse guard in a Gilbert and Sullivan opera.' offered Penelope.

'What with stiletto heels and a whip?' replied old Mrs Thing.

They both looked at each other with raised eyebrows and pursed lips.

The suspender hoard was augmented by a no longer white, seen better days set, with only one pale blue mini bow remaining.

'I wonder,' observed Penelope Jones. 'If they used to be all pale blue?'

'I was wondering,' mused young Tollemina. 'What happened to the other bows?'

'I expect they'll be in the washing machine filter along with the hair clips and shredded tissues,' said Constance. 'They used to be Mum's,' she added with a look of profound disgust.

'That's what happens when you mix your colours in a wash,' sighed Jonty Bullock the butcher's wife, in a supportive sort of way.

The following morning, Tollemina and Constance were lounging about in Tolly's bedroom. Constance liked being there, no squabbling siblings, the house was light and airy despite voile drapes at the windows and it was good for people watching. Not that you

The Blackney Swans

could see many as the house was tucked away from the main village green and there wasn't a road through which led to anywhere. It was even more limited, though with Tolly's Mum's National Trust binoculars, you could sometimes catch deliveries at the back of the shop. Handy to know when the new delivery of cider was made by Zak. Glancing at Tollemina before resuming her watch, Constance asked. 'So why don't you want us to put the fancy corset on the tree?'

Tollemina looked up from her book. 'Well, I would find it embarrassing for one thing, I am sure my mum wouldn't see it as she hardly ever goes out and definitely not up to the sacred spring but I think it would be disrespectful for the spirit too. I think it's Nimue isn't it who is goddess of all the waters in Britain? And I'm not sure the tree would be happy either, it's one thing putting ribbons and beads of offering and thanks on its branches but you never know what some perv might get up to.'

'I think we should make a May Queen, a display of flowers coming out from the top of the corset, that would look nice, branches of spring blossom with tulips and forget-me-nots,' observed Constance as she moved her binocular inspection to the hedges and back gardens.'

'And we could put some from below like a big skirt, so it looks more like a ball gown than a corset,' enthused Tollemina. 'Brilliant idea Conny, let's go over to the rectory and see if Mrs Fairweather is in, she might have an idea how we can manage it; it would look great by the tea tables or the garden club tent.' The girls dashed down the stairs and Tollemina put her head into the kitchen. 'We're just going to the rectory for a few minutes, Mum.'

'Ok dear,' her mum smiled, 'It's just salad for lunch, no problem. Will Constance be coming back?' Tolly leaned back and looked at Constance waiting by the front door, who was nodding enthusiastically.

'Yes please.' And then they were gone. Samantha carried on preparing the meal, she was so pleased that Tollemina had found a friend. It had been a very difficult time moving house, having to change schools, keeping it all very hush hush, changing names even, she wasn't really cut out for all this cloak and dagger stuff. Tollemina had coped very well and settled into the village life, she didn't seem to miss London at all in fact. Tollemina seemed happier now than before and didn't mention her Father, though that was to perhaps establish a habit, so as not to slip up outside. She wrote an occasional duty letter, very cleverly not giving away anything about where they were, just enough to let him know they were Ok but of course he couldn't write back. She hurried on with the salad, taking the eggs off the cooker and plunging them into cold water and, as she had already set the table for three, poured herself a glass of white wine and went outside to feel the sun on her face.

Constance rang the rectory bell and the Vicar answered the door.

'Is Mrs Fairweather in please Vicar? We have had an idea for the May Day flowers and stuff.'

'She's busy in the kitchen but I'm sure if you go through, she can chat, she's just making sandwiches for lunch.'

'Oh sorry,' said Constance. 'Shall we come back later?'

'No, no, you carry on through, I'm sure she will be happy to hear your ideas.'

The girls went to the back of the hall and down some steps. It was an old Georgian house and the kitchen was below stairs, only a few but it was a demarcation point in times gone by.

'Hello, Mrs Fairweather,' the girls chimed excitedly.

Sally Fairweather looked up from buttering bread. 'Hello ladies, what can I do for you?'

'We have had an idea and wanted to see what you thought and ask advice about making it.' said Tolly. The girls explained their corset into ball gown with flowers notion and Sally was very impressed.

'I'll look in the attic to see if there's still an old wicker dressmaking form, if not I will ask around. I suppose if all else fails we could cut some withies and mock one up ourselves. I did a basket making workshop years ago and think I could manage to make something. What a lovely idea girls, and with hedgerow blossom too.' Sally beamed at them.

The girls excused themselves to go home for lunch, calling 'Bye Vicar,' as they let themselves out.

'What was that all about?' asked the Vicar as he came down to the kitchen.

'Those two,' said Sally, pointing towards the hall with her butter knife. 'Are your next generation of Church flower ladies and thoroughly nice girls too, enthusiastic, sensible and caring.'

'And you wouldn't be biased in any way?' teased the Vicar.

The Blackney Swans

'Not in the least,' replied Sally. 'Crusts on or off?' The Vicar gave a passable Gaelic shrug as Sally made a decisive diagonal cut.

The week that followed was filled with finding and cleaning the Maypole and ribbons, and with laundering and ironing table cloths for the afternoon teas and white sheets for the village show trestle tables. There was much stealthy grooming of petals and vegetables and of peering over back garden fences eyeing up the competition. Midnight torch and salt bucket forays into the garden undergrowth, though some went in for a more instant despatch of slugs and snails, not only nature can be red in tooth and claw. Though strangely, cats were kept in and humane mouse traps deployed.

The day before the First of May most of the village was galvanized into action. The Maypole, Marquee and tables were put up on the green and bales of straw made a large circle. The 'Well Dressing' committee gathered their unusual offerings of suspenders, flowers and ribbons from the village hall and went through the Church yard, along the bridle path, climbing up gently to the Well Spring with the Cluty tree standing sentinel by it. They stood around the stone water cistern each offering their silent thanks for the blessings received in the year past. They scattered petals and each in turn removed their last year's offering and placed their new ones onto the Cluty tree. Ribbons, bows, pieces of lace and silk flowers attached by the assorted suspenders. In their own time, each dipped their hands in the sacred water. Some drank, some sprinkled it on their heads or patted it onto their faces, some double dipped and others put the water on their tree favours, many had been dipped before being placed on the tree.

The woodland scents and blackbird songs filled the air, the bluebell colour amazingly intense in the twilight. The stillness was wonderful and timeless.

'Ladies, we had better leave now or Lesley and the St Cygnus swan people will be here and like their bird muses, can be cross as well as beautiful.' There were a few giggles and sneers, Jane 'shushed' them as the ladies reluctantly left and made their way down the path.

The Blackney Swans

'Can you hear geese?' asked Tolly.

'They will be from the paddock,' said Jonty Bullock, 'Sounded nearer though, sound travels funny sometimes.'

'That Josh Summers has some in his garden,' said Mrs Thing.

On they went through the wicker gate and church yard beyond, round to the playing field where a small Beltane fire had been lit already for the young people. There were sparklers for the children and balloons, the Morris Men were saving their dancing for tomorrow but the fiddler, penny whistle and tambour players made merry for a short while. Everyone was jolly and relaxed. The party didn't go on too late as there were children to put to bed and they had to be up bright and early to finish preparing for a busy May Day. As the fire died down, the youths showed off jumping the last flames. There were some who sneaked off to the woods and fields whilst they thought no one was looking, though Mrs Thing and others never missed knowing exactly where everyone was and who they were with. 'That's what Beltane was all about in the old days,' she mused to herself with a smile. Sally Fairweather nodded in agreement.

The May Day team had all retired to the Black Swan, tired but mostly happy that preparations had gone according to plan. Though there was always the odd worrier who felt they had forgotten something. Sally had made sure the Vicar was on orange juice, but she allowed herself a port and lemon. Mrs Thing had a snowball and most of the others were on half ciders. Samantha Clarke had been persuaded to come because the girls wanted to be with the grown ups, eager to absorb the chit chat. 'So, I've heard about May Poles and Morris dancing but I don't know about Beltane,' said Samantha.

'It's all to do with the Celts and the old ways,' explained Sally, 'pre-Roman. Beltane is a time when the veil between the worlds is thin, like Halloween except where Halloween, which is called All Hallows Eve by the Church, is about death and the spirits gone before us, our ancestors, Beltane is about new life and creation. It marks the Great Rite, or wedding if you like, when the Goddess and

The Blackney Swans

the God get together. She takes off her mantle of maiden and becomes a mother.'

'So, the May Pole is a phallic symbol and as the ribbons wrap around the pole, the flower crown descends. The celebration of new life, the crowning of the goddess and god, or May Queen and Green Man, new growth of plants and trees. In the old days before calendars came into being, it would be timed by the May blossom coming out.'

'So, you look after yourself and these two girls.' said Mrs Thing emphatically, 'We'll see you home, we don't want any lads who have had too much drink bothering you on your way, and we don't want any more little Cridges. He thinks he should be treated like a god but he's not to be trusted.' Mrs Thing nodded to the assembled ladies, grim faced, to emphasise her words.

'Goodness really?' exclaimed Samantha, very shocked.

'I'm afraid so,' agreed Sally. 'He's already put some in the family way.'

'I told him, gelding was too good for him,' put in Jonty Bullock. 'I said I better not catch him sniffing around my daughters.'

'But they're only twelve and fourteen,' exclaimed Penny Jones.

'I wouldn't trust him with a sheep,' snapped Jonty, as surprised as everyone else by her proclamation.

'Ugh,' they all agreed with a shudder and pulling faces.

'Erm, so going back to Beltane,' asked Tollemina, in an effort to diffuse the atmosphere and shake off the unpleasant thoughts.

'Ah, that started with people driving their livestock through the thick smoke of herbs strewn on the fires to get rid of parasites and I suppose, it would make them more fertile if they were healthier. The fires were lit to the god Bel. Then the people went through themselves. Smoke is still seen as spiritually cleansing in many cultures, it might also have made them uninhibited or a way of communicating with the gods. Some jumped over the fires as dares, to marry, that or jumping over the broomstick; all rights of passage,' summed up Sally.

'You know an awful lot about this for a Vicar's wife,' commented Tollemina.

'I like to know about all religions,' smiled Sally. 'Just because I'm married to a Vicar doesn't mean I don't respect other people's beliefs.'

The Blackney Swans

'She's an archaeologist,' put in Mrs Thing.'

'A dig at Skara Brae, Orkney, that's where I met him,' explained Sally, nodding towards the Vicar sitting with the men folk.

Lucifer came and sat on Mrs Thing's knee. 'Have you got any hot tips then boy? Are you fit and fast?' She continued to stroke him and he purred like a hubble-bubble pipe. She leaned into Penny Jones and whispered, 'I think he's getting too mellow for the chase now, there'll be more than one winner tomorrow.'

The girls and Samantha welcomed the offer of walking towards home with the others. Constance was staying over with Tolly and Samantha tonight and after the talk about Cridge they were rather nervous. Sally extricated the Vicar from a heated discussion about miners' strikes. He'd just nodded here and there, trying not to take sides despite his own views. Mrs Thing came too and they all walked along chatting and enjoying the spring night and quiet. They saw Samantha and the girls to their gate and continued along north of the village green towards the rectory.

'That's the first time Samantha Clarke has been to the pub,' Mrs Thing pointed out.

'Yes, she's quite a nervous sort,' agreed Sally.

'Hmmm,' agreed Mrs T. 'We don't want Cridge opening a can of worms there, or we'll have all the big boys from both sides of the law swarming all over the village.'

'I think if I can persuade the Vicar to have a chat with the Chief Constable about Cridge's woman from the levels, we might be able to avoid him being around here for too much longer,' said Sally, pointedly making eye contact with her husband.

'Good idea Vicar, night, night, see you both in the morning.' Mrs Thing waved and went in through her gate.

'Night, night Thingy, sleep well,' they replied

Sally linked her husband's arm and they continued on home to cocoa and an early night. Sally smiled to herself thinking about her new nightdress, dark as night with little spangles like stars.

All whilst certain other people of the village were starting on their annual night of worship.

Chapter 9

The air was heavy with the smell of burning embers and herbs, a mixture of scents that made the small group of Blackney Forloren villagers feel alive and connected. The twilight seemed to stretch on forever as they danced and sang around a bonfire, their arms outstretched to honour the sacred swan. Suddenly, a figure in a diaphanous cloak with a suggestion of wings and a beak emerged from the small pond waters, leading an even stranger procession, a sky clad man and woman, wearing nothing but flowers in their hair, making their way slowly toward the Beltane celebration.

The Cygnus group were entranced by the strange sight before them, two people without clothes or any sense of shame. This handful of villagers dressed in every shade of white or cream, some who carried candles, coloured inks, talisman or drums and other musical instruments, while others sported swan feathers and coloured ribbons in their hair, stood very still and waited. As they approached, a chant began to rise up from within the crowd: 'We come in peace with gifts for thee! Welcome us at thy sacred feast'

A hush fell over the gathered crowd as they watched these people approach. A few had never seen anything like it before. There was something almost magical about this gathering; it seemed to be calling them home to something greater than themselves. They drew nearer and nearer until finally they reached the edge of the firelight where everyone could see them clearly. In that moment, something shifted within each person present, a deep knowing that these two represented not only another way of being but also an ancient wisdom kept hidden away for centuries. They embodied the 'soul' of a voyaging shaman, a glimpse of the highest heaven or the purest stanza of grace and beauty.

Lesley stepped forward from among them and bowed deeply towards the sacred couple. She carried herself with grace and dignity as she asked permission to join in their celebration and offered her sacred gifts as a token of gratitude for allowing her this honour. In her hands were a miniature crown, sword, sceptre and spurs to help anchor the Swans' blessings. With reverent eyes, six more figures followed in her wake, carrying gifts such as flower petals, herbs, fruits, seeds and stones – all things that were used during ancient Beltane rituals for Honouring Mother Nature's bounty.

They spread out amongst those gathered around the bonfire offering blessings for health, fertility, peace, prosperity and joy. And then came one last gift…a single white swan feather taken from one of their own sacred birds. This act marked the end of what had become known as 'the blessing of swans' or 'the annual Cygnus ceremony' – a cherished tradition based on a remarkable Beltane celebration held by a group of naked villagers for many, many years.

The night ended with promises made between those present – promises to always revere the swan and what it represented; promises to remember how special it felt when they all joined together under starlit skies to honour the swan ancestors' ways; promises never to forget or forsake a swan. Little did anyone know on that fateful evening what powerful forces lay dormant for now.

Little did the sky clad ladies also realise that their secret ceremony had been under surveillance. In fact, the whole of the rest of the village knew what they were up to and a large number of them had hidden in the undergrowth to watch, ranging from teenage boys who wanted to see naked women to older villagers who just wanted to be voyeurs or even have a bit of a laugh.

Russ and Josh were two of the audience and had spent most of the time trying desperately not to giggle and spoil the whole ambience of the evening. Once they were out of the woods, they made their way back to Josh's house.

'So, we need to get her all provisioned up,' Russ said as he contemplated the burger van.

'First thing in the morning,' Josh said. 'A couple of hours kip now I think.'

The Blackney Swans

The previous week had been hectic for both of them but they knew it would be worthwhile. This was one of the times of the year when most profit could be made. A special brew had been prepared based on elderflowers this time and was now already in the van ready for surreptitious sale. They had set their mouse traps and captured a good population of potential winners which had been safely delivered to the pub. Their biggest problem had been getting Tom Bullock the butcher on side.

When Russ had explained what he wanted to do, at first, things had not gone well.

'You want me to do what?' Tom had exclaimed when the idea had been suggested. 'Now look, passing on the odd bit of deer is one thing but you know how bloody obsessed this village is with swans. We'd be tarred and feathered, by everyone from those loony ladies to the Vicar and everyone in between. Have you two lost your marbles or what?'

Russ had anticipated the reaction. 'Hold on a second Tom, it's just a code name and the taste is what we are after, just try this.' And he opened an insulated box he had brought with him. In it was a burger which he handed to Jim.

'Is this what I think it is?' he asked suspiciously.

'Only in name. Come on Tom, when have we ever let you down?' Josh said encouragingly. 'Give it a try.'

Tom took a tentative bite and swallowed. A strange look came over his face and he quickly took another mouthful. Within seconds the burger was gone. 'Bloody hell, you two are right, that was the best burger I've ever tasted.'

'Chicken burger Tom,' Russ said. 'Best chicken burger you've ever tasted, alright?'

Tom nodded but then a concerned look came over his face. 'Alright, I get it, and maybe we can do a deal for the May Day party but I know you two crooks. What's your real plan?'

Russ and Josh had decided that they really needed Tom on side for the bigger plan so they had already decided to confide in him. They told him the whole idea, the farm up in the old chapel which was technically legal, about all the other side products like swan down for bedding, and feathers for craft work, and how it could all be made profitable, very profitable. In the end, they cut a deal. Tom would prepare the meat and take a cut of the profits but that was all, any other activities would be the sole responsibility of Russ and Josh.

So in the morning, they loaded up the van with their product as well as more conventional fare acquired from the Cash and Carry in Bridgwater and set off to get a good site overlooking the green.

Chapter 10

Morgana awoke with a start. She looked around for a moment wondering where she was. In fact even wondering for a few seconds who she was. The sun was pouring in through the thin curtains causing her to close her eyes again. Her head hurt. Maybe that extra glass of wine last night had been a mistake, especially as she had to be up early......

She had to be up early! May Day! She looked at the time, leaped out of bed, which she immediately regretted and staggered to the bathroom, where she tried to turn herself back into some semblance of a human being.

A little later, after a breakfast of strong coffee and paracetamol and some very rapid dressing in whatever was to hand, she rushed out to deal with her goats. They were not co-operative, which didn't improve her mood or her headache, especially as she was simultaneously trying to remember the list of things she needed to take with her for her stall at the May Fair.

'Now you two, be good girls and I'll see you soon,' Morgana gave each of them a little piece of carrot as a treat and dashed back to her cottage. She grabbed her pull along trolley full of beautifully crafted swan items. She told herself that's what they were anyway, and trundled along to find her stall.

She was a bit disappointed when she saw the location but swallowed the feeling of irritation and decided to make the best of it. At least she was on the Village Green, even if it was a little obscured by the trees and bushes and rather closer to the village shop than she would have liked. Not that they were exactly competition, she laughed to herself. It was conveniently near her cottage though, so that was useful. She set out her goods and waited for people to turn up. The events would be starting soon! It would all be very successful and great fun!

The Blackney Swans

Eight in the morning and Daisy was briskly checking that everything was ready for what she hoped would be a good day, with plenty of customers. By contrast, Violet, yawning and complaining at having to be up early, was moving things around in a desultory manner, most of them items Daisy had already arranged to her liking the day before. She glanced at the clock again.

'What is the matter with you? Why do you keep checking the time? Expecting someone, are you?' Daisy looked at her sister impatiently.

'No, of course not. I just want today to be over and I was working out how many hours I have to get through.' Violet's voice was filled with misery.

'Well, keep busy and the time will soon go. And I'll be here so you won't be alone.' Most of the time anyway, Daisy thought to herself.

Through the shop window, she could see PC Cridge parading past.

They were almost ready to open at 9, when there was an urgent tapping at the door. A man they didn't know was peering in anxiously.

Daisy opened the door a little, 'Morning, we're not really open yet you know.'

'Oh please, it's an emergency. I know I'm not a regular customer, but I have a problem and I hope you can help.' The man looked at her hopefully.

'Well, you'd better come in then. What's this urgent problem?'

He looked embarrassed. 'It's my wedding anniversary today, ten years, and I completely forgot. My wife will never forgive me if I don't have a present for her. You must have something!' He looked despairingly at the array of dusty bottles, boxes and trays of limp vegetables and then at the special display of May Day goods. He groaned. 'Oh dear, can you suggest anything? And please don't say chocolates. She's on a diet again and that will just make her depressed because she's trying not to eat so many.'

The Blackney Swans

As he spoke, Violet had emerged from behind the counter and was looking around the shop thoughtfully. Her face suddenly lit up and she leaned towards Daisy and whispered rapidly in her ear. Daisy turned to her in surprise. 'That's actually not a bad idea! My sister has reminded me that we have some very attractive picnic sets, complete with a rug to sit on. What about one of those? You could buy some nice treats and take her for a romantic picnic and then spend the afternoon at the May Fair?'

The man smiled with relief. 'You're a genius,' he said to Violet, the first and probably only time in her life she would hear those words addressed to her. She blushed deeply and hurried into the back room as Daisy dealt with the sale and saw the happy customer out of the shop. Well, she thought, May Day magic!

The colours floated in the early morning breeze. There were multiple shades of greens and yellows along with a baby blue, cerise pink and dark crimson red ribbon. They hung from the tall maypole on the village green like a vertical rainbow above the Blackney Forloren villagers' heads. A wind caught June's flower crown – one made of daisies and carnations with lace and ribbons, as she emerged slowly from the wooded area bridle path astride a Shetland pony. Balanced precariously on her head, it visibly wobbled. Some of the villagers thought this was the first sign of the chaos to come.

An older boy laughed at the bizarre sight before him. An overweight thirteen-year-old wearing a white gown. To him, she looked not so much pure and angelic but more like his sweet-toothed younger sister in a cut down of one of Grannie's old nightgowns. The previous night, he had watched the shenanigans from the corner of his eye. June stood in her knickers whilst his mother held the long, white cloth along with her scissors and a needle and cotton. A little after June and her mount had passed the village church and the pub, and were within steps of the horse trough. The wickedness came out in him. He had a carrot in his pocket, something the small pony could never resist.

The Blackney Swans

Jane from the big estate, and one of the swan ladies who had volunteered to be the Green Man or in this case, the Green Lady, had a pained look on their faces. The May Day queen approached her ceremonial row of rowan, birch and hawthorn trees standing at the edge of the village green at a good trot. It was clear she was out of control and about to get faster. It was as if the Green Lady's druid guise had somehow warned her this would happen or the stag's antlers on her head acted like an antenna. The parade faltered and lost its stride. A group of small fairies and magical sprites became naughty, and both the fertility Goddess Ostara and the God Bel were so hung over they had difficulty keeping any of the smaller children in order. When June passed her brother, something had changed. The Shetland pony became more Thelwell than horse of the year.

The boy held out his hand and stroked the pony's ears, letting him scent the carrot. Then he simply loped off towards the May Pole. June screamed abuse, her crown slipped down over her eyes and the hem of her gown got caught in a stirrup. The pony cantered after her brother, head down and intent on eating. With the strange knowing of an under five-year-old, several sprites followed in hot pursuit. They were far more interested in food than magic or a celebration of warmth, flowers, greenery and new life with the start of summer.

The villagers spread out. Some jumped over the bonfire embers in an effort to catch a sprite. One held onto the May Pole to stop its crown of apple blossom along with blue bells and tulips, coming loose and falling to the ground. The twins from the village shop who had taken a five-minute break to watch the parade held each other's hands whilst June, the villager's official May Queen or Queen of May sat weeping in a steaming pile of pony poo and Ostara looked like she may be quietly sick.

The Blackney Forloren parade ended in chaos, no one honoured the gods and goddesses and June refused to lead the May Day dance or to make her speech. The Green Lady was silent and broody. Little did the villagers know the disastrous parade was an omen of things to come. There were peculiar happenings in the village, mischief afoot and someone was intent on working out exactly what that was.

Chapter 11

Morgana missed it all and was now feeling decidedly fed up. There had been very little interest in her stall and she had hardly sold anything. By contrast, people had been constantly popping in and out of the village shop. Still, the kids' races in the playing fields would be over soon and then more Village Green events would be happening. There would be more people wandering around looking at the stalls. Things would pick up. In fact, she could see Lesley and one of the other swan Ladies heading her way now; time to put on her welcoming but professional smile.

'Good day ladies, I hope you're enjoying your day?'

The two women looked at the items on display, swans made from instant drying ceramic, white feather dream catchers and one or two things that could have been almost anything. They exchanged glances and Lesley struggled not to laugh.

'What exactly are these meant to be? And were they made by the children in Reception Class at the village school?' asked the other swan lady with a disdainful expression. 'Of course, it's very kind of you to sell them on their behalf. Fund raising for the new playground equipment perhaps?' By now Lesley was definitely laughing.

Morgana felt hot with embarrassment and anger.

'Certainly not. They are hand-made by me and represent the beautiful swan traditions we love here.'

At this, Lesley choked back her laughter and said 'Oh, I'm so sorry,' but in such a pitying tone Morgana knew that it was not an apology. They turned and walked away, leaving Morgana mortified. Which of course, had been their intention.

To console herself, she took a break and bought a burger from Russ and Josh's van. She was a bit dubious about it, but as she was starving decided to take a chance and to her surprise it was delicious.

The Blackney Swans

A little later, she strolled back and waited for a few minutes until they weren't so busy.

'Hey you two, just wanted to say I really enjoyed the burger. It was one of the best I've had in ages!'

Josh looked surprised. 'Well, I'm glad you enjoyed it. It's a new venture for us and a um, special recipe of our own.'

Morgana smiled. 'I'll tell people how good they are if in return you maybe send a few customers in my direction?'

'OK,' said Josh. 'I guess we could do that. Can't promise results though...' he looked enquiringly at Russ, who shrugged.

'Thanks, it's a deal then. Worth a try,' and Morgana sauntered back to her stall.

In the distance, she could hear announcements over the loudspeaker in the Flower and Produce Marquee. Good, not long now! She'd been for a brief wander in there earlier while eating her burger. The displays actually looked pretty good. Lots of beautiful flower arrangements, carefully placed fruits and vegetables and delicious looking cakes. People had obviously gone to a lot of trouble.

The flowers were picked and the Floral Lady made, she was quite spectacular, with fruit tree blossom and blackthorn, lots of fresh young greenery and masses of bluebells, tulips and buttercups. The Withy and Flower May Queen with her fixed crown was set up outside the marquee.

'You hardly see the suspenders at all,' said Sally Fairweather. 'Well done girls, I will ask you to help with the flowers next time we have a wedding in the church.'

Although the girls were happy to be praised, they were a bit alarmed to be recruited for dressing the church. There were children to help find where to put their posies in saucers, and iced buns in the marquee. Ladies sailing in like galleons with Victoria sponges, jars of jam or chutney and interesting flower arrangements. It was mostly the men who brought home made beer, wine and liqueur classes, operating a bit of a closed shop. Jane from the manor and the Vicar were judging these classes and Sally had made a mental note to keep a watchful eye on him after the Harvest festival incident. He was such a trusting soul.

The chalk board by the burger van announced free cider to over 18's with each burger or hot dog. There was no way Cridge could stop them from doing that, those boys would run rings around him. They even had their answer ready for where the booze had come from, donated by an anonymous benefactor. Of course, the charge for the booze was in with the burgers, but Cridge couldn't prove that, and of course the meat didn't cost them anything at all.

Jonty Bullock was selling smoked eel buns, very upmarket with mayonnaise and salad. Well, you have to cater for all tastes. Daisy Coombes had roped Russ into carrying buckets of ice with lollipops in and the tea ladies were filling the urn. Parents were starting to arrive with their offspring in party dresses, not all of which were May Day relevant, circlets of flowers meant to be fixed in their hair. Only a couple of little boys had been recruited, the rest thought it all sissy, wait till they grow up! The deputy head teacher Vivian, tried to marshal the excited children in one place near the May Pole and keep them clean.

The Morris men practised without their bells, clashing their sticks as the hobby horse man circled this way and that. The W.I. Ladies set up their stall with jam, cakes, knitted goods and plants. And at half past ten, the judges closed the entry to the marquee to begin their deliberations. The early bird helpers began to queue at the burger van for a late breakfast as the smell of cooking food filled the air.

'Ooh, smells like chicken,' sighed Mrs Thing.

'Definitely poultryish,' sniffed Penny Jones, 'Maybe goose?'

'Whatever it is it's making me feel hungry,' sighed Constance.

'Me too,' said Tolly, 'Come on I'll buy one for us to share.'

The butcher had a stall selling taxidermy he had made, birds on branches, a stoat with little dark eyes crept over stones and moss. A couple of foxes, one looking cute the other in hunting stance and the centre piece was a magnificent swan, which was said to have flown into a power line. The 'Swan Ladies' were really not happy, but as he said, 'I couldn't just bury it, it seemed disrespectful somehow, it was so beautiful. He secretly hoped Lesley and Jane, the squire's wife, would get into a bidding war over it.

Tom Bullock explained, 'All the creatures have been brought to me, the results of accidents. You can't do much with roadkill, sometimes manage to use the odd pheasant, as once you've made an armature from a shot one, you can make another for a knocked down one.' There was a tiny harvest mouse with a wheat nest and another dressed in a little jacket, sat on an anchor cotton reel.

Cridge was loitering about the stall, looking at the creatures and asking too many questions.

'They have stuffed mice in the skittle alley,' he announced, watching Tom Bullock intently.

'Ah yes,' Tom didn't miss a beat. 'Janet has managed to deprive her Lucifer of an odd catch now and again, has them immortalised so to speak.'

'Is that so,' said Cridge.

'Ay, tricky the little'uns are too, take just as long if not longer to do than bigger items, them being easier to handle.'

'Is that so,' repeated Cridge, 'Funny hobby for a butcher all the same.'

Tom decided to steer the conversation toward philosophy and bamboozle Cridge.

'I may be a butcher, Mr Cridge, but I always dispatch my animals humanely and only for consumption by other people. I do think all creatures deserve respect, and showing them lifelike and in their prime, they're a thing of beauty and not to be looked down on or disparaged. In their own ways they're as clever as thee and me Mr Cridge, else they wouldn't be walking the earth the same time as us.'

'They can't send men to the moon though, can they,' said Cridge.

'With all due respect Mr Cridge, sir, neither could thee or me,' replied Tom

Cridge breathed in to reply, but unable to come up with a riposte, sidled away. The Vicar, who had been admiring Tom's work, waited till Cridge had made a hasty retreat, leaned in closer and congratulated Tom. He was having great trouble keeping a straight face. Tom mopped his brow, watching the retreating policeman, but then indicated with his head and eyes urgently at the Vicar, who turned to see Cridge accosting Samantha and Tollemina

Clarke by the W.I. Stall. The Vicar nodded to Tom and advanced towards the group beaming, with his hand outstretched, helped by the home made wines and liqueurs he had judged.

'Ah there you are Mrs Clarke, Sally asked me to look out for you.' The Vicar shook Samantha by the hand and whilst saying, 'Do excuse me for interrupting sergeant,' segued it into tucking her hand in the crook of his left arm, thus turning their backs on Cridge and walking the ladies away, exclaiming surprisingly loudly. 'How delighted that he and Sally are that you come to church so regularly.' Short of telling Cridge to leave them alone, he wasn't sure what to do. The man was immoral, fancied himself as an alpha male, it wasn't just lock up your daughters but any other female too. Gosh, he had drunk too much, and what had he heard Mrs Thing say to Sally, 'In my young days he'd have bromide put in his tea.' Not a bad idea really. Where would one obtain bromide nowadays?

Chapter 12

While the exhibits in the Marquee were being arranged ready for judging, and tension began to build, a little bit of excitement had been happening in the world of Sybil and Gertie, Morgana's goats. In her rush to leave that morning, Morgana had been careless about securing the paddock gate. Goats, being more clever than they might appear, are surprisingly dextrous at opening gates, and Gertie was an expert. She was also easily bored and often fiddled with the latch on the gate to see if it would open, and on May Day, it did!

She and Sybil were soon triumphantly free and meandering down the lane towards the interesting sounds and smells coming from the Fair, stopping to nibble at plants, having a nice little rest in the shade and finally reaching the school playing field just as the children's races were taking place. Some of the parents were in the field, leaning on the post and rail fence watching and exuberantly cheering on their children. Sybil grazed happily on some especially tasty weeds near the fence and then noticed something very tempting, a light cotton skirt worn by one of the mums. She tried a little taste, found it good and then chewed more enthusiastically, tugging and nibbling as she pulled more and more cotton into her mouth. The owner of the skirt suddenly became aware of being touched in a rather friendly manner, prodded her husband and glanced at him flirtatiously. He looked at her, puzzled. She swung round, saw Sybil, and screamed. Sybil let go of the shredded skirt, now covered with green saliva and mashed grass and fled in panic, with Gertie clattering delightedly after her. They trotted briskly towards the Marquee, the sound of hysterical screaming fading in the distance.

As it was a warm day, the Marquee had some of the side flaps open for ventilation, so it was easy for the goats to slip inside, just as the prize winners were being announced by Jane from The Manor, with the Vicar in attendance. She suddenly faltered in her speech and looked rather distracted, gazing fixedly at the table where the flower arrangements were displayed. She was sure one of them had just moved. Imagining things, must be the heat. At that point Gertie jumped nimbly and rather gracefully, she thought, onto the table so she could devour the winning flower specimens more easily. Sybil, meanwhile, was helping herself to a delicious Victoria sponge cake, and rather rudely, bleating with her mouth full.

Bedlam ensued, both goats running up and down, on and off of the tables, snatching mouthfuls of anything in reach, including, and this was spoken of in hushed tones much later –Sally Fairweather's Hat. Oddly, no one seemed prepared to try to catch them, although calling for PC Cridge was mentioned and immediately shouted down.

Back on the Village Green, a few people were wandering around the stalls and Morgana was beginning to cheer up a little, although the derogatory comments made about her swan items by Lesley the Witch and her friend had been rather upsetting. Deciding she had to 'move on' from that, Morgana was smiling, rather rigidly at some potential customers when the sound of screaming, shouting and general uproar began to filter across from the Marquee. Well, someone's making a lot of fuss, laughed Morgana to herself, maybe they didn't get first prize. Her smile became more genuine but froze again when she heard the bleating. The bleating, which was much too loud, much too close. She hardly dared turn around but knew she must.

It was coming from the Marquee. She rushed there as quickly as she could, to be confronted with chaos. She started dashing here and there, her purple and black attire flapping and billowing. She dived below a trestle table and emerged without her hat and its accompanying hair! Now everyone was staring at her and ignoring the goats. More than one person was reminded of a vulture rather than a crow with her face as red as a beetroot and her own real hair tied tightly up. She put her hand over her hair and ran out of the tent, dodging the amazed visitors, thus ensuring everyone knew something very odd was going on in there.

'Well,' said Penelope Jones in her best Miss Marple fashion. 'Discretion is certainly not her middle name.'

Jane's husband, his Lordship, was sat in his wheelchair roaring with laughter and clapping his hands on the armrests. He sent

The Blackney Swans

Colonel and Hildegard, his chocolate Labradors, to round up the goats but Gerty and Sybil were having none of it.

The goats decided to scarper and now pursued by Morgana, headed for the Village Green, zigzagged through the stalls, crashing into one or two of them and made for the shop, skidding to a halt outside. Gertie peered in through the window and bleated enthusiastically. Loud screams came from inside.

Earlier that day, life in the shop had been disappointingly quiet and rather boring in Daisy's view and quite busy enough, thank you in Violet's view. After Violet's triumph at suggesting the anniversary present, there had been only a trickle of customers, the most interesting one being one of the Swan ladies, coming in looking a little flustered and embarrassed.

She explained 'The top of my white costume had been ruined by a bit of an accident with some red wine. Can you do anything to help?' Her face indicated that asking how this might have happened would be unwise.

After searching around among the boxes and pile of goods, Daisy held up one of the festival T-shirts (white with a design of just a few flowers) and a pair of net curtains. 'What about these? I'm sure you could improvise something quite lovely?'

This suggestion was reluctantly but gratefully accepted and the purchase made. After she left, Violet and Daisy had a fun conversation speculating on who spilled the wine on her and in what circumstances and also laughing at how she was going to look in her new outfit, bearing in mind the difference in size between the T-shirt (small) and the Swan lady (large).

The morning dragged on for Daisy. Eventually, she could take no more and told Violet she would just pop out to have a quick look at the stalls and get them something for lunch. She returned with chicken burgers, which they agreed weren't too bad and that Russ and Josh must have put some extra spices or something in them as they had more flavour than any burgers they'd had before.

The Blackney Swans

They had just finished eating when they heard a bit of a commotion outside. Violet went and peered through the shop window and screamed loudly.

Outside the shop, the goats were wrecking the table display of goods, knocking over stacks of drinks and crisps, while Gertie was experimenting with the taste of a flip-flop. Inside, Violet was now hiding behind the counter but Daisy strode outside and began waving an umbrella at the animals. Morgana appeared, breathless and panicky, with her now exposed red hair, loose from its ties and flying around wildly. She reached out and managed to get hold of Sybil's collar, calling for help, and shouting out desperately, 'has anyone got any rope or something, please!'

Across the Green, in the burger van, Josh saw what was happening and without really thinking about it, rushed over and flung himself at Gertie, getting his arms around her and tried to remove the flip-flop from her mouth. After a brief wrestling match, he got hold of her collar, extracted the now revoltingly slimy flip-flop and flung it onto the ground. He picked up a belt which someone had taken off and helpfully thrown in his direction. He slipped it through her collar, fastened it and heaved a sigh of relief. Gertie stood still, head down and panting, looking a little subdued. At that moment, he became aware that Morgana was watching him open mouthed, an expression of combined amazement and admiration on her face.

He handed the end of the belt to her, which she took silently, still holding on to the now docile Sybil's collar and gazing at him as if she had never seen him before.

'Thank you. That was incredible. If she had swallowed that flip-flop, it could have killed her. I don't know how I can repay you.'

'Well,' said Josh. 'I'll probably think of something.' He laughed, a little embarrassed and headed back to the burger van, looking over his shoulder as Morgana led the goats away.

On the far side of the village green Janet was taking a well-earned break with a fag and a cup of tea behind the skittle alley when the commotion started. She'd dealt with the lunch time drunks, most of whom were now snoring contentedly on straw bales scattered around the lane outside. She'd had to ban Old Seth, yet again, after he got carried away with Russ and Josh's batch of May Day Special gin and she caught him peeing up against the wall round the side. Again. He'd had the grace to look ashamed.

'Shorry Misshush. I didn't mean to… shupposhe you mighn't overlook… let me back tonight…'

'No, I mightn't and I won't. I've other customers to think about. You're banned until tomorrow evening. And that's that.'

But it happened most May Days. There'd be no hard feelings. If he'd managed to get home at all he'd probably need till tomorrow to sleep it off. And if he hadn't, well, he'd spent more than one May Day night snoring in a ditch during his years of serious Beltane boozing.

And since he'd gone there'd been no other disruptions to the regular routine. The under-sevens' white-mouse-racing had gone without a hitch precisely at half past eleven. Only six entrants this May, but she'd keep it on. For years, there'd been mums and dads, who'd raced their own pets bringing the next generation for a go. Some of them had even left the village now and lived over to Bridgwater or Taunton, but they still came back. You couldn't disappoint them.

In any case, Janet herself always enjoyed watching those little faces peering over the side of the table-top race track, noses twitching, while their pets scampered across the plastic turf towards the line of nuts on the far side.

And now there was the under twelves at four and then she might treat herself to a sizz before evening opening. At least there were eleven taking part in that. Quite a lively-looking field stacked up in their cages well out of the way by the back door. She'd laid on a decent spread of cake and biscuits for the owners and parents, after running out last year. In fact, when she thought about it, she had a lot to be grateful for. People might not like her much, but then she didn't like most people much herself. Any more than her parents had.

She could still remember Dad sitting her down when she left school and saying, 'Janet my girl, there's a few things you need to know about running a pub like me and your mum. I'm telling you now because when the time comes, we're both hoping you'll take over and keep the Duck going the way it always has been. And Number One is, most of your punters will most likely be a giant pain in the arse. Some'll talk down to you, some'll puke in the toilets, some'll bend your ear for hours with stories about theirselves, and they'll all expect you to remember what they like to drink. But you'll put up with it. And why? Because it's them pays the bills.'

She stubbed out her cigarette, swallowed the last of her tea and looked at her watch. That was odd. The first of the under-12s should have turned up by now. Better go round the front and see if something had happened to delay them.

Everything looked the same as usual on this side of the green. Not many people about, but there weren't the stalls to bring them. It seemed, though, that something was happening on the other side of the duck pond. There were shrieks and yells, and as she watched, the Vicar came running through the trees towards her, shouting, 'Get back. There's a herd of animals on the loose. Causing total mayhem. And Cridge is nowhere to be seen. I have to go and lock the church door.'

Chapter 13

The three judges looked down from the village podium at the line of swan like figures stretched out before them. One by one, their eyes met with each of the hopeful entrants as they looked them up and down. There were eight small children in all, two swans came as Odette from the ballet Swan Lake, one couple were dressed as the six swans from the Grimms fairytales, a couple were regular white swans and two were just unrecognisable. The fancy dress outfit of the child on the far left looked more akin to an elephant. He had a white sock tied over his nose, large flappy ears and something that looked like a small tail pinned to his trousers, whilst the small toddler in the centre had strewn his outfit across the grass in a temper tantrum.

The villagers were also rather taken by the sight before them. There were feathers of every hue and from a range of birds. In fact, several were so colourful they looked like they had come from a parrot. One child was wearing a collar of crow feathers around her neck and claimed to be a black swan. Two sported three papier mâché swan's heads a piece, on a plastic tiara stuck to their heads. Some villagers clapped but from the back there was a loud shout of, 'get them off.'

The judges called for order. The village swans of Blackney Forloren had worked hard, and for the younger ones, their parents had helped to cut out cardboard and glue on feathers deep into the night. It looked like a couple of old wedding dresses had been donated to the cause, giving a gauzy and silky white appearance to at least one outfit. Each of the judges had at some time done the same. They were all very proud of their ability to make something wonderful out of jumble sale items.

Lesley stepped off the podium and called for silence. She moved slowly, attaching a ribbon to one outfit. The swan wept copious amounts at the pleasure of winning, smudging her black mascara. The black protuberance at the base of her cut-out paper bill was ruined. On her feet were two orange slippers and a white feather had been glued to each of her fingernails. A tutu like affair finished off her swan effect. All of it was now splattered with black dots and mucky marks where she had tried to wipe herself clean.

Unfortunately, the fancy dress entertainment didn't end there. Bedlam ensued as several of the losers undressed in front of the judges as a protest against their decision. They thought they deserved to win, not the silly swan that had been awarded first prize. Two stood there stark naked whilst one other had kept her knickers on. Lesley enjoyed it all. She had no problem with a few sky-clad behaviours.

As the day wore on Charles Cridge grew more and more dispirited. He'd been so sure that he'd find someone committing an arrestable offence at the May Day celebrations in Blackney and had talked his sergeant into sending him there for that very reason.

'You know what they're like out there in the back of beyond,' he'd said. 'Up to all sorts. And I think you should give me a car, too,' he'd said. 'So I can bring the criminal straight in.'

But the sergeant had drawn the line at that. 'If, and only if, you catch somebody in the act and put the cuffs on them, you can phone in for back up,' he'd replied. 'Otherwise, it's a bike for you, sunshine.'

So, he'd got there bright and early, and gone peering about in odd corners looking for evidence of illegal goings-on, but without success. And now the main events were over, and though Charles was aware that not everything had gone entirely to plan, he hadn't actually witnessed a crime. A bit of mayhem at the costume judging and a couple of goats temporarily on the loose, apparently, but that's what happens when you let the local yokels organise their own events. Even those two shady characters Russ and Josh had done nothing doubtful. On the contrary, they'd spent almost all day doing a roaring trade at that new burger van of theirs. Hardly surprising that, given the quality of their wares. Charles had joined the queue so he could check out what exactly they were selling and finding himself peckish, had bought one to try, but it tasted totally above board to him. He'd even gone back for a second one just before they sold out.

So, as the church clock struck six he decided to call it a day and cycle home. He wasn't more than a mile or so out of the village when a couple of four-wheel drives loaded up with lads rounded the corner in front of him at speed. He held up a hand and pulled them to a halt. Peering at the driver of the first car, he recognised Pete Sturrock, president of the Young Farmers.

'Evening,' he said. 'And where might you be going in such a hurry?'

'Oh, you know, just out for a Bank Holiday drink.'

Charles leaned in closer to see if he could smell alcohol on the other man's breath. Perhaps he could do him for drink driving. But he couldn't detect anything.

'Well, you behave yourselves,' he said. 'And if I hear there's been any trouble, I'll know where to come.'

He waved them on, and then wondered if he shouldn't perhaps follow them back into the village in case any trouble broke out. But it had been a long day and he never felt comfortable in Blackney. Most of the villagers made no secret of their feelings about him. So, he got back on his bike and carried on his way.

He was almost home when it suddenly struck him. A lot of the kids in the cars looked as if they might be under 18. It was hard to believe they'd just stick to Fanta and Coke when the rest of the gang were going at the beer and the cider, or worse. Or maybe they'd be doing pills in corners, uppers. If he snuck after them now, he could catch them at it and Precious Janet Grinter could be done for illegal sales and allowing her premises to be used for illicit drug-taking. That'd show them back at the station.

Chapter 14

By teatime, with everything sold from the van, the two entrepreneurs were sitting outside the pub.

'I really need this,' Russ said as he held his pint up to the light to inspect it before taking a long swig. 'That was a hell of a day.'

'Couldn't agree more,' Josh said. 'One of the more eventful May Day celebrations I think I am safe in saying.'

'Well, if you mean by that, the marvellous May Queen, the best dressed swan and Morgana's famous goats, then eventful is definitely one word that springs to mind. Oh and I noticed some looks between you and the statuesque Morgana, got your eye on her goats, have you?'

'Sod off old chap, but she is quite striking, I might need to make a closer acquaintance at some time. Anyway, what about the chicken burgers? They sold like hot cakes, we could have sold twice as many,' Josh said as he put his pint down. 'I was really worried when we started, as they didn't seem that popular. Then the word seemed to get around all of a sudden.'

'I wonder what would have happened if Lesley, our senior witch, knew what we are calling what people were actually eating,' Russ said with a grin. 'Mind you, she came back for seconds.'

'Oh well, looks like we are really on to something,' Josh said. 'Just the evening's entertainment to look forward to. You know I wonder how it all got started, we've been doing it for longer than I can remember.'

'Ah, I can probably answer that,' Russ replied. 'I did some research a while back. The answer is Wolves.'

'Nope, completely lost me there, old chap.'

'Right, go back hundreds, even thousands of years ago, before they drained the levels. All the slightly higher ground was used for settlements like this one. That's where the word 'Ney' in our village's name comes from, it means little island. Anyway, around here the levels dried out a bit in the summer and supported quite a large wolf population which migrated to higher ground in the autumn and then back to the levels in the spring.'

'Ah, so the villagers had to defend themselves because they were in the way.'

'Exactly, it became a test of manhood to kill a wolf. Eventually, it became a sort of competition. It seems that over the years it slowly changed.'

'Not the least because they killed all the bloody wolves, I suppose,' Josh said.

'Exactly. It seems to have been caught up in the Beltane mythology as well. So when they ran out of big shaggy dogs they started using alternatives like foxes and then rats and over the years it seems to have slowly become more of a gambling competition than a test of manhood.'

'Hmm, I can't see chasing a small rodent as being much of a test of anything.'

'Oh, I don't know, remember when the Vicar's wife saw one in church the other Christmas and ended up standing on top of the altar with a broom in her hand shouting hysterically?'

'Oh yes, and we all saw what sort of underwear she likes.'

Both men stopped for a few seconds, recalling the moment.

'Anyway,' Russ continued. 'That's where we are today. We have our mice and our cat and our competition, all because of big old shaggy dogs of days gone by. At least we don't chase bloody great cheeses down ridiculously steep hills like some of the other lunatic villages.'

'Good point and as we supply the rodents, we get to keep book for the evening. Looks like this is going to be a very lucrative day.

So, a little later the two men went back to Russ's place and retrieved a large box. Inside were six field mice.

'It seemed much harder procuring these little sods this year. I suppose it was a hard winter. I still say it would be easier to go to that pet shop in Bridgwater and just buy some.' Josh said.

'We've had this discussion before. Firstly pet mice don't look the same and secondly, it would quickly get suspicious if we bought six the same time every year.'

'You really think the punters would notice and anyway we could go further afield even as far as Taunton.' Josh said. 'But I suppose you're right, it's an ancient tradition and we should stick to that.'

By six thirty, parents with young children were taking them home after a full day of excitements, some scheduled and some decidedly not. But nobody had got hurt, and if you went to a village like Blackney on May Day you expected things to be a bit rough round the edges.

Inside the pub, Janet was breathing a sigh of relief. In the end, the under twelves race had gone particularly well this year. Some new faces and promises from everyone to come back next May Day. You had to keep the old traditions going. Proper Somerset treats for the kiddies. Not all this Beltane nonsense.

She looked at her watch. A minute to opening time. Everything was ready for the evening. She'd checked the cellar and the toilets. She'd put the big blackboard in the skittle alley for the odds later and checked the course was firm. She'd even made sure Lucifer looked the part by getting any tangles and drool out of his fur. He might be losing his edge, but to the average mouse, he'd still look like a force to be reckoned with. There was a hammering at the door.

'All right,' she called. 'I'm coming.'

The moment she drew back the bolts, the door was pushed firmly open and she stepped back to find the Sturrock kid standing with his hands on his hips, while a gang of younger lads assembled behind him.

Janet glared at him. Young Farmers indeed, going on about their good works and what not, like they were a choir of angels. But when it came to basics, boys growing up in the country hadn't changed much since she was a teenager herself. On a night out, they still wanted to grope a girl and get legless. Also, to sing loudly, rattle dustbins and generally disturb the peace.

Before the Sturrock kid could speak, she walked straight up to him and put a hand on his chest. 'More room outside,' she said. 'You all find yourselves somewhere to sit and I'll take your order in a minute.'

The Blackney Swans

For a moment, Pete considered arguing with her but he didn't know who else might be in the pub, listening. Outside would be better, in fact. He could make sure they weren't being overheard, because it was very important that he talk to Mrs Grinter about various things. He had a proposition to make and there were other people involved. People were waiting to hear not only that she'd agreed to everything they were offering this year, but also that she was open to the idea of repeating the arrangement in future. The sort of people you didn't mess about with and who wanted an answer as soon as possible.

'All right,' he said and smiled. 'Thank you.'

Chapter 15

By the time Cridge got back to Blackney, he was sure he was about to make an arrest. But before he'd even parked his bike, he spotted Pete Sturrock and his companions walking towards their cars, and not one of them looking pissed. He ducked behind a wall. There might still be a few of them indoors. He could still catch them at it.

He waited a few minutes, then nudged the door open to find Janet staring at him from behind the bar and a couple of the younger lads finishing what looked suspiciously like Vimto.

'Oh, it's you again,' she said. 'What do you want this time? I thought I saw you leaving the village a couple of hours ago.'

He swaggered over.

'I did. And then I met young Sturrock and his crew on their way here. And though I carried on, the more I thought about it, the more I began to wonder. What are they doing out here heading for the Duck? Not their sort of place at all. No jukebox, no pretty barmaids. Had they got something lined up to do here? Were they planning to cause a ruckus in a nice peaceful little place like Blackney? So, I turned round and came back. I have my duty to do.'

Janet smirked. 'Course you do, but …'

'… and my duty is to uphold law and order.'

'Well, they've gone now, so I won't need you holding anything up this evening, thank you Charles. Or perhaps it wasn't them you wanted to check on but me, making sure I wasn't selling liquor to under 18s, for instance.'

Cridge looked away. How could she know what had been going through his mind?

'As if,' she went on. 'I intend to hang onto my licence, thank you. Or was it a small glass of something you fancied yourself? I've got a nice single malt in. I wouldn't have had you down as a Scotch man, necessarily. But this one… And on the house of course, to

The Blackney Swans

show my appreciation for you pedalling all the way back here. That's real policing, that is. I've half a mind to ring your sergeant and tell him what a good copper you are.'

Cridge began to back away from the bar. 'No, no, don't worry. All part of the job.'

'Well, thank you, Charles. Goodnight then.' She came out from behind the bar. 'Remember me to the family.'

And before he knew what had hit him, she had a hand on his arm and was guiding him out of the door.

After he'd got on his bike, she hung around for a short while, watching him make his way out of the village. What a fool! Never in the right place at the right time. But, after that, thank the Lord, unlikely to be back tonight.

She couldn't help smiling as she resumed her position behind the bar. Well, well. The big money people were interested in the Dirty Duck special, were they? And the Sturrock kid had turned out to be quite business like when it came down to it. After everything he said, she'd had to agree to let the Young Farmers put their own mouse in for the race and somehow she'd have to make sure it won. But after all these years, that shouldn't be a problem.

And if this worked, if Sturrock was right, she'd be getting a very generous cut of the bookie's takings. In another few years, she'd be able to retire in comfort. Never mind Mum and Dad and their 'you'll take the Duck on for the family, won't you' speech. She could think about a new life. Leave Blackney behind. Nobody would miss her and she certainly wouldn't miss them. She could take Lucifer with her and let him live out his last years in the sunshine. She'd never been abroad yet, but people said Spain had a lot to offer and there were plenty of other Brits already there to show you the ropes.

The church clock struck eight. Extraordinary how your whole life can change in just a couple of hours.

Russ and Josh went back to the pub which was now starting to fill up and went into the skittle alley, which was being set up by

The Blackney Swans

Janet. The course was already set up and she was just arranging the seats for the judges and clearing the other furniture away.

'Got the contestants here,' Russ said. 'Did you get the secret ingredient?'

'Over there,' Janet said indicating a table off to one side. On it was a small pot of something. 'I put it through the blender so it should rub on easily.'

The two men went over to the table and started rubbing the green compound onto the fur of the mice. Which all had a number painted on their backs.

'Sure this will work?' Josh called across to Janet.

'He got a whiff of it this morning and I had to stop him from trying to shag the blender so yes I'm confident it will be fine,' Janet replied. 'So, we start in ten minutes if you are ready?'

'Yup, time for some ancient country traditions,' Josh said.

'And some modern country gambling,' Russ added.

Right on time, the doors were opened and the crowd pushed in, all talking excitedly. But as they started to spread out around the large central table, a group of young men pushed to the front.

'Janet, we are the Young Farmers and we would like to enter our own competitor into the race,' one of them said in a stentorian voice.

The noise of the crowd stopped immediately.

Janet pretended to be completely taken aback. 'I supply the mice,' was all she managed to get out before the farmer spoke again.

'Says who? We've got a potential champion here and why shouldn't he enter the competition?' he held out a beefy hand. Inside was a fit looking field mouse.

Russ leant over and whispered into Janet's ear and said something.

'I don't see there is any reason why not,' she said but you will get the same odds as all the others.'

'Fair enough,' the man said. 'Where shall I put him?'

'Over here,' Josh said and indicated the large box with the other mice in. 'Just pop him here, I'll get my felt tip and put number seven on him.'

When he got a second, Josh turned to Russ, 'What the hell? How are we going to set odds now?'

Russ grinned. 'He's the only one without the special addition, he's just about guaranteed to win. We've just got ourselves a sure bet.'

Janet overheard them and grinned to herself in silent agreement.

Chapter 16

The moment had almost come. The air was full of tension, the room was hot, crowded, and filled with a miasma of assorted alcohol fumes, plus the aroma of over-excited people overlaid with a hint of the musty smell of mice. It was noisy too, bets being placed, speculations being voiced about which of the runners would win and one or two doubts muttered about whether Lucifer would perform his duty.

'He looks a bit past it, if you ask me,' said Daisy to Violet, sniffing loudly.

'Well, I'm not asking you and I don't want to watch, it's horrible,' protested Violet. 'I just want to go home. There are too many people and they're already pushing and shoving and the race hasn't even started yet.'

'Oh, you are such a party pooper, why don't you...' at that point someone bumped hard against Daisy, spilling her glass of cider all over the Swan Lady who had visited their shop that morning to buy a replacement for her wine stained white top.

'Oops,' said Daisy and Violet burst out laughing, then quickly put her hand over her mouth, her bad mood forgotten for a moment. The Swan Lady turned round crossly, about to let fly at the sisters but a loud clanging cut through all of the noise, and people began to fall silent.

Janet put down the handbell she had been ringing.

'Evening everyone, welcome to this year's Special May Day Event, the Mucky Duck Mouse Racing. Now, I expect you all know how it works but for any who don't, or have forgotten, it's very simple. This year we have seven runners, each numbered, all freshly caught and raring to go. Our hero Lucifer has been training hard...'

At this point a voice from the audience called out 'What, by either eating his head off or sleeping all day?' This was met with an

The Blackney Swans

outbreak of laughter, jeers, and shouts of, 'he'll still do 'is job,' 'yeah he's past it' and other helpful contradictory comments.

'All right, thank you,' Janet looked a bit put out but soldiered on. 'As I was saying, everything is ready, the mice are waiting to be released, as is Lucifer. He will catch the mice, the last one to be caught is the winner. So simple, even you can understand it.' This was addressed to the first heckler. 'You have five minutes to finish placing your bets, getting drinks or whatever urgent things you have to do, then we start when I blow this whistle,' she said, waving it in the air.

Amid cheers, more laughter and general hubbub, there was total chaos as drinks were bought, bets placed and places near the race track jostled for.

Then everyone quietened. Janet held the whistle up high again and one of the helpers, or Stewards as they liked to be called, delegated to release the mice from their box, leaned over the race track. He set the box down, keeping the door ready to open on the signal. The other Steward lowered Lucifer further down the track, carefully holding him facing the box, so he could see and leap into action as soon as the mice were released.

The air almost crackled with excitement. Everyone holding their breath, eyes fixed on the racetrack.

Someone sneezed loudly into the silence, making everyone jump, including the Steward holding Lucifer, who nearly lost his grip on him.

'For goodness' sake!' said Russ to Josh, both of them intent on what was about to happen. The sneezer muttered an embarrassed 'Sorry' and laughed nervously.

'Lucky that wasn't a few seconds later.' warned Janet. 'Right, are we all ready? Absolute quiet now, so the racers can concentrate.'

'Blimey,' thought Morgana to herself, not daring to speak out loud. 'You'd think it was the start of the blooming Olympics.'

Janet blew the whistle. The door of the box opened. The mice stayed inside. The Steward tipped up the box, so they fell out. Two of them scurried off immediately, the others huddled together for a while, except for the largest, donated by the Young Farmers. He sat up on his hind legs and began washing his whiskers, looking rather cute if a little over-confident given his circumstances. None of them appeared to have noticed the cat. Yet.

The Blackney Swans

Lucifer, on being released, also sat down and looked around in the regal fashion that cats can do so well. He looked almost bored, if a little put out by all of the noise, which was now rising as the onlookers became impatient, shouting advice to Lucifer. 'Go on you lazy moggy, get on with it' being typical. Others shouted encouragement to the mice, especially those wearing whichever number they had bet on.

Suddenly, Lucifer rose to his feet, arched his back in a stretch, his tail straight up and quivering. His eyes widened and his whole being focused on the little group of mice. His movement attracted their attention and they all froze for a few seconds, then scattered at high speed.

Lucifer leaped, pounced, grabbed. There was a squeak; one mouse down. Turning rapidly, the cat pounced again and demolished another racer. Two more victims were dispatched equally quickly. One of the remaining three made a bid for freedom, dashing along the edge of the track but Lucifer could dash even faster and hooked him with an outstretched paw, tossing the little creature into the air, then catching him in his mouth.

The crowd were going wild with excitement. 'Well, he's just showing off now,' shouted Jonty Bullock to her husband. 'Still got it in him though,' he shouted in reply. 'Good job he got going or he'd be the next one for my taxidermy freezer.'

Now there were only two mice left, one of Russ and Josh's field mice, number five and the Young Farmer's unscented specimen, number seven. Both mice were now frantically running around, appearing to try to go in several directions at once. Number seven was jumping at the barrier at the side of the track, attempting to escape. Number five, who was very small and probably not full grown, seemed to be especially adept at changing direction suddenly. Lucifer stopped running after either of them, for a breather perhaps. He wasn't as young as he seemed after all. He had found the catnip so irresistible, and it had been fun, but rather tiring. However, there were still two left and one of them smelt of that wonderful stuff.

He watched Number five carefully, crouching down, tail extended behind him, the tip of it twitching and flickering, his jaw chattering. Then, just as he was about to launch himself at the mouse, someone threw a handful of his favourite cat treats in front of

The Blackney Swans

him, cat treats that no cat can ignore, more desirable even than a mouse smeared with catnip. Also, the treats didn't run away and he was absolutely exhausted.

Lucifer settled down to eat, ignoring the mice. Number seven had succeeded in his jumping technique and had escaped over the top of the barrier around the track. Number five had disappeared into a corner of the track and somehow, in the way that mice can, wriggled through a hole apparently too small for any mouse.

The noise level from the watching humans had reached a crescendo. The race seemed to be over. But who had won?

There was a cacophony of voices, with shouts of 'There goes one of them. Try and catch it, Stop pushing,' and other useful suggestions, accompanied by people scrabbling around searching for the two escapees. Lucifer had finished his treats and was now sitting calmly in the middle of the race track, washing his whiskers.

A loud shriek rose above the mayhem. Rather surprisingly, it came from one of the Young Farmers. The small mouse, number five, had run up his leg. he had grabbed it and it had promptly bitten his finger. Being a brave and determined young man, in spite of the shriek), he managed to hold on to it, shouting excitedly, 'I've got one.'

Meanwhile, someone had crawled under a table in the corner and captured the Young Farmers' mouse. 'Me too!' A cheer went up and then Janet rang her hand-bell for silence.

'Right,' she said. 'Let's finish this. Put them both down at the same time. One of the Stewards get Lucifer in place please.'

They readied themselves. The spectators were breathless with anticipation and the after effects of shouting and shoving. The mice were released, and Lucifer, having had a bit of a talking to and having no treats left, began twitching his tail and watching both mice. The Young Farmers' mouse ran straight past him but the cat leaped over it and grabbed number five, still redolent of catnip. It was all over, or the spectators thought so. But at the same time as number five was being snacked on, the exhaustion of racing followed by the shock of being jumped over by a large cat was too much for the other mouse, which collapsed. Frustrated howls arose from the watchers, especially those with money at stake.

Lesley had purposefully stood to one side of the mouse racing track. She was conscious of movement but discreetly glanced aside.

The Blackney Swans

Her focus had pivoted when Lucifer was dropped into the centre of activity. She turned to Jane who still had a patch of green paint daubed on the side of her face. 'I can never decide if I love this or hate it!'

Jane answered in the typical hunting, shooting, fishing response of the landed gentry. 'Chin up, old girl.'

The noise inside the track grabbed their attention but they continued to watch silently. 'Jane, what do you think of those Young Farmers bringing their own mouse?' Lesley asked.

'Below the belt, not pukka. They're outsiders.' She sucked in a breath and with an explosion of air through her nose, followed up with. 'It's just not a Blackney Forloren type of thing to do.'

Lesley shook her head in disbelief. The words 'not pukka' caught her attention. It was about then that the atmosphere in the skittle alley changed as accusations and counter accusations started to fly around. It took on an electrified air as if something was about to happen. Lesley gasped

'Watch out, Jane! The big guy on your left is angling for a fight.'

Jane had only just replied, 'let's move to the other side of the skittle alley,' when a contented purr came from inside the mouse racing track.

What happened? No one knew. Was Number five still alive? Was the Young Farmer's mouse dead or just resting? But by then it was too late. The first blow had landed on the other side of the racetrack and that corner of the Black Swan skittle alley was alive with angry exchanges.

Immediately alert to the strong energies, Lesley took Jane softly by the arm and led her friend away from the melee and into a Blackney Forloren starlit night. The winner's decision had little to do with them. Jane was too grand and had little need for money and Lesley, well she was a witch and had an inkling all would not end well in the skittle alley.

At that point, the young farmer who had caught number five started shouting something, very angrily. His voice rose above the others, the word 'cheating' catching people's attention.

The noise died down. 'Yes, I said cheating,' the young farmer, red-faced with anger held up his hand. 'Look at my hand, covered in something green from that mouse. Well, I sniffed it and I know what it is. It's catnip! Cheating!' And whoever threw the cat treats on the race track was in on it too.'

'You outsiders don't come in here and think you can say that kind of thing,' shouted one of the Blackney locals.

'Just try and stop me, I'll say whatever I...' That was as far as he got because a punch landed on his nose. The other young farmer retaliated by swinging his fist randomly at everyone around him and in moments there was pandemonium. Fists connected, sometimes, where they were aimed. Hair was pulled, drinks thrown, pent up feelings released, more shouting, more and more people joining in and those trying to escape getting dragged into the brawl anyway.

Someone fell on a table, which broke, taking several bystanders and their drinks with it. They promptly joined in the fight, which by now had spread from the skittle alley into the rest of the building. Moving like a human tsunami, the tangle of panting, hitting, struggling, swearing people was heading towards the main entrance of the pub, carrying everyone and everything in its path with it and leaving a wake of detritus behind.

Chapter 17

Cridge was still unhappy, something was niggling at the back of his mind. Those bloody villagers were up to something, he was sure. For the first time in his life, he decided to carry on working even though he was now officially off duty. He had been taking his time but now turned back towards Blackney Forloren, trying to pedal furiously but failed to make much progress, having never fully mastered the art of using gears. The switchback roads added further to his discomfort when an adverse camber launched him into a roadside rhyne. When he had worked out which way of him was up and spat out the dubious water, he looked around for his custodian's helmet. There would be hell to pay if he lost that and he would never hear the last of the ribbing, his fellow officers were especially delighted to make his life a misery at the least opportunity. He spied the helmet, although filled with water, floating level with the surface a few yards off thanks to its cork infrastructure. Struggling with the water weed and underwater debris, he doggy paddled boisterously towards it, alarming yet more wildlife. Eventually he succeeded in retrieving it, poured out the murky water and weed, after minutely inspecting the interior for wildlife he reluctantly replaced it on his head, as he needed both hands to climb out of the ditch. Several attempts, loud splashes and helmet retrievals later he succeeded in returning to the road, recovered his bicycle, which now sported a wonky front wheel and was sadly missing its bell, he mounted it hopefully and made his now even more precarious way toward the iniquitous village, with the light flashing weakly like an exhausted strobe, exactly matching his own weariness.

But he had sworn to uphold the peace even if he had to do it in his own time and those mean-spirited villagers would not best him, so it was with squelching boots and quivering lower lip that he arrived in the village as all hell erupted from the Black Swan Pub. Those Young Farmers, Russ, Josh and other villagers were having a

The Blackney Swans

right set to. Insults and fists flying and more locals joining in, spilling out of the lighted doorway, it was like the wild west. Despite his bedraggled state, he adopted his best John Wayne/Dixon of Dock Green persona and waded in with a vision of braid and shoulder pips at the forefront of his mind.

Attempting to grab Russ, he accidentally collided with a blow thrown by a farmer, landed on the Vicar, totally winding him and so incensed the dainty Sally Fairweather, she of the exciting lingerie, that she grabbed the cider jug clutched protectively by Mrs Thing, and raised it to, well, smash it over Cridge's head. Before she could execute her intended retribution, she was relieved of the jug by a strapping farmer who quaffed freely from it before Mrs Thing brought him down to her level by kicking both of his shins, so she regained the jug and walloped Cridge with it.

It's been a long time coming to you but I did so enjoy it." She grinned at Sally and they began to haul the Vicar to his feet and find a safe place to revive him.

Somehow there seemed more people, strangers, joining in.

'You seen her, mate?' A man with a London accent asked.

'Not yet.'

Another two villagers accidentally hit one another before realizing their mistake, apologising, shaking hands and then standing back to back to rejoin the fray.

Suddenly, there was a piercing scream, which for a second or two stopped the mayhem as everyone turned to see Samantha Clarke, grasped by a burly stranger being dragged off towards a blacked out car. Tolly and Constance were in hot pursuit, hitting and kicking the assailant but were themselves being harried and pulled off by another stranger.

Jonty Bullock nudged her husband Tom, pointing and rallying him to their aid. The two well made country folk had right on their side, defending fellow villagers from kidnap. Tom, light on his feet for a big man, caught up with and tackled the one holding Samantha; 'Be light as a butterfly and sting like a bee,' he murmured to himself as he rearranged the man's nose and ribs, causing him to drop Samantha and double up. Sam flew to aid Tolly and Constance as Tom Bullock finished his villain off with a Karate chop. All the women were on the second man, ripping his tie off and tying his

The Blackney Swans

hands behind his back. Tom did the same with his conquest, though he didn't think he would be coming round any time soon.

Samantha thanked them profusely and Jonty smiled, eyes sparkling at her husband.

'A man of hidden talents is my Tom,' she beamed at him, 'You didn't hurt your hand love did you.?'

'Not at all,' he reassured her. 'You all alright girls?'

'Yes, we're fine,' said Sam looking round at the other women.

'What was that all about then, know them did you?' Asked Tom.

'Yes, I'm afraid so, they were some one time associates of my husband and won't accept their money was lost in the stock market crash, they think it's stashed away somewhere. He's in prison, for insider dealing, they think I have it, or can make him talk by threatening us.'

'Right then, I think it's the cold store for these two while I call the police,' announced Jonty. 'Not having them putting women at risk, no way, nor messing with Blackney folk.'

'I haven't seen Aunty Mo, do you think she will be all right?' Tolly asked her mum.

'I don't know dear, I didn't see her in all the kerfuffle at the Black Swan, she has taken this keeping her distance very seriously, so people don't know we are connected.

'Aunty Mo. Do you mean Morgana? Is she your Aunty? But you don't speak.'

'Yes, she's my dad's sister but as this gang were looking for three women together, we kept it a secret.'

'Goodness me, dark horses, cloak and dagger stuff, it's like living in a TV drama,' pronounced Constance.

'It's not very nice being in the middle of it though,' said Sam, 'I hate having to tell lies and keep so many secrets.'

'Well, it's all out in the open now,' pointed out Jonty, 'Best let's go and warn everyone the police are coming and have a good clean up, we don't want any unnecessary village business brought to their attention, do we?'

As the group headed towards the Butcher's shop, conveniently near the Black Swan and village green, they saw the rumpus, though still going on, was quieting down, with more bodies on the ground, and much holding of heads and faces. The ones still slogging it out had forgotten what it was they were fighting about and were almost propping each other up in order to take or give another punch.

Once the men were locked up, they all quickly adjourned to the Swan, righting tables and chairs, sweeping up glass and debris. Janet had removed any trace of the mouse racing, save for the contents of a lidded tureen in the fridge upstairs.

The last thing to be tidied away was Cridge, the large Young Farmers bumping him before a final toss into the village pond. Everyone left him and went about their own business.

Janet began serving coffees and offering packets of crisps to soak up the alcohol and sober people up before the police arrived. She wasn't best pleased and was worried about her licence. She reminded customers sternly that mice and betting were not to be mentioned on pain of being barred. Russ split the mouse racing takings with the Young Farmers and it was agreed that any visible injuries had come from a May Day friendly Rugby match. They in turn promised Janet regular custom and a contribution to any breakages.

On the other side of the pond, in the village shop, Violet and Georgiana the cat, were hiding upstairs and peeping out of the bedroom window. Violet terrified and Georgiana thoroughly enjoying the spectacle. Violet was horrified to see a man and woman struggling near the front of the shop, she so wished Daisy were here. It looked like that horrible Morgana woman, but she had long red hair and the man she had never seen before. She really didn't like Morgana and was secretly glad that someone was teaching her a lesson. Then Georgiana sat bolt upright and stared in the direction of the big tree on the village green, there was someone there. Violet followed Georgiana's gaze and saw a man and what appeared to be the long barrel of a gun at his side.

Georgiana leapt from Violet's knee, shot downstairs and out of the back door cat flap, streaked down the side of the shop and took up her observation place next to the post box.

The Blackney Swans

Josh called from behind the tree. 'Let her go or I will shoot,' he could see the handgun at Morgana's head. He had seen it in its holster when the stranger's jacket had flapped open in the melee at the pub and had snuck home for Russ's old gun and a pocketful of ammunition. He was happy with booze and a punch up, skirting the law and running circles around Cridge, but this was something else, real violence, guns and hurting women, you had to draw a line. The man was backing away with Morgana as a shield.

'I said leave her or I will shoot,' called Josh again. The man kept stepping back with Morgana in his grip. Josh fired at the ground by their feet, the man paused, the bullet had caused a plume of dirt to rise before it bounced up, hit the post box with a loud ping and landed just behind the strange man. Georgiana's trance was broken by the noise, the ping above her head and the dust plume caught her attention and she suddenly spied the bright shiny thing behind the stranger. She pounced soundlessly and as she reached to bat the pretty shiny thing, the stranger stepped back onto her paw. Georgiana let out a series of blood curdling howls and as the man lost his concentration, she sank her claws and teeth into his leg, doing that clutching thing with her front paws whilst raking her back claws repeatedly down his leg, like she did when killing Daisy's slipper. He lost his balance, falling backwards, his arms flying up and out. As his body hit the ground the gun went off harmlessly into the night sky. Josh ran towards Morgana as she lunged for the handgun, just as a large and very angry white swan landed on the man, one wing seemingly damaged by the stray bullet, the good wing repeatedly banging the man's head.

Josh gave Morgana the rifle to keep the prisoner under control whilst he held the swan to stop it from injuring itself further. With the swan safely in Josh's arms, Georgiana gained her bright shiny object, retaking her place under the post box to play. The cars with blue flashing lights and sirens blaring screeched to a halt outside the Black Swan where all was calm and bright with friendly chatter. Morgana enjoyed forcing the man up at gun point towards the waiting police.

'Put your gun down madam,' they called as they ran forward to handcuff the man and retrieve Russ's dad's gun. Morgana saw Josh's face fall when the gun was taken and said to him kindly.

The Blackney Swans

'Thank you Josh you're a hero. They will probably let Russ have it back eventually, but he will need a licence for it from now on.'

Josh nodded.

'And there will be a reward for catching this man, you can buy him a new one if necessary and take me out to dinner in Langport, if you like.' Their eyes kept contact for an extra few seconds, which spoke volumes. Not quite a Pride and Prejudice at the piano moment but not far off. If he hadn't had hold of the angry swan, he might have ventured to put his arm around her shoulders. Bloody swans.

Fellow officers retrieved Cridge and his wonky bike from the village pond. The Vicar, speaking discreetly to the senior officer, mentioned that Cridge seemed to be suffering from amnesia and possible hallucinations. Perhaps a desk job might be more suitable for him in future? The officer sighed heavily and nodded.

'He doesn't seem suited to country policing, or any sort of policing for that matter, I'm afraid. We will see what the medics have to say.'

Epilogue

'Well, that went well,' Russ said.

Russ and Josh were sitting on the edge of the now somnolent duck pond which no longer contained Young Farmers, villagers or an unfortunate Police Constable. The men were sharing one last large glass of illicit hooch.

'Well, I've lived here all my life and never seen a May Day like that one,' Josh said. 'I wonder what would have happened if we hadn't shot that swan by accident all those months ago.'

'Well,' Russ said. 'The parade would still have ended in chaos, closely followed by the fancy dress. The flower and produce tent would still have been eaten by feral goats and the mouse racing would still have gone completely up the spout and ended up in a riot. Mind you, on the plus side, the Vicar didn't end up in the produce this time. Then some thugs from outside the county would still have ended the evening like a scene from the Sweeney. There are going to be some awkward questions in the village about that tomorrow.'

'All true I suppose,' Josh said in agreement. 'We may not have won much keeping book on the mouse racing but without our 'burgers' we wouldn't have ended the day in profit. And look how well they were received, that confirms our idea that there is a real business opportunity for the future.'

'True, true and hopefully we won't be seeing that damned nosey Constable again.'

'Hmm been thinking about that,' Josh said. 'If they replace him, they might actually get someone who knows what he's doing and isn't a complete pain in the arse.'

'Oh, I hadn't thought of that,' Russ replied. 'Good point, let's not worry about it too much, eh? Tomorrow will bring what it will, including a rather plump, red haired, hippy lady. Who you are getting to know now mainly due to our accidental connection with swans.'

The Blackney Swans

Josh decided not the rise to the bait, instead he changed the subject. 'Alright, now I have to ask, where is it?'

'Where is what?' Russ asked in an innocent tone.

'You know exactly what I mean.'

'No sorry old chap, you've lost me.'

'I gave it to you when you finally arrived and you disappeared for ten minutes before the police collared you about that rifle.'

'Oh, you mean the injured swan?'

'Yes, as you very well know. Come on, where is it?'

'Back at my place, the wing wasn't badly hurt. He's tucking into supper as we speak and he can come and join the ladies out at the chapel. We needed a good male to make us some baby swans. I would say he's probably come out of the day better than most of us.'

Josh lay back and looked up at the stars. '

'You know I think you might just be right and maybe getting half pissed, tripping over with a loaded rifle and shooting a poor innocent swan wasn't the worst thing that could have happened to us.'

The Pink Swan

A 'pink swan' is the definition of a complete cock up that could easily lead to all sorts of problems for the people who made it in the first place.

Chapter 1

Russ and Josh were celebrating a return to normality.

'I dunno, we've always complained that nothing exciting ever happens around here and then look what went down last week,' Russ said.

'Yeah, well let's hope that's an end to it,' Josh replied. 'I'm quite happy with the quiet life.'

The two men were sitting outside the shed that hid their illicit still amongst other things.

'The last thing we need is bloody outsiders snooping around,' Josh continued. 'Our little enterprises keep us well occupied and in credit, we don't need any interference.'

'I understand but it was rather exciting,' Russ agreed. 'It'll keep the village gossiping for months. Anyway, what's this brew we're on today?'

'Elderflower, rather good if I say so myself.'

They sipped at their glasses for a while and contemplated the vista of the Somerset Levels in front of them.

'You know, I think we should go to Glastonbury with some of this stuff, I bet we could sell it at a premium.' Russ said as he held his glass up to the light to admire its quality.

The Blackney Swans

'Eh, why Glastonbury?' Josh asked. 'Nothing but a rather boring High Street and that silly hill behind it. I went there once, nothing special.'

'Not the town you twit, the music festival.'

'No sorry, no idea what that is.'

'Bloody hell man, where have you been all your life? No, don't answer that, I know quite well you've hardly stirred from here.' Russ said with a smile. 'Some years back, they started a music festival at some farm not far from Glastonbury and it's become very popular. They get all the good rock bands and thousands of people show up. By all accounts, there are loads of illicit drugs and booze, just our sort of place.'

'Not drugs old chap but we do have rather a good stock of hooch,' Josh said. 'But are we short of cash? Could be a lot of work.'

'You really are a lazy old sod you know,' Russ said. 'What about our entrepreneurial spirit? Anway, those damned swans, geese and chickens are not cheap to keep in food and we're going to have to shell out quite a lot to feed them.'

'I thought you said you had taken care of that, some dodgy mate of yours had access to supplies from a wildlife park, wasn't it?'

'Well, yes but I still have to pay him and as I said, we can't start supplying any real quantities to Tom Bullock for some time yet. Anyway, Glastonbury is meant to be great fun. You could even invite that hippy girlfriend of yours.'

'She's not my girlfriend,' Josh exclaimed with rather too much insistence to Russ's mind.

'Oh yeah? And what were you doing the other night when I came around your place then? I heard some very strange noises from inside and you didn't answer the doorbell.'

'None of your business.' Then Josh clearly decided that his friend would never let up and anyway why not tell him? 'Oh well yes, we are getting on alright, you'd find out sooner or later but she's had a bit of a hard time in recent years so we both want to keep it low key, you know tongues wag in the village.'

'Good point but what happens if she finds out about our little enterprise in the woods, isn't she into Swan mythology and all that stuff?'

The Blackney Swans

'Actually, not as much as you might think and nothing like those loony witches who she really doesn't like. Until she came here, she was working in an office. She also has a bit of an entrepreneurial streak, I'm pretty sure she'll be no problem.'

'Alright but let's not let her find out anything that we don't want her to know, not for the moment anyway.'

'Fair enough,' Josh said, quite glad his friend wasn't making too much of a fuss. He was getting quite fond of Morgana but would hate for it to affect his friendship with Russ. 'Anyway, it's time we moseyed out to the chapel and fed the livestock, is it not?'

'Indeed and as the Police have given me my rifle back, maybe we can see if any deer accidentally come into view.'

'As long as you let me check it's not loaded before we go.'

'Of course.'

The two men made their way across the flat fields towards the raised ground of the woods where they were keeping their stock of swans. 'Old Dinsdale seems to have settled in well,' Russ said.

'Who the bloody hell is Dinsdale?' Josh asked.

'Oh sorry, it's what I'm calling the new male that we acquired the other week, the one that was injured. He's almost healed but probably won't be able to fly for some time yet. He's quite the bossy type.'

They entered the woods and made their way to the remains of the old chapel which was now their farm. As they turned the corner, both men stopped and stared in shock.

'What the hell?' Josh asked.

In front of them were their swans, cygnets, along with some geese. The young cygnets were still mainly in their brown plumage but with some white showing or what should have been white. The adults should all have been white as well.

'Russ, how on earth have we got a flock of bright pink swans?' Josh asked. 'What the hell have you done?'

'Me? Why are you blaming me? I haven't done anything.'

'Where is this stuff you've been feeding them? Are those the bags of it over there?' Josh asked, pointing to a large wooden box frame they had installed. He went over and pulled out a bag of feed and examined it.

'This is bird food but it's got Beta Carotene in it and I know exactly what that is. I read about it some time ago.'

The Blackney Swans

'Ah and what exactly is that then?'

'It's for Flamingos to keep them pink as they don't get their natural diet in this country and would turn white otherwise. Your dodgy contact must have nicked the wrong stuff.'

'I wondered why it was so cheap,' Russ said. 'But hang on, so we have pink swans, so what? Apart from the colour, they look healthy enough on it don't they? And who knows selling pink feathers later on could be quite a novelty.'

Josh looked at the birds and was forced to agree, they all looked in good condition and quite content despite their bizarre appearance. Just to be sure he went around and checked all the families.

'Er Russ, you have a good point I've checked them all and they all seem fine, more than fine actually but we've got another problem.'

'Oh, wassat then?'

'Where's Dinsdale?'

Chapter 2

Dirk Thrust had been up early. His day had started with a number of Sun Salutations on the balcony of his glossy hotel room in the West End. He had sipped a wheatgrass smoothie before meditating for an hour. Now he was relaxing in the lounge of his penthouse suite. He contemplated himself in the full length mirror in front of him. He looked so much better now that he was on the straight and narrow. Tall and thin, with a shock of blonde hair that, despite his age, had no grey in it, he looked like the archetypal rock star. Now that he was on the wagon, he had shed the pounds of middle age that had threatened his figure. He felt good, he felt in control and vowed it would stay that way from now on.

His entourage drifted in. He was perusing a report one of his minions had prepared for him. He had a complete listing of his band 'The Pistons,' his albums and hit singles from the last thirty years of fame. Also, there were envious tales and press cuttings of his sell out concerts around the world, and many stories of his drink fuelled excesses.

His interest was more than just idle curiosity. The Thrust family had been based in Somerset back to the mists of antiquity, and there he had grown up in genteel poverty. Given a remarkable voice and an extrovert personality, he had not looked back since leaving university.

His manager strode in, his strident voice breaking across the low hum of conversation, and Dirk's reading. 'Dirk, my boy, how are you doing? All set for Glasto?' Dirk looked up. 'It's confirmed, then? I'm headlining?' The manager looked triumphant. 'At a record breaking price, you are headlining alright! You'll never need to work again and neither will I. Three weeks tomorrow!'

The manager threw himself back into a deep chair next to Dirk and pulled out his cigar case. 'We have something to celebrate. Joe.' He turned to an acolyte. 'Order champagne, and lots of it!' Dirk remained serene and spoke softly. 'I will not pollute my body with

The Blackney Swans

alcohol, or any other unnatural substance. And I would prefer that you did not smoke.'

The manager returned his cigar case to his pocket. 'Alright Joe, champagne for us and mineral water for our Dirk. Well done, boy.' Quietly, he wondered how long the effect of the latest rehab would last. It had been astronomically expensive and had taken Dirk off the road for no less than six months. But the boy was unrecognisable. For all that, the manager was sceptical. He had seen it all before. 'As long as you stay clean for Glasto, that's all we need.'

Dirk smiled gently. 'I am reborn. One day at a time, my life is renewed. I do not need any substance to interfere with the purity of my body and spirit.'

'So,' the manager proposed. 'Where do you want to spend the next two weeks? Nights on the town? Las Vegas for the casinos? Or Bali for some R&R?'

'What I want,' said Dirk firmly. 'Is a trip to Somerset. On my own.'

'On your own apart from the guys, you mean?' The manager was puzzled. 'You'll need a driver, and the lads to look after you...'

'No,' Dirk was calm. 'I have things to do. I'll meet you in Glastonbury three weeks today.'

Dirk got his own way. It had never really been in doubt. The manager was mightily concerned but in the end, he had to give way. 'You will stay off the booze, won't you?' the manager begged.

Dirk was unconcerned. 'My soul is pure. I have no need of artificial stimulants.'

Dirk had left the main routes and was threading through increasingly narrow and muddy lanes in the depths of rural Somerset. His black limo, complete with darkened glass, was automatic and easy to drive, which was just as well, as he had not driven himself for some years. It was rather large for the lanes, though, and took up all available space. He had spotted Glastonbury Tor a little way back and was making his way towards it, regularly thwarted by unexpected bends and oncoming tractors requiring him to back up.

Dirk's thoughts were full. Back in rehab, he had started to research the Arthurian legends associated with his birthplace. On delving deeper, he had found rumours of a knight of the Round Table with a name that could be something like Trust or Thrush who

The Blackney Swans

could only be his forebear. Slowly, the pieces had fallen into place, and he had realised that this heredity made sense of his whole life. He had been searching for something, and at last, it was in grasping distance. When he found the Isle of Avalon, he would finally be home.

He had made so many twists and turns, that he could no longer see the Tor and the levels surrounded him with no signs of life. He shivered, and for the first time, wondered where he would sleep that night. Over the hedges, he caught sight of another mammoth piece of farm machinery headed his way. To his left, a small turning signposted 'Blackney Forloren' opened up, and he swung his limo to take the turn.

Russ and Josh had been searching for Dinsdale since dawn. They had found plenty of swans, but none of the required roseate hue. His wing had evidently recovered. As they plodded back towards the cottage, Russ spotted something totally unexpected. A black limo, with darkened glass, was trundling slowly up the lane. 'Hellfire!' shouted Russ. 'It's the Excise men.'

As Russ and Josh ducked behind the hedge, Dirk became aware that he was entering a village. He smiled, seeing cute cottages arranged around a traditional village green, complete with duckpond. As he glanced back at the road, in front of him stood a huge, pink, swan.

Dirk was accustomed to hallucinations, but there was something scarily real about the way the swan stood its ground, stretching its long neck towards him and hissing. And it really was very bright pink. He swung the steering wheel frantically and the limo trundled across the village green, coming to rest nose down in the water of the pond, to the consternation of the ducks.

He flung himself out of the limo and emerged from the pond, hung about with waterweed like a Christmas tree with tinsel. He stood dripping and gaping as the swan followed a short, tubby figure armed with a bucket down the lane.

Russ took his arm. 'Steady there,' Russ said. 'Are you hurt?'

'Did you see that swan?' cried Dirk frantically.

The Blackney Swans

'Swan? What swan?' replied Russ as Dirk fainted dead away.

Josh returned and between them they half carried the Excise man back to Russ's cottage. As he started to come around they revived him with a glass of their strongest brew. Some familiarity caused Dirk to ask if it contained alcohol, but Russ reassured him, 'Oh, no, that's pure Elderflower juice, have another.'

Chapter 3

'Jimi Hendrix?' Russ asked.
'Never heard of him,' Josh replied.
'Eric Clapton?'
'Nope.'
'Pink Floyd?'
'What the hell is that?'
'Sheesh. Mick Jagger?'
'Nope again.'
'Bloody hell Josh. John Lennon?'
'Oh yeah might have heard the name, wasn't he something to do with insects?'
'No, he bloody well wasn't.'
'Led Zeppelin?'
'Oh come on now you're just taking the piss.'
'Pete Townshend and Roger Daltry?'
'Who?'
'At last, we're getting somewhere.'
'What?'
'The Who.'
'The what?'
'Not the What the Who.'
'What?'
'The rock band the Who.'
'Never heard of them.'
'Jesus Josh, didn't you ever listen to pop music as a kid?'
'Not really, not my thing really.'
'Right, well, if I was to tell you that this chap,' he indicated the comatose body on the sofa. 'Was in the same category as those people I've just mentioned, it clearly wouldn't mean much to you but this guy is a rock legend in the same league. His name is Dirk Thrust, I didn't recognise him at first as he always makes himself up when he performs but I've checked his wallet and his driver's

The Blackney Swans

licence confirms it. So, I think we have an enormous opportunity here but also a potentially massive problem.'

'What's the opportunity?' Josh asked.

'Well, someone's got to get that girt great limo out of the duckpond, it must be worth a fortune and I know where we can borrow a tractor from to pull it out. Rock stars like this chap have money to burn and we can charge a reasonable rate.'

'Good thinking there. And the problem?'

'He saw Dinsdale. I know you caught him and got him back to the farm but we will have to convince him he saw nothing strange. We don't need our little enterprise discovered, do we?'

'Ah yes,' Josh said. 'I wonder how we will be able to do that.'

Just then the body in question decided to groan, roll over on its side and throw up all over himself and then the floor.

'Oh come on,' Josh said. 'I only got that rug from Trago Mills a few months ago.'

The body then opened one eye, closed it, and then opened both. 'Jesus Mary and all the saints, what the hell was that rotgut you gave me?' it croaked.

'Purest Elderflower old chap maybe with a tincture of home brew added,' Russ said.

'Oh Christ, I've just come out of rehab. You stupid sods. Do you know who I am?'

'Dirk Thrust, Rock God and pisshead by all accounts. Glass of water?'

'Please.' He sat up and saw the mess on the floor. 'Sorry about that but it's your bloody fault. Now where the hell am I?'

'Blackney Foloren,' Josh said as Russ went into the kitchen for a glass.

'And where the sodding hell is that?'

'Well, here really. Oh sorry yes, Somerset, nearest town Bridgwater, out on the levels.'

Russ came back with the water and passed it over. 'Do we call you Dirk or Mister Thrust?'

'Well as you clearly know who I am, call me Dirk. Christ, I've just remembered. There was a swan, a bright pink one. What the hell was that all about?'

'No idea old chap but you did drive your bloody great car into our duck pond.' Russ said. 'We do get swans around here but they're

The Blackney Swans

all white as far as I know. Sure you weren't, you know, doing some Rock Star drugs or something?'

'No, I told you I was in rehab, I haven't touched booze for months, until you bozos fed me your home brew that is.' Dirk said through mouthfuls of water. 'Hang on, did you say Blackney? I've heard that name before, something to do with my family's past.'

'Can't help you there old chap. Now would you like us to pull that great big car of yours out of the water?' Josh said, trying to change the subject.

'What? Oh yes if you would. I presume you will want money for that?' Dirk said immediately suspicious.

'Well, someone has to pay for a new rug,' Josh said. 'I'm damned if I'm going to try and clean that.'

'Fair enough, now tell me more about the village and I could really do with a large black coffee.'

It was immediately clear to the two men that something they had said had sparked an interest in Dirk's head. They gave him a potted history of the village such as it was. He seemed to get quite animated the more they told him.

Two cups of coffee and one removed rug later, Dirk realised he was wet and the contents of his lunch, which strangely seemed to consist of tomatoes and carrots, neither of which he had eaten for years was down his front. 'I don't suppose you've any dry clothes? Mine are still in the car.'

Josh went off and came back with an old T shirt that actually had belonged to an old girlfriend, a pair of jeans that had seen many a better day and some ancient Wellies. 'Sorry, this is all I have to hand. We'll get your bags out as soon as we can.'

Dirk put them on, feeling somewhat awkward but at least they were dry and relatively clean. He then clearly came to a decision. 'Right, you two I've got some time before my next performance at Glastonbury. Is there anywhere to stay in this backwater? I think I might look around for a few days.'

'Well, we have a pub. You could probably talk the landlady into renting you a room but don't expect any Rock Star treatment. Most people in the village won't have a clue who you are. And there is a village shop where you might get some better temporary clothes, they seem to sell most things.'

The Blackney Swans

Dirk was inclined to be surprised and for some reason annoyed. Being recognised was the bane of his life these days but he sort of always expected it. 'Right, tell me where they are and if you two could drag my car out of its watery grave and recover my bags as well, I would be quite obliged. Oh and here are the car keys.'

They told him how to find the shop and the pub and then set off in search of a certain tractor.

'Do you think we got away with that?' Josh asked.

'What, the swan sighting? No idea but it will be our word against his.'

'As long as Dinsdale stays put.'

'Good point.'

Chapter 4

Cassie Cridge awoke and found that Charles had already left for work. He was so wrapped up in trying to find the residents of Blackney Forloren getting up to no good. He hardly seemed to be home, she thought. But this was alright as she was only really married to him so she could get the inside knowledge about investigations he was involved in.

After her shower, she decided to go for a bike ride and head into Blackney for a little shopping. It was a beautiful morning, the sun was trying to come through the low lying fog that usually consumes parts of Somerset just before a beautiful day. Everything seemed fresh with the early morning countryside smells. After reaching the village, she parked her bike up and walked through the playing field, approaching the church, picking wild flowers as she was going. She was nearing the heart of the village but she still wanted to avoid people as much as possible, they always had questions, sticky beaks. The clean smell was suddenly interrupted from the back of the Black Swan pub, a smell of stale alcohol from the spent kegs waiting to be collected.

She could hear a commotion somewhere nearby, the noises got louder the closer to the corner of the pub she came. She could see a little of the green so peered around and saw the back end of a black limo sticking out of the duck pond with Russ and Josh helping a man who had obviously been driving. She could not make out who he was. She saw them heading to Russ's cottage. She would do her shopping and then come back later to take a look at what was going on.

Cassie arrived back at the cottage just as the man was asking for a black coffee. She crouched down under a window to listen to what they were saying, the man had recently awoken from a stupor due to their 'Elderflower Juice.' Her heart began to race when she heard it was Dirk Thrust, the rock star. She had read that he was headlining

Glastonbury Festival this year in the paper, but never thought she would ever meet him in person.

The sun was getting stronger, the mist had finally dissipated and as predicted, a gorgeous day was beginning. New day, new ideas. She had read of an investment opportunity in the business section of the paper, but on a policeman's salary, there was never much money to play with, but there could be a way that she could get some from a certain person staying at the Black Swan. She had questions going around her head. What were Russ and Josh up to? They were always scheming and what was the deal with a pink swan? Was it code for something?

Cassie would have to make sure that she had a chance meeting with Dirk, where she would be able to be in the same place at the same time. She had also overheard that he was going to stay at the Black Swan. She wondered if they had any job opportunities now that they had a paying guest. She would talk to Charles, as it was very much about time she was taken to the pub for an evening drink.

Morgana was deep in thought. So much had happened over the last couple of weeks that she felt emotionally confused, beset with brain fog, even more than usual and strangely tired and headachey. It was a bit like jet lag, or a hangover, but without the excitement of travel or the enjoyment of alcohol, so she was out for a walk to try to clear her head.

There were all of the revelations about who she was, that moment of real danger. Her heart raced at the memory and of course whatever it was that was going on between her and Josh. She knew she needed to make some decisions about the future, although she had already made one, she was going to keep her new name. Everyone here knew her as Morgana Crowe and it certainly sounded a lot more interesting than Maureen Grey.

As she passed the village pond, she became slowly aware that something was different and dragging her attention back to the present, she noticed that there was a car half submerged in the rather murky water. Now she had seen it, it was hard to ignore, a large black and very expensive looking vehicle, draped with pondweed, splattered with mud and with a couple of ducks sitting on top, one nonchalantly preening and the other fast asleep. Morgana stared at the idyllic rural vision and was just thinking 'Who the hell does that belong to and how did it ....' when she was interrupted.

'Oh, er, hi there.'

It was a tall skinny man with a lot of long hair. He was wearing a slightly odd and rather ill-fitting combination of clothing, jeans which were too baggy and too short, what looked suspiciously like a woman's top and a pair of ancient looking wellies. Morgana regarded him with distaste. Although he looked vaguely familiar. One of the Young Farmers from the recent incident at the pub perhaps?

'Yes?' she said abruptly.

'Do you live around here?' he asked. His accent was a bit strange, Morgana thought, a tinge of slightly fake sounding American. She felt her suspicions aroused and glared at him.

'Why else would I be here? It's not exactly on the tourist trail.'

'Oh, well, sorry,' the man looked embarrassed and a bit confused. 'I was just wondering if that,' he said pointing across the Green. 'Is the only shop around here? I'm a stranger here you see.'

Morgana sighed. 'Yes, it's the only shop for miles but they do sell all kinds of stuff. Depends on what you want, but it's worth giving it a try.'

'Thanks,' and Dirk, for of course it was he, plodded sadly on, the wellies scuffing the ground as he walked. It gave him the air of a rather sulky toddler, not his usual cool image. At least, he thought, no one seems to know who I am around here. He'd have to decide whether it was an advantage to remain incognito or to let these bucolic types know who he was.

Dirk arrived at the shop and peered through the smeary window. A large cat gazed back at him inscrutably. He groaned inwardly. He found cats unsettling and perhaps a bit threatening. He really didn't like them and it seemed to be mutual. With his newfound interest in the more mystical side of life and then the apparition of the pink swan, his exploration in the west country had got off to a rather different start than what he had imagined. Now there was this enormous moggie watching him.

The Blackney Swans

He took a deep breath, opened the shop door and jumped at the loud jangling of the bell just above his head. The cat stood up and did that arched back stretching thing which Dirk particularly disliked. He hoped it would stay put as he walked around looking at the amazing collection of objects displayed haphazardly on shelves, in boxes and stacked on the floor. Georgiana followed him closely, tail waving languidly and sitting next to his leg when he stopped to look at the contents of one of the boxes.

He looked towards the rear of the shop. There was a counter, also covered in an assortment of objects and lurking behind that, two women. They looked identical, even dressed the same. Dirk found this disconcerting too.

'I really must get a grip,' he murmured to himself. 'Been reading too much weird stuff.' He wondered what it was about this place that was getting to him. The village felt strangely familiar but not in a particularly pleasant way.

Daisy and Violet watched their new customer with interest. Then he looked in their direction and approached the counter. Violet expected Daisy to do her usual 'Can I help you routine?' politely or not depending on who it was and what mood she was in that day. This time however, she just stood there, staring at the customer as if she'd seen a ghost.

Dirk had found some of the things he needed, some toiletries, socks, a couple of men's shirts and some flip-flops. He'd hoped to find some shoes and jeans or trousers but these would have to do for now.

'I'll take these please,' he said. 'But I couldn't see a price on them.'

Daisy still stood unmoving and silent, her mouth slightly open. Violet nudged her, but it had no effect. Crossly, she muttered a price, which Dirk couldn't hear.

Good grief, he thought, what is wrong with these people? 'What was that, I couldn't hear you?' he said loudly and very slowly.

Violet shouted the price and then, having shocked herself, quickly put her hand over her mouth. Then, she felt herself smiling. Shouting like that had been rather liberating, even fun.

'Sorry,' she said in a normal voice. 'That came out louder than intended. Here, let me find a bag for those things for you.'

Dirk handed over some money, Violet thanked him, gave him change and smiled at him pleasantly.

'Haven't seen you around here before, are you on holiday in the area?'

Dirk responded to her friendly manner with some relief. At least one person around here seemed normal.

'Just here for a while.'

'Well, enjoy your visit, pop in any time.' She stroked Georgiana who was now up on the counter purring and trying to look loveable.

Dirk raised a hand in farewell and escaped.

Daisy hadn't moved and appeared to be in some kind of state of shock.

'Are you OK? What happened? Was it something about that man? I thought he seemed very nice, looked a bit familiar somehow? And it was really strange because I didn't mind talking to him.' Violet looked at her sister, puzzled and concerned about her but also a little bit proud of herself and how she had dealt with the emergency.

'I recognised him,' said Daisy. 'I remember him and you should too.'

Chapter 5

Cassie was hidden by clothes racks in the store, listening to Violet and Daisy talking about the new visitor to the village, but it seemed not a new visitor after all, someone who had escaped and chose to return. She would have to discover more about Dirk, as this could be something she could use to emotionally blackmail him into helping her invest in the land opportunity she had seen. She tried to get closer but only succeeded in moving a clothes hanger that scraped on the rail, making an awful noise. She looked up and saw the sisters staring at her, wondering how long she had been standing there.

Cassie smiled at them saying, 'you've got some nice stuff in here.' They tentatively smiled back as Cassie left the store. She needed to get back home to see if the people were available now, to talk about the land, she could almost see the future, a housing development, with the sale of plots to a developer to build, she could make a huge amount of money.

As she was cycling back, she recalled all she had seen and heard that morning. She was thinking of the Pink Swan, maybe it's not code, maybe it's what they have called their Elderflower Juice, Pink Swan Elderflower Juice, had a nice ring to it. She thought. But it's moonshine. What if they are selling it at the Black Swan? I bet Janet is making a killing from it when the Young Farmers come in after a busy day. Cassie wondered if her husband knew anything about it. She would have to mention it when he got home, if nothing else it would sow the seed in his mind, which would no doubt instigate a night out for the two of them, just so he could take a look for himself. Charles would be intrigued about the limo in the duck pond too, she had so much to talk about when he finally came home.

She was a bit tired when she finally sat down at her kitchen table with a cup of coffee, she was looking through the paper looking for the advert about the land for sale. 'Ah here it is,' she said to herself with an air of excitement. She picked up the phone and

The Blackney Swans

dialled the number, it seemed to ring for ages but eventually an answer machine kicked in, so she left her details and told the machine to only call during the day and on weekdays. She had to be sure that Charles did not answer, she wanted her potential windfall to be a secret. After making the call and drinking her coffee, she still felt tired so went upstairs to take a nap before getting the dinner ready.

She lay there for what seemed an age, she couldn't sleep as her mind was turning over and over, it was too busy to shut down. Just then, the phone started to ring downstairs. She jumped up and ran down to answer it.

Ten minutes later the plan was firming up

She replaced the receiver. She was glad she had a response so she could think about how much she could get out of Dirk now she had something on him and a possible way of getting Charles to take her to the pub.

It was late afternoon and Cassie was starting to prepare dinner, marinated steak and potatoes tonight, something simple. She heard the keys in the door echoing down the flagstone hallway. Charles was home early for once. He came up behind her, put his arms around her waist and kissed her head.

'How was your day?' Charles asked lovingly.

'Yes, not bad really, found out some juicy gossip from the village this morning,' she replied with an air of mystery.

'Oh yes, tell me more,' he asked.

She told him all about the black limo in the duck pond, the new temporary resident and finished with Russ and Josh's 'Pink Swan Elderflower Juice' and that Janet may be selling it in the pub. At this, Charles put down the newspaper he was reading and looked at her.

'What did you just say?

'I said, Russ and Josh's moonshine is called Pink Swan, Janet must be selling it under the counter to the Young Farmers,' she added.

'Well, we'll see about that, it's been a long time since we have had a night out, fancy going to the Mucky Duck for a G and T?' he said, looking like the cat that got the cream.

'Oh really, what a great idea Charles, when, tonight?' She asked as if it was not her plan all along.

'Well, no point in letting it sell out and it get called something different,' he stated sharply.

'Oh, yes I can see your point, yes of course,' she said as she smiled at the marinated steak.

Chapter 6

Russ and Josh found their tractor. It belonged to Gerald a local farmer. He didn't use it much as there was little land to plough around Blackney. A promise of a barrel of Elderflower had sealed the deal and Gerald even offered to drive it for them, which was gratefully received as neither men had a clue how to.

On the walk over, the two men had been chatting about opportunities.

'I've got an idea,' Russ said.

'You always have ideas,' Josh replied. 'And I have it on good authority that some even work sometimes and don't land us in the crap.'

'Thanks for that, anyway this Thrust chappie, what does he do?'

'Well, you said he sings songs, must have been doing it a while because he looks a bit of a worn out wreck.'

'That's the Rock God look these days. But why does he sing songs?'

'I dunno, because he likes to?'

'For God's sake Josh, what are we going to drag out of the pond?'

'A bloody great expensive Limo.'

Russ reckoned he could actually see the tumblers dropping as the gears ground around in Josh's head. 'He sings because he makes money?'

'Give the man a banana. Yes, he makes money, lots and lots of it. Great piles of it. Shining mountains of the stuff. And we can tap into that because, as I said, I have had an Idea.'

'Go on then,'

'Well, he makes his money from people either paying to buy his music or actually coming to watch him and his band play live and what happens every summer solstice in Blackney?'

Josh thought for a second and then the penny dropped. 'You mean get him to come along with the Blackney Junior School

The Blackney Swans

Recorder Group and the Young Farmer's Ukulele band? Not sure he would be up for that. We only go as it's a good time to sell hooch.'

'Yes but think of the crowds of people who would come if he was there with his band. Think of the opportunities to sell tickets and more burgers and all sorts of things.'

'Alright but how do we talk him into that?'

'Leave that to me. He seems pretty taken with the village and is staying for a few days, I'm sure we can come up with something. Once we've talked him into it, we will have a licence to print money. What could possibly go wrong?'

Assorted inhabitants of the village had begun to drift towards the pond, their curiosity aroused by the presence of the limousine sitting in it and a few minutes ago, the arrival of a tractor. Russ and Josh had supervised the attachment of various chains and hooks to the underneath of the car, giving strict instructions to the tractor driver not to damage it. The onlookers, all experts in such matters presumably, were offering helpful advice and one or two had even brought folding chairs to sit on.

Morgana had heard the noise from her cottage and now ambled over to join Josh and Russ, who were standing supervising the slow emergence of the dripping vehicle.

'Where on earth did that come from? And of course, I'd have known you two would be involved in some way.' Morgana laughed.

'We're just helping a stranger in trouble,' said Russ, with a look of total innocence.

'Well, it's certainly drawn a crowd, nearest thing we've had around here to the Raising of the Mary Rose a few years back. I'm surprised you're not selling tickets.' Morgana followed that with giving Josh a little dig in the ribs, to which he responded by grabbing her and trying to tickle her.

'Oh for goodness sake you two,' Russ sighed.

'Who's Mary Rose?' asked Josh, brow wrinkled.

'Not who, what,' said Morgana. 'It was a ship built for .....oh never mind, I can't face it. You really do live in your own world, don't you?'

The Blackney Swans

She reflected on how different she and Josh were. She had become very fond of him but he had never *been* anywhere. In her former life, she'd lived in a city, travelled a bit, been to big music concerts. At that point, a realisation dawned on her. The big car, the oddly familiar stranger who'd spoken to her! She knew who it was. Dirk Thrust! She'd had a poster of him on her wall, looking a great deal younger and much more glamorous. She had even bought several of his records.

She turned to Josh. 'Am I right in thinking this car belongs to Dirk Thrust? He's actually here, in Blackney?'

'Oh, yeah, Russ said he was famous, but I've never heard of him. We rescued him.'

'I see,' said Morgana slowly. 'Can you introduce me then?' She smiled, linked her arm in his and looked up at him persuasively.

'I suppose so. Can't think why you'd want to meet him, but if you want, why not?' Josh shrugged.

Hearing this exchange, Russ looked thoughtfully at Morgana but said nothing.

Chapter 7

Meanwhile, in the Village Shop, Violet and Daisy were watching the goings on through the window.

Daisy said quietly, 'We need to talk about earlier, that stranger.'

'Yes,' said Violet, 'It was so odd. I talked and you didn't! But it seemed OK somehow.' She sounded puzzled.

'You didn't recognise him then?'

Violet shook her head.

'Well, I did. Remember when we were at college, having fun, going to concerts, we chatted to everyone, real party girls? Before everything changed?' Daisy looked at Violet, waiting for her to remember, to realise.

'You mean when I had Zack and Mum and Dad were furious, and my life fell apart.' Suddenly Violet buried her face in her hands. 'That man, was he….?' her voice faltered.

'Yes, I'm pretty sure that was Dirk Thrust. That's why I was lost for words and you thought he looked familiar. He certainly would be to you. You had such a crush on him, you even liked that ridiculous name of his and when we hung around and finally got backstage after that concert. Well I did warn you. And it was my life that fell apart too, trying to look after you.'

'But they'd only let one of us in backstage and you went off in a huff. You've been in one ever since really.'

Both sisters fell silent and glared at each other.

'I never understood why you were so naïve,' said Daisy. 'You were at first, anyway.'

'And I never understood how you knew so much but didn't tell me what I actually needed to know. You just vaguely told me to be careful.' Violet was pink with anger.

They hadn't spoken of this for so long, almost afraid to disturb the truce. Violet of course, had coped by retreating into fear of people and not speaking to them at all. But now this man had appeared out of the blue and they were again confronted with the reality of the past, the upset, the shame and the anger.

'And then, there was no stopping you, was there?' Daisy said, also pink and angry. 'After your very brief encounter with Mr Thrust.' She almost spat out the name. 'You had so many little flings that when you found you were expecting, you didn't know whose it was.'

'I was so hurt and upset, I thought Dirk really loved me and we'd be together forever. I suppose the other boys were to take my mind off him and make me feel that someone still wanted me.'

Violet was becoming tearful. Daisy relented, as she always did and being the older, even if only by thirty minutes and more sensible sister, she put her arms around her and said softly, as she always had, 'It's OK, it will all be fine, don't worry. We'll stick together and deal with whatever happens.'

From the vantage point of her bedroom window, Janet watched as the crowd around the duckpond grew. She'd already seen someone looking remarkably like Dirk crossing the green to the shop and she'd wondered if the rumours were true and he really had fathered a baby on shrinking Violet all those years ago. Nobody was supposed to know about it, of course, but there'd been talk at the time even if it was something that never got mentioned now.

What was the man doing in the village? He surely hadn't come to see her. She doubted his mum would have ever told him where she spent her childhood. Only too glad to leave the Swan at Blackney behind. It had almost broken Dad's heart at the time.

Janet must have been about ten when her Auntie Lizzie dropped the bombshell. It was one evening, just before opening time. She'd announced that firstly, she was now engaged to be married to a Thrust from over to Street. Secondly, that she'd be leaving immediately to live with her fiancé's family until the wedding, because they didn't want her working behind a bar any more. And thirdly and finally, that she'd be grateful if everyone in the family would call her Elizabeth in future.

It was all Dad could talk about for weeks, especially when he'd had a few.

'And would you believe it?' he'd say to anyone who'd listen, 'She only had her bag already packed. It turned out the fiancé, young Robin Thrust, was waiting outside in his sports car and off she went, there and then.'

Even years later, when Janet was a teenager, Dad would still moan on about the Thrusts, and how they thought they were so grand when everyone knew that back along the family were common or garden thrusters, pig-stickers hiring themselves out to whoever'd pay them to look after the swine.

'Good honest trade, thrusting,' he said. 'Nothing wrong with being a thruster, or a grinter come to that. Only there's not much call for either of us now. Nothing to be ashamed of, though. And yes, those Thrusters struck lucky and went into the meat canning business and changed their name by deed poll and made a few bob. But you won't catch me calling my little sister Elizabeth. And I never want her name mentioned in this house again.'

Which was ironic, when you thought about it, seeing that he was the only one who ever brought up the subject.

More recently though, once Dirk's singing career had begun to take off, Janet realised who he was and had kept up with his doings, though she never told anyone they were related. She'd read in the papers about his success and his problems with alcohol. She'd heard the customers talking about how he was on the wagon now and would be performing at the festival over at Glastonbury this summer. Not her sort of music, but the kids liked it.

Sometimes she'd even thought about coming out with it when the kids went on about his success. 'He's my cousin, that Dirk Thrust, you know, on my father's side.'

But then she'd remember how his mother had denied her own as if they were trash. Who'd want to be associated with that kind of behaviour? Mind you, if that big black car in the pond was his, as everyone was saying, you had to wonder what he was doing driving around out here on his own. Might he even be wanting to discover his real roots?

The Blackney Swans

Some of the crowd around the pond were beginning to drift over towards the pub. She'd better get back downstairs and see if she could find out if anyone knew anything.

Chapter 8

Later that day, Lesley the witch had scattered salt crystals around the perimeter and settled herself on her circular rug. She had made it herself from a kit, it depicted a circle of swans on a blue background. She asked the great entities to guide and protect her, regulated her breathing into a relaxed rhythm and opened her mind.

At first, she saw nothing very much, hazy, then mist coming off water, clearing to two pink lines with red bumps halfway up, she couldn't work out what it was. Then an eye, yellow, looking straight at her but the head it was in seemed the wrong way up, and pink.

'Hello,' she whispered, have you come to tell me something?' Still not understanding what she was seeing. She tried very hard not to think, in case she led the visions and made something of them herself instead of waiting for it to be revealed to her.

She heard a whole lot of honking and 'Geese' popped into her head, Curiouser and curiouser and then BAM it hit her, of course, Alice in Wonderland, the pink upside down head and red knees belonged to a flamingo. The pink feather she had found that morning near the pond must have come from a flamingo of course but what on earth was a flamingo doing in Blackney Forloren? Would St Cygnus be displeased to share the village with a flamingo? If it stays here, it will need a mate, but where could it have come from?

Too excited to continue with any meditation, her mind buzzing with possibilities, Lesley quickly thanked the great entities for their amazing insight, closed her circle, grounded herself and rushed off to investigate the village pond for further signs of more pink feathers. Seeing lots of people going into the Black Swan, she followed, curiouser, and curiouser herself.

Word was seeping around every nook and cranny of the village that there were exciting developments afoot. An expensive limousine had been extracted from the pond by the chaps with the not so secret still, and a very oddly dressed, aged rocker was taking up residence, albeit temporarily, in the Black Swan.

The Blackney Swans

Thus it was that the pub was getting full, everyone pretending to mind their own business but actually minding everyone else's.

Lesley, was excited, thinking that the feather was a sign and wondered if the change in colour was a first stage of metamorphosis into a half human, half supernatural being. She decided to meditate on it by the pond and wondered if she should use a bit of tie-dye colour on her group's stock of feathers and costumes, or would that offend St Cygnus?

After sitting a while meditating by the pond and watching what was going on at the pub, she scouted around the pond and church yard for more evidence but wandered home empty handed and musing to herself. Where would a flamingo come from if not a miracle? She had no idea, she needed to find someone who would know and resolved to write via the BBC to the famous naturalist Sir Peter Scott. He would know. They could forward the question to him. She liked his wildlife programmes. Yes that's what she would do, straight away and put it in the early post.

Twenty minutes later, the pub was full and the bar was awash with gossip.

'There's them says he's fallen off the wagon,' said one customer. 'Muttering on about seeing a pink swan and getting such a shock he drove his car into the pond.'

'So how come it's Russ and Josh first on the scene and organising a tractor?' said someone else. 'I wouldn't trust either of them two. They're up to something, you mark my words. Wouldn't trust them further than I could throw them. Have you heard what people have been saying about …'

'That's quite enough tittle-tattle,' Janet interrupted. 'You going to buy another drink or what?'

'Just a half this time. Ought to be getting back to work.'

The conversation had died almost to nothing when the door swung open to reveal a long-haired middle-aged figure in a grubby T-shirt, scruffy trousers and wellies, clutching a carrier bag. Ignoring

The Blackney Swans

the stares of the customers, he came straight over to the bar and leaned across it.

'I'm told you might have a room I could take,' he said to Janet. A waft of something met her nostrils, something suspiciously like Russ and Josh's elderflower spirit.

She smiled. 'I'm sure I can fit you in. How long would you be wanting to stay?'

'Definitely tonight,' he said. 'And after that it depends.'

He didn't offer any explanation as to what it depended on, and Janet didn't ask. It was him all right, Lizzie's boy. And if what everyone said was right then he was rolling in it. He might like to make a contribution to her pension in return for her keeping quiet about the connection, not to mention what she'd smelled on his breath.

She smiled. 'As it happens, I do have a space at the moment. Not en suite, I'm afraid, but the bathroom's at the end of the passage. Is that all your luggage?'

'For the time being, till I rescue my case from the car. I don't suppose you'd be able to do some washing for me?'

Janet smiled again. 'I'm sure I can arrange something,' she said. 'For a consideration. Will you be wanting lunch?'

At the thought of food, Dirk's stomach heaved. Whatever those two chancers put in their hooch it packed a powerful punch.

He dredged up a smirk. 'Not just at the moment,' he said. 'Perhaps you could show me the way to the room.'

At two o'clock closing time, Janet chased the stragglers out of the bar and locked the door. She tiptoed upstairs and gently opened the door to Dirk's room. He was splayed on the bed, flat on his back and fast asleep. He looked as if he'd be there some while. She reckoned she'd have plenty of time to get over to the shop before he woke up.

As she let herself out of the back and started across the green, Lucifer joined her. She wondered whether she should take him home and lock him in. He was always hanging around the moggy at the shop. Virginia, was it? No, Georgiana, for heaven's sake. What sort of a name was that for a cat? Those twins thought they were so grand, but she knew better. No, let him come too.

By now the crowd round the pond had cleared, the car had been towed away and there was no sign of either Russ or Josh. She'd have to speak to them soon and find out what Dirk had told them. She also wanted to check out what people had been saying about a pink swan being seen on the road.

What was it Violet had called her boy? Zack, that was it. Janet hadn't thought about him in years, poor little mite. Born out of wedlock and to a girl who couldn't wait to give him away. Well, the Coombes sisters wouldn't be looking down their noses at her any more.

Chapter 9

Morgana was a bit of a groupie when she was younger and used to drag Sam along to Concerts. Sam wasn't very keen on going but safety in numbers, their mum always said, so she went. The safety in numbers hadn't really worked out because Sam ended up with a posh boy who turned into a suave insider dealer currently in jail, while Morgana was footloose and fancy free. Well, they both were really since the bad guys who had forced them to hide at Blackney, were also in jail. Hence, now that Dirk has turned up in the village and Morgana has been enlightened by Josh, she was keen to be nosy. She tried to involve Sam and Tolly in a night at the pub.

'No thanks,' said Sam, putting both her hands up to protect herself from further entreaties and Constance just thought he was a naff old rocker and pretty disgusting.

'Josh and Russ won't have time to sit with me because they are obviously up to something, involving their hooch and a money making project. Morgana said.' So they were eventually persuaded to go with her for a drink to find out what is going on.

The Vicar and Sally used to be keen music scene aficionados, both sets of parents had dreams of San Francisco but settled for the Isle of Wight, smoked a bit of pot, depending on your idea of a bit, and wore flowers in their long hair. They wore hippy, flamboyant, floaty clothes and at times when they were 'far out' wore not a lot. They avoided psychedelic visions but they were fairly open minded considering their ecclesiastical turn.

Sally grew up listening to her mum singing Joan Baez's 'There but for fortune,' 'Plaisir d'amour' and Bob Dylan songs. Her dad, the Animals 'House of the rising sun' and Procul Harem's 'Whiter Shade of Pale,' even Lonnie Donegan's 'Stewball' and remembered Dirk and the Pistols.

But as is often the case, although a bit liberal in their own space, they became more establishment and mainstream as time wore on.

The Blackney Swans

Mrs Thing had relayed the news to Sally, who only vaguely remembered him, while Mrs Thing hadn't the faintest idea who he was and why everyone was making a fuss.

'Give me Matt Munro any day of the week,' she sighed. 'This one's off his head going on about pink swans and Arthurian legends, still it'll be worth a port and lime to eavesdrop in the Black Swan, so are you coming Sally?'

'I think so Thingy, I'm sure I can persuade the Vicar to walk us down.' She replied with both eyebrows raised.

Jonty and Tom Bullock were not star struck either, though Tom mentioned he was interested in the idea of a pink swan, what it might taste like and thought it would be spectacular in a glass case. The more he thought about it, the more he suspected Russ and Josh were up to something, so they had best go and keep an eye open in the pub tonight.

Unlike, apparently, most of the population of Blackney, Daisy and Violet decided not to go to the pub that evening. They were both feeling a bit shaken up by their encounter with Dirk and their conversation following it so by unspoken agreement they stayed upstairs in their flat above the shop.

Violet sat near the window, lurking behind the net curtain so she could see what was going on, without being seen. She gave a running commentary on who she saw coming and going. Daisy, ensconced in her favourite armchair on the other side of the room, kept sighing and fidgeting. Eventually, she threw down the book she was pretending to read and said, 'for goodness sake Violet, will you stop that, it's really annoying. I know you're just hoping to catch a glimpse of that man again.'

They had now heard on the village grapevine that it definitely was Dirk Thrust but at the moment Daisy couldn't bear to say his name. After a few minutes of thought, she made a decision.

'Okay, come and sit down over here. We need to talk. We have to work out how we are going to deal with this.'

The Blackney Swans

'What do you mean?' said Violet rather crossly. 'I don't think he recognised us and no one in the village knows about Zack. Surely all we need to do is keep quiet, which I'm rather good at,' and she gave a little laugh at her own uncharacteristic joke. 'And of course, we can avoid him as much as possible and if we do see him, just behave as if we've never met. He's probably only going to be here for a day or two until his car's fixed.'

'Do you really think that will work? You know that lot out there,' said Daisy, jerking her head in the direction of the window, 'will be turning his presence here into a three ring circus. They'll either be behaving like idiotic fans, all over him like a rash, or trying to find a way of cashing in, which will mean delaying the car repair as long as possible.' Daisy sighed again.

'Well, what do you suggest we do then? Invite him round for tea, tell him everything and show him a few snaps of Zack, so he can see....' Violet's voice tailed off. 'Oh,' she said quietly, the sarcastic look fading from her face.

'What?' asked Daisy, anxiously.

'I've just realised something, seeing Dirk again after all this time. You know you used to make comments about not knowing who Zack's father might be and I went along with that because I was too ashamed and embarrassed about how I behaved to even think about it? Well, now I know for sure. Did you notice Dirk's face, his chin, that deep dimple? I'd forgotten about that over the years, but Zack has one exactly the same. And the same eye colour. Now that Zack's grown up, you can see the resemblance. Dirk must be Zack's father.'

'I think you're right.' Daisy fell silent for a moment. 'So maybe we should do as you suggested, say nothing, keep out of the way even more than usual and hope that he's not here for very long. Let's give that a try anyway. And I'll make sure that Zack doesn't come anywhere near Blackney. He rarely does anyway, especially as he thinks we're just a couple of eccentric friends of his parents who are useful for buying some of his less attractive stock. Thank goodness his market stall is in Bridgwater.'

'All right, agreed,' said Violet quietly. 'I'll put the kettle on, I think we could do with a cup of tea.' She went into the kitchen, her head full of disturbing thoughts.

The Blackney Swans

She was followed by Georgiana, who meowed and twined helpfully around Violet's legs as she went to get cups out of the cupboard. Violet bent and stroked her. 'You can't be hungry again, I've fed you. No wonder you're getting a bit tubby around the middle.' She looked at the cat thoughtfully and as she went back into the sitting room with the tea said. 'Daisy, do you think Georgiana's getting a bit fat? We'd better keep an eye on her I think.'

'Ok, but that's the least of our worries at the moment,' laughed Daisy.

Chapter 10

Janet had never seen her pub so busy, not even when the annual mouse racing was underway. All the regulars, all the Young Farmers and quite a few people she barely recognised were there waiting for her to open up. Dirk had yet to put in an appearance but she expected him soon. As soon as she had the thought, the door at the back of the bar opened and in walked the Rock God and this time he looked the part. Skinny jeans with cowboy boots below and a tye dyed t-shirt above. His long hair had been combed and reached down to his shoulders. Nobody in the room appeared to notice, except that of course they were all staring as surreptitiously as they could. Dirk came over to the bar, the crowd parting as if Moses was there.

'What can I get you?' she asked as he came up.

It was clear that he was having an internal debate about the answer to that. After some hesitation, he looked at the beer handles and pointed to one, so she pulled him a pint. As he turned around and took a pull at the beer there was an almost sub audible sigh from everyone. Dirk didn't seem to notice.

Russ and Josh had been waiting for just that moment. If they left it too long and the ice melted, the poor man would no doubt be inundated with questions and autograph requests.

'So Dirk,' Russ said. 'Your car is fine. I had a local mechanic come over and check it out. But I have a proposal. Why don't we forget about any bills for recovering it? We know you will be starring at Glastonbury soon but how about a warm up here? The Blackney music festival takes place on mid summers eve. It's quite ancient. Records show it's been held for hundreds of years maybe even more. Some local music to start with and then you and your chaps to finish the evening off.'

Dirk looked shrewdly at Russ. 'And no doubt you two chaps will be involved in managing the whole thing?'

'Yes and why not? It's what we do around here and you would be in good hands.'

The Blackney Swans

Before Dirk could answer, the main door opened and in walked Charles Cridge and his wife. This time the sigh that went around the room was definitely audible. If the Cridges heard it, they took no notice. Cassie was mainly ignored and slowly made her way through the crowd to be in an ambush position as soon as Russ and Josh left and gave her the opportunity she wanted.

All eyes followed Charles as he made his way to the bar. Even Dirk seemed to catch the mood and stayed quiet.

'Evening Janet,' Cridge said in what he hoped was a convivial tone. 'Looks busy tonight.'

'What can I get you Charles?' Janet asked, ignoring his statement.

'I hear you've got some celebrity staying. I guess that's him over there? The hairy scruffy one?'

Janet bit her tongue, ignoring the remark. 'What do you want to drink Charles?' She repeated.

He looked back at her and said deliberately in quite a loud voice. 'What I would really like is a large glass of Pink Swan.'

'Janet looked non plussed. 'We've got Tribute, Doom Bar and that local stuff from Bridgwater, charmingly called Bat's Piss but no Swan I'm afraid.'

'Oh come on, Janet I know all about it. Just give me some Pink Swan.' Cridge demanded in an even louder voice that cut through the conversation in the pub, which having restarted, immediately stopped.

Dirk had clearly heard what was said and immediately headed over to the bar.

'What did you say about Pink Swans?' he asked Cridge. Maybe he would at last get some sort of answer about what he was sure he had seen.

'What's it to you?' Cridge replied, clearly annoyed at being interrupted.

'Well, I saw one and ended up crashing my car into the duck pond.' Dirk replied.

'What? You were drunk and crashed your car. I'll have you know I'm a policeman. That's a very serious thing to admit.'

'No, I wasn't drunk, I don't drink, er, well not until later. No, I saw one.'

'Eh? What are you talking about? How can you see a drink?'

The Blackney Swans

Dirk was getting more and more confused and also starting to get angry. This idiot didn't seem to be able to understand simple English.

'I didn't see a drink, you idiot, I saw a Pink Swan and swerved to avoid it.'

By now Cridge was also getting worked up, his simple plan to wrong foot Janet into admitting she was selling moonshine was clearly failing and now he was having a surreal conversation with this moron. He decided on one last attempt to get to the bottom of what was going on and turned back to Janet.

'Come on Janet, I know what Pink Swan is. Come clean or I'll be here tomorrow with a whole team.'

Dirk did not like being ignored and put his hand on Cridge's shoulder. 'Hey you, I was talking to you, don't you bloody well turn your back on me.'

Cridge spun around, shaking off Dirk's hand. 'I'll deal with you in a minute. Just because you are some sort of music star doesn't entitle you to flout the law.'

Russ, Josh and Pete Sturrock had been watching the exchange with fascination. Once again Cridge was making a complete idiot of himself but now it looked like it could get ugly. The last thing Russ needed was Dirk being upset.

The three men surrounded Cridge. 'You on duty then Mister Cridge?' Pete asked.

Cridge looked at the three of them. 'Not tonight but the law never sleeps.'

Russ burst out laughing. 'If you're not on duty then you have no police authority.' And turning to Janet. 'Is this customer bothering you Janet?'

'Too bloody right. I've no idea what he is wittering on about and he's upsetting my most important customer. I don't suppose you could deal with him?'

'In the traditional Blackney Foloren manner?' Josh asked.

'If you wouldn't mind,' Janet replied with a wicked grin.

'What?' Cridge said in alarm. 'You wouldn't. I'm a policeman.'

'Not tonight you aren't,' Pete said. He and Josh picked Cridge up by the arms and lifted him bodily off the ground. Russ opened the door and then helped the other two take the protesting man outside.

The Blackney Swans

The door closed and a complete hush descended over the pub. Dirk was about to say something but Janet put her finger to her lips.

A few seconds later there was a distant cry and the sound of a large splash. A cheer went up as the three men came back in.

'Sorry about that Dirk,' Russ said. 'Now where were we?'

Cassie was furious. There was no way she could approach Dirk now. She stormed out of the pub, took one look at her wet husband climbing out of the village pond and got in her car. As she drove away, she wound down her window. 'You can bloody well walk home,' she shouted.

Chapter 11

Later on, Morgana and Josh were having a Conversation.

'I was not flirting with him.'

'Well, it looked like it to me. You had a really silly grin on your face when I introduced you and he said that Morgana was a wonderful name.' Josh looked decidedly fed up.

'Ah, that's because Dirk's researching Arthurian legend, especially as it's all centred around this part of the country,' explained Morgana. 'In fact, he asked me if there was a special reason why that's my name and if I was connected in some way with the stories.' She gave a rather superior smile. 'So maybe he was genuinely interested in me.'

'You didn't tell him it's not your real name and that you've only lived here for a short time though, did you?' said Josh crossly. 'That might've dampened his enthusiasm a bit. And how do you know he's into all that King Arthur rubbish anyway?'

'I overheard him talking to someone else about it and it's not rubbish, it's part of our mystical local history. As for not telling him about changing my name, that's my private personal history and anyway, I'm making the change permanent. Maureen Grey no longer exists as far as I'm concerned. Well, except for my red hair, it's such a relief not to be wearing that wig. Also, I may not have been born here but I feel it's where I belong. When I was finding a special place to begin my new life something drew me here.'

Josh looked at Morgana suspiciously. 'Oh no, you're not going all mystical on me are you? Or is it just so you keep him,' stabbing a finger in Dirk's direction, 'interested in you?'

'Don't be so small-minded,' hissed Morgana. 'You're just jealous.'

'I am not jealous of that, that …' Josh had turned very red in the face and his voice was getting louder.

'Keep your voice down. You are behaving like an idiot and I'm not listening to any more of this,' and Morgana turned her back on

Josh and threaded her way across the pub to where Dirk was surrounded by admirers.

'Excuse me,' she said, pushing her way through. 'Dirk, just letting you know I have to go now but if you need any competent assistance with your historical research, I'd be glad to help. I live in Cobweb Cottage, just across the Village Green. Bye for now.'

As Morgana left, she glanced back at Josh standing on his own, looking like a dog which had been kicked by its owner. She felt a little glimmer of compassion, but soon got over it.

It had been a day like no other Janet could remember, and as the pub clock crept towards midnight she perched on a stool at the back of the bar and slipped off her shoes.

Perhaps she should have thought twice before agreeing to any kind of lock-in but Russ and Pete Sturrock from the Young Farmers had been very persuasive.

'You're going to make a fortune,' Russ said. 'Word spreads fast when someone like Dirk winds up staying in your spare room. Once you've officially closed, me and Josh can supply small quantities of the very same elderflower cordial with which we revived the great man. They'll get a chance to shake his hand and maybe get him to sing. A lot of fun will be had by all.'

'And twelve o'clock is fine,' added Pete. 'You don't need an all-nighter. Most of them'll be half asleep and gone home to their beds by eleven in any case.'

But Pete hadn't reckoned on the different responses to the cordial in the drinkers. Some got very merry almost immediately. There had indeed been singing and dancing, and several semi-conscious bodies slumped in their seats well before eleven. Janet didn't dare go and check what condition the Gents was in.

She had looked around to tackle Pete about it. He was already on his way over. He'd been keeping an eye, he said, and he'd noticed what was going on.

'I don't want to fall out with you,' Pete said. 'Dirk's unexpected visit, just before Glastonbury and everything, that's one thing. But

The Blackney Swans

the Swan's been the Bridgwater Farmers' favourite pub for years and there's no way I'm risking a ban. I'll make sure they get taken home. Or at least sleep it off somewhere else.'

And he'd been as good as his word. He had some control over the lads. When the clock struck, there wasn't going to be any difficulty emptying the bar

As the last calls of 'Night, Janet,' and 'Nice one, Janet,' echoed across to her, she put her shoes back on and locked and bolted the door. She watched Dirk go up the stairs, turned off the lights and let herself out to her quiet spot behind the skittle alley for a last cig before bed.

What an evening! Around six there'd been faces here you only normally saw at the WI or at church. Even the Vicar showed up. He'd had a good look round before he sat down at the bar, with his back to Dirk, and ordered a port and lemon.

After a sip at his drink, he leaned across to her and said, 'I won't stay long. There's a shepherd's pie in the aga. Is that him, then, in the corner?'

And when Janet said, 'Yes,' he went on. 'I wonder if you'd be so good as to introduce us. He's bound to be interested in my researches. I've heard on the grapevine that he's looking for his roots. So I spent an hour in the library at the Vicarage this afternoon and I think I may have found his family crest among my heraldry books. Not to mention what I might be able to unearth from the rest of the shelves. I have access to written references as far back as the Domesday Book, you know. You'd be doing him a service.'

Probably after an autograph for one of the grandchildren or a contribution to the church roof fund, Janet had thought. But she'd come round and pushed a way for the rev to get to his quarry.

'Let the Vicar through, folks. Show a little respect.'

And Dirk had smiled at him and nodded and seemed to be pleased to see him. He'd been doing that a lot, all evening, as if he were enjoying being there and meeting the locals. She wondered why. He had to be after something.

As she sat there, Lucifer scrambled over the wall. 'Where have you been, you devil? As if I don't know.'

She threw away the cigarette butt, picked him up and began to stroke him. 'There'll be no prowling about upstairs for you, tonight,' she said. 'We've got a guest and we don't want him upset. The

Vicar's not the only one around here with proof of this and that. My auntie Lizzy's birth certificate is still in the desk where Dad left it. And I dare say there are marriage records at county hall with her maiden name on. If cousin Dirk's so interested in where he came from, he might like to buy a share in the family business. Or even take it over entirely. For a consideration. A nice little pension pot. I'd be able to take early retirement.'

Dirk finally managed to retreat to his room at half past twelve, wondering if the opening hours would still have been so flexible if the pompous copper had not been removed. His escape was fraught with peril, especially as many of the ladies present and even some of the men felt that only a thorough kissing could demonstrate how pleased they were to meet him.

The room Janet had allocated him had been described as the best in the house and the epitome of luxury and style, but the only aspect which seemed to Dirk at all luxurious was the price quoted. Not even an en suite, he thought, turning a slow circle on the bedroom rug. Heavy drapes, not quite meeting in the middle, a dog eared armchair, and a double bed, which Dirk investigated and found to be furnished with sheets and blankets topped by a very grubby eiderdown. Notable was the smell of damp and black mould climbed the floral wallpaper in all corners.

He turned off the central light and flopped onto the bed fully dressed. He propped his cowboy boots on the end of the bed and stared into the blackness. Yes, he had been recognised, courted and feted for his celebrity status, but as many locals as had identified him had not, but gaped at him blankly before asking if he came from Marsh End. Dirk was in the habit of sighing and rolling his eyes over the crowds of screaming women who met him wherever he went, but after years of adulation, he had rather come to expect it and to be blanked was not to his taste.

He mused on Josh's idea for him to bring the band and perform at the village festival. Not a bad idea to have a warm up for Glasto and what better way of establishing his status for the doubters. He'd

The Blackney Swans

have those sisters from the village shop who cold shouldered him mobbing him with the rest. The plan would also give him longer to investigate Blackney Forloren. Intriguing hints of magic and mystery drew him to the place, rumours of witchcraft abounded and even this forthcoming Festival was excitingly pagan. And of course, he'd seen that pink swan with his own eyes, and that was before they fed him that elderflower hooch.

The thought of hooch drew his attention to the slow circling of his visual field in the gloom and the more energetic unrest from his stomach. How many had he had tonight? Best get some rest.

Chapter 12

The next day

Unlike, apparently, most of the rest of the population of Blackney, as they had agreed, Daisy and Violet had avoided the goings on at the pub but they were only too aware of the curiosity generated by Dirk's presence. They had heard snatches of over-excited conversation and learned that he was, unfortunately, planning to stay for a while.

'It's no good Violet,' said Daisy firmly, the next morning while they were opening the shop. 'This isn't going away and neither is Dirk. Zack will be coming here this morning. He said he has some shop stock for the Festival and he'll be having a stall on the day as usual. I think we need to tell him who he is. It's obvious he's Dirk's. The resemblance is quite striking, as you pointed out. You've shown that you can speak out when you want to, so now you're going to have to be really brave.'

Violet took a few slow deep breaths with her eyes closed.

'What *are* you doing?' said Daisy impatiently.

Still with her eyes closed, Violet replied quietly 'I'm preparing myself. I read about how to deal with anxiety and this is meant to help. And I'm extremely anxious, look.' and she held out her hands, which were shaking.

'Well, I hope it works quickly, 'cos I can hear Zack's van arriving around the back right now.'

The sisters walked together through to the storeroom and unlocked the back door.

'Morning Zack,' said Daisy cheerfully. 'I'm glad you're early. Come in and sit down for a minute, Violet wants to have a little chat with you about something important. I'll go and put the kettle on.' She gave Violet a significant look.

The Blackney Swans

Violet took another deep breath. It wasn't helping much but it was all she had.

'What's this all about then Violet? Nothing wrong I hope?' he smiled at her gently and Violet suddenly realised that actually she wanted to tell him. He was basically a good lad, well, most of the time and she was really fond of him and he was always kind to her.

'Um,' Violet began, at the same time thinking, how on earth do you do this?

'I have something to tell you and it might come as a bit of a shock. I know you've never known who your birth parents are, although maybe it's never troubled you.'

'Oh but I've always wondered,' broke in Zack. 'Mum and Dad never talked about it and I didn't like to ask as it seemed a bit of a forbidden topic at home. Do you know then?' He looked at Violet, a mixture of emotions crossing his face.

'Yes. You see,' Violet paused for a moment, took another deep breath and took his hand. 'It's me.' Her voice shook but she managed to continue, 'I'm your birth mother.'

There was long, a very long, silence. Zack withdrew his hand from Violet's and stared intently into her eyes.

'I'm so sorry,' she continued. 'For waiting so long to tell you, for not bringing you up myself but you seemed so happy with your lovely foster parents and I'd have been a useless mother.' Her voice faltered and stopped.

Daisy came in rather tentatively with cups of tea.

'Zack, I know it's difficult, but please try to accept that we thought it was for the best at the time.' Daisy put her hand on his shoulder.

Zack stood up. Then sat down again. He ran his hands through his hair, then shook his head. Stood up and sat down again.

'Ok,' he said decisively after a few moments. 'I need time to think about this. I'm going to unload the van.' He gave a little laugh, shook his head again and went outside, leaving his tea untouched. The twins sat in silence for a while. Then Violet picked up Zack's cup, went and made him a fresh drink and took it outside, where he was leaning against his van. She held it out to him.

'Thanks, Mum.' He took the cup and when Violet began to cry, set it down and put his arms around her.

'It's Ok, it will all be all right. In fact, I'm glad it's you, I've always felt there was, I don't know, something about you?' He smiled at her almost shyly. 'But there is something I'm wondering about. Why are you telling me now? And who's my Dad?'

'Ah, um, yes.' Violet stopped speaking and sighed. 'Look, this is a lot for both of us to deal with for now so how about we have a bit of a break to think about everything? Let's talk again soon and I'll answer all of your questions, I promise. Maybe come and see me later today?' She blew her nose and dabbed at her eyes.

'Yes, of course,' said Zack, looking slightly relieved. Perhaps, he thought, some time to absorb all of this before hearing the rest of the story would be best. He drank his tea, gave Violet a quick hug, jumped in his van and drove off.

She watched him go, feeling relieved, anxious and to her surprise, a little bit excited. She tried not to think about the many comments and complications probably about to head her way.

After tidying up the bar, Janet decided to go and wake Dirk. He'd been putting away Russ and Josh's hooch like there was no tomorrow last night, not to mention several pints of bitter. So much for what she'd read in the papers about his recovery from addiction and his current clean living. They said he was a changed man. But apparently not so you'd notice.

He'd also clearly been revelling not only in the attention he'd had from what felt like the entire village but also in all the Vicar's claptrap about his aristocratic pedigree and the Arthurian connections. But now the new day was with them it was time someone told him a few home truths, and that someone was going to have to be herself. Apart from the fact that nobody else knew the facts, it appeared that they were all deeply impressed by his career and his fame. The Young Farmers in particular had been thrilled about meeting someone who was going to be headlining at Glastonbury in a few weeks.

He probably wouldn't be up to a full English, but she could at least take him up a tray with a pot of strong tea and perhaps a couple

The Blackney Swans

of biscuits to settle the stomach, or an offer of Alka Zeltser if the thought of eating was too much for him.

There was no response to her tap on the door, so she put the tray down on the window sill in the corridor and let herself in quietly. To her surprise, he was already up and dressed and pulling on his boots.

'I found the bathroom,' he said. 'Your plumbing could do with an update.'

Janet bristled.

'It suited your mother well enough, though I don't suppose she ever told you about where she grew up.'

'My mother? What do you mean?'

'This was her home when she was a child.'

'What? The village? I thought the name on the signpost rang a bell. Maybe she brought me here when I was little. I have a vague memory of coming this way with her.'

'Not just the village, the Black Swan. Your mum was a Grinter born and bred till she got ideas above her station.'

'You're kidding.'

'No. She was my aunt, my Dad's little sister, Lizzie. She used to help out in the kitchen here and with the cleaning to earn a bit of pocket money at the weekends and in the school holidays. But she always had her eye on new horizons, better opportunities. And then she took up with the Thrusts when she was in her teens. Dropped the Lizzie, moved out and kept very quiet about her real family after that. We weren't good enough for her, apparently.'

'So, what are you saying? That we're related in some way?'

'Yes, we're first cousins, you and me.'

He stared at her. She couldn't resist a smile.

'Didn't reckon on that, did you? So if this place isn't good enough for you, maybe you could fork out for some improvements.'

'Well, I suppose I…. no, forget that. What are you doing here in my room? Is there something you want from me?'

'I brought you some tea, in case you're interested.'

She went out to fetch the tray, but when she carried it into him, he said, 'I'd rather have a shot of that elderflower, if there's any around. Good way to kickstart the day.'

'I don't think that'd be wise.'

The Blackney Swans

'Maybe not. But I'm the customer, and the customer is always right. Isn't that so, cousin? And you don't want someone with my influence slagging off your Dad's pub now, do you?' He smirked at her. 'Especially when I only need to put in a few good words about the local hostelry to get the crowds flocking. Who else knows?'

'About what?'

'About my mother and where she came from.'

'Well, I suppose one or two of the older people might. But it was all a long time ago now. I doubt any of them will have put two and two together.'

'Fine. In that case, I suggest we keep quiet about it. And you can forget the tea and find something more stimulating to start the day. Off you go.'

As Janet retreated down the stairs, she tried to put her finger on what it was about the man that had taken the wind out of her sails. She'd been so sure he'd be a pushover once she told him who his mother really was. But somehow he'd turned the tables on her. It wasn't like her to give in so easily. Perhaps when you got to be rich and famous you could throw your weight around and people just went along with it. She wasn't finished with him yet, though. If he was staying around for the village Midsummer festival, perhaps she could find some way of profiting from their relationship after all. She'd have to give it some thought.

Chapter 13

When she had finished dealing with her goats, Morgana decided to go for a little walk. A bit of fresh air would do her good and as it was a nice day she'd changed out her scruffy goat wrangling clothes and was dressed in one of her favourite flowing black and purple dresses. She knew she was looking her best and if she did happen to bump into Dirk, she was sure he'd talked of exploring the village in the morning, that would just be a coincidence.

Over the other side of the pond, she heard voices. It was He. Oh, unfortunately he was walking with the dreadful Lesley and apparently deep in conversation. Morgana quickly trotted back along the path, waited for a moment behind a tree and then casually reappeared so that they all met.

'Morning Lesley,' said Morgana, immediately turning away from her. 'Dirk, how lovely to see you again. I wondered if I might bump into you because I've been thinking of our conversation last night. About local history and customs and so on.'

'Well, actually,' began Lesley, trying unsuccessfully to insert herself between them.

'I have so much information about the ancient past and the people in this area,' continued Morgana, as if Lesley hadn't spoken, indeed didn't exist. Morgana smiled happily, this new assertive version of herself was very effective. Her old incarnation, Maureen Grey, would never have dared be so confident.

Lesley looked furious, Dirk appeared intrigued, it was all going so well. Then Morgana heard her name being called and glancing round, she saw Josh, rather red in the face and carrying a very large and apparently heavy sack. She swore under her breath. She'd forgotten about this.

'Oh, um, hi Josh,' Morgana made a half-hearted attempt to look pleased to see him.

The Blackney Swans

'As promised, here's your bag of feed for the goats.' Josh put it down with a thump and a cloud of dust, and nodded briefly to Lesley and Dirk.

'Come on then Mo, let's get it round to your paddock.' He looked her up and down. 'Blimey, you're a bit dressed up for goat keeping! Anyway, let's get going, I've got things to do.'

Dirk looked somewhat bemused and Lesley was struggling not to laugh. In a very loud whisper, she said to Dirk. 'That's Mo's boyfriend. I think you've met? We'd best leave them to it, I think. Now,' taking his arm. 'I was explaining about the mystery and significance of swans in this village.'

As Dirk and Lesley walked away, Morgana turned to Josh, fuming, 'How could you? I've told you not to call me Mo, well, except in very private moments and now Lesley's doing it. Also, that was terrible timing. And please don't comment on what I choose to wear.'

Josh looked amused. 'Actually, I thought it was brilliant timing! That sack was getting really heavy and now you can take the other end and help me carry it.' Privately, he thought the timing was great for other, Dirk related reasons. He chuckled to himself and with Morgana complaining bitterly, they picked up the sack and headed for her cottage.

The twins had, outwardly, a normal day in the shop, in other words, with not much happening, although both were a little on edge and carefully not talking about the one subject that preoccupied them.

When it got to closing up time, Zack still hadn't appeared and Violet was getting rather twitchy.

The phone rang and she jumped, then fluttered her hands around. Daisy picked it up, listened for a couple of minutes, said, 'Ok, yes, I'll tell her. See you soon,' and hung up. She turned to Violet.

The Blackney Swans

'That was Zack. He said everything's fine. He's just taking a bit more time to think things over and is also very busy with work. He said he'll see us on Festival Day and sends you his love.'

'Festival Day.' said Violet. 'Oh dear, well we'll just have to make sure I tell him about Dirk as early as possible before there's any chance of them meeting.'

Dirk had agreed to call at the Vicarage to look at the Parish Records and the Vicar's collection of coats of arms relating to the local gentry.

The Vicarage was a typical substantial house from the days when people had large families. The garden was a colourful riot of flowers, not what he had expected at all. Grasping the old pull bell, he heard it ringing in the distance and was surprised when the Vicar answered the door almost immediately.

'Come in, come in,' urged the Vicar, 'I saw you from my office window,' indicating to his left. He led Dirk through the hall to his office and offered him a seat at his desk, which had several large and heavy ledgers, some looking pretty moth-eaten at the edges. On a lower table between two armchairs and a sofa, rested some black metal boxes. The room was lined with bookshelves, more like a library. As this was the first time Dirk had been in a Vicar's office, he wasn't sure if this was typical. There was a discrete knock at the door and the Vicar's wife came halfway in. 'Coming for a sneaky look at the celebrity,' thought Dirk.

'Would you like tea or coffee?' asked Sally, 'Or I have peppermint, green tea or ginger if you prefer?' They both looked at Dirk expectantly. He would like another hair of the dog to be honest but knew he needed to keep himself together.

'Coffee, decaffeinated if you have it please,' he reluctantly replied.

'Me too, thank you Sally,' chimed the Vicar. 'You met Sally in The Black Swan didn't you Dirk?'

'Yes, we did briefly,' Sally answered for him. She thought he was pretty tipsy so wouldn't remember faces and names. She gave a slight smile and exited the room. So not a fan, decided Dirk. The Vicar brought him back with a bump by suggesting they map out a family tree, asking for his parent's names and where they were from.

'The thing is Vicar,' he sighed, 'I have just found out some information I don't want in the public domain, at least not yet,'

'That's fine,' said the Vicar, 'Vicars are like doctors, we hear a lot and know even more about parishioners and it would never do to be indiscreet, what you have to tell me will not go further than this room.'

'OK then, I will have to rely on your guarantee.' Taking a big breath, he was just about to blurt out what Janet had told him, when Sally returned with a tray of coffee mugs, sugar, milk and chocolate digestive biscuits, dark ones Dirk noted, which he suddenly realised was quite welcome, especially the biscuits, his mum always had dark chocolate ones too. Sally gave a brief nod and left straight away. Perhaps she's a bit straight laced he thought. Taking a biscuit, Dirk began again. 'Janet at the pub has just told me we are cousins. My mum was her dad's little sister and I had no idea.'

Well, that's quite a surprise,' said the Vicar, 'But a big help because the parish records here will be much easier to search and if they are a village family, we might get a few generations back, quite exciting.'

Dirk was being buoyed along by the Vicar's enthusiasm and they were soon side by side at the desk, working through the records. The Vicar drafted out a basic tree and began to add names and dates.

Sally was busy preparing lunch and decided to make plenty as the Vicar would probably invite Dirk to eat with them and it would be better for him than a liquid lunch at the pub. She would do pasta to help soak up the previous night's elderflower hooch. Really, Josh and Russ's stuff could be lethal. Quite a while later, the kitchen phone pinged a couple of times and Sally picked it up.

'Yes, that's fine, I was expecting he might stay, ten minutes, I've done Pasta with ham and cheese sauce, is that ok? Yes, apple crumble. No Booze,' she announced, 'Are you happy eating in the kitchen?' The Vicar relayed the menu to Dirk, who asked to use the bathroom first, the Vicar gave him directions and went to lay the table.

Dirk went to find the loo and hearing them talking and pots rattling downstairs, decided to have a nosey round upstairs. He was

The Blackney Swans

quite surprised on opening one door to see a wicker dress form wearing a Jean Paul Gautier corset and decided one shouldn't judge Vicar's wives by their public persona. There is a lot more going on in this village than he ever would have thought. Quietly, he closed the door and went down to lunch.

Dirk liked the Vicarage, he liked the look of it and the ambience, it reminded him of his old Uni house, only more homely and it smelled better too. No bikes cluttering up the hall or piles of mucky washing up or washing in the kitchen. They seemed nice people and he genuinely enjoyed his lunch and the conversation. If he lived near here, he could be friends with them. They didn't fawn over him or want to exploit him, just good people.

Dinsdale was still mad at the cat for redirecting the bullet at him and had sworn revenge, though perhaps the cat had secret powers and it was best to be cautious. He didn't like the men who had imprisoned him. They smelled like a cider factory and didn't seem to respect swans or his status in the swan hierarchy.

After his last aborted bid for freedom, his wing felt much better now and he exercised it as much as possible but the pen in the wood was a bit limiting. He was able to untie the round turn and half hitch that Josh used to 'secure' the swan enclosure. Dinsdale hadn't grown up on the waterways for nothing. He had pretended to play dumb and let the men blame each other for not fastening the gate. This time, he would bide his time till all the humans were preoccupied before making a full attempt at freedom. After his narrow escape with the big black car, he would keep well away from humans and their vehicles and take off as soon as he could. He couldn't use the recreation ground, they were organising it as a car park and the village green was being set up for some sort of event, perhaps the paddocks behind the butcher chappies might give him enough runway for a take off?

He really hadn't liked being pink, no self respecting swan would, not even those at Barbara Cartland's estate. He didn't know how it had happened, was it the medicine? It couldn't be dye, there

The Blackney Swans

was no coloured water, perhaps it was that weird food? Swans like their fresh green duck weed and grains but prisoners planning to escape had to eat well to maintain their strength. Thank goodness he had turned white again.

He would bide his time and choose his moment.

Chapter 14

Festival day

Daisy and Violet were up especially early, getting the shop ready and setting up a stall outside too. Zack had arrived, also early to their relief, for, he said, 'a cuppa and a bit more chat.' They had just settled down on the stools behind the counter when the door opened with a loud clang of the bell and Dirk strode in.

'Morning ladies,' he began. 'I thought I'd better let you know that your cat is behaving very strangely down among the trees near the pond, and I'm certainly not going to pick it up.' His voice tailed off as he came face to face with Zack. Violet had turned bright red. She had let her hair loose, having normally tied it back in an unflattering style, but had decided that things were changing and so should she. At that moment, she was trying to hide behind it.

Dirk regarded her thoughtfully, then stared at Zack, then back at Violet. Pennies dropped, almost audibly. 'Hang on a minute,' he said. 'I think I know you, we met, years ago. I didn't recognise you when I came in here before, but you look different now.' He stopped, frowning. 'Your name's Rose or something like that?'

'Her name is Violet,' said Daisy coolly. 'And you should remember her, you knew her rather well for a short time. There were ...consequences,' She looked pointedly at Zack.

'You, you're the consequences?' Dirk frowned.

'Yeah, well I've been called a few things, but never that,' Zack said. 'Thanks *Auntie* Daisy.' He looked angry and upset. Violet said nothing, but her eyes sparkled with tears.

'How long have you known about this?' asked Dirk coldly.

'Since about five minutes after you came in and I thought I was looking at my future self in a mirror,' said Zack rather shakily.

'I was about to tell him,' Violet whispered still hanging her head.

'Look, I think you three need to talk,' said Daisy. 'I'll go and take care of Georgiana, find out what's wrong with her,' she left hastily.

The new little family exchanged embarrassed glances. No one seemed to know what to say or do.

'Right,' said Dirk wanting to get back some semblance of control and privately thinking, 'What is it about this crazy village?'

'I suggest we meet and talk later. I have to prepare for a gig and my band are arriving soon. I'll come and find you. When I'm ready.'

Violet and Zack nodded silently, both currently beyond speech. Dirk headed for the door, opened it for Daisy who entered holding the cat, and then walked briskly away.

'I think I know what's wrong with Georgiana,' announced Daisy. 'The poor little thing is about to have kittens.'

That afternoon, Dirk sat on top of a five barred gate which provided a view of the village Green. He was observing the erection of the stage on which he would later triumph if all went according to plan. He had never previously seen such an informal approach to the job as that taken by the Young Farmers and their pals. Quantities of baler twine had been applied to the shaky structure, and a shortage of planking had been dealt with by the insertion of a few hay bales, too rotten to provide forage for anything but a hungry goat. The construction effort appeared to be entirely fuelled on cider and not a visibility jacket or safety helmet was to be seen.

Despite that, Dirk was charmed by the rustic simplicity on display. For too long, he had been searching for a place or community to complete him. His fame and celebrity had always meant that very little that attracted him was off limits, and he had sought his personal nirvana across the hotspots of the world, in the arms of beautiful women and consistently at the bottom of a bottle. At the end of another hectic, star spangled night though, an internal void had awaited him too many times to count. Here, now, was it possible that Dirk had come home? Could it be that the sullen villagers, many who knew nothing of his fame would still be there

The Blackney Swans

for him after his tattoos had sagged and his golden voice had gone croaky?

A substantial portion of Dirk's youth had become clouded in his memory by his heroic intake of vodka, but even so, he retained a grasp on family relationships and once he discovered that Janet was a cousin, a number of family occasions with her had come back to mind. Being able to claim an authentic villager as a relation suggested that Blackney Forloren could offer him the roots he craved. Janet's hints that he could take over the pub had astonished him at first, but on reflection, he could rather see himself as mine host, genial and beloved, pint mug always to hand.

As for the episode at the village shop, could that young man really be his son? He could see a bit of a resemblance to his younger self, though not as good looking of course and he very vaguely remembered Rose or Violet or whatever her name was, but there had been so many girls. Could it be true? Or were they just out for what they could get from him? Wouldn't be the first time! Well, he'd have to park it for now. There were far too many other things to do and think about, for a start, all of that amazing stuff about swans.

Dirk's village tour with Lesley and Morgana had only built on his initial beliefs that some mystical energy was calling to him from the area. Vague ideas about ley lines and ancestral voices had now been overlaid by Lesley's proclamations about swans and St Cygnus. After all, he'd seen a pink swan himself, although Lesley had challenged him as to whether it could have been a flamingo. Witchcraft as a current lifestyle choice had shocked Dirk to the core, to the deeply hidden place in which he treasured the memory of coming top in his Sunday School Annual Quiz at the age of nine. None of his publicists had seen fit to broadcast this triumph of his youth, but Dirk had always been quietly proud of it. And here was Lesley, apparently normal and sane, accepted in the village, but a practicing witch. Dirk couldn't help feeling that with his almost satanic reputation in some quarters, becoming a practicing warlock could only enhance his image.

He shifted on his perch atop the gate. These jeans really were a little tighter than comfort required. The stage appeared to be complete and a gaggle of Young Farmers were now debating the electrical provisions with an ancient guy holding a bunch of cables.

Dirk shuddered and made a mental note to ensure the wiring was properly checked before he touched it.

The Vicar passed by, on his way home for lunch and stopped to greet Dirk. The two of them had got quite cosy over the Vicar's extensive collection of myths and legends from the area. The Vicar had entered wholeheartedly into the search for Sir Thrust of the Round Table and had even prayed for the success of Dirk's research. Finding Dirk at leisure, the Vicar was keen to pass on a rumour of a knight's memorial being found at a disused church nearby. Dirk wanted all the details, and the two of them were absorbed in speculation when a thunderous diesel engine split apart the peaceful morning. Dirk fell off the gate in shock and was caught by the Vicar, who clutched him in a compromising pose which didn't go unnoticed by the occupants of the gigantic bus approaching. Hoots of the horn, revving of engines, and howls of laughter arose, as the bus halted at the gate and disgorged the members of Dirk's band, together with his team of roadies, his backing singers, and of course a sample of his most ardent groupies. Behind the vast bus, a cavalcade of similarly oversized vehicles drew up.

A riotous assemblage of noisy and wildly dressed rockers surrounded and gathered up Dirk and the Vicar. 'Hey man, where's the booze?' was the cry. Close on a hundred rockers marched on the Black Swan with single minded purpose as the village gawped after them.

Janet, seeing their approach, had steeled herself to announce that the pub was closed. She found herself engulfed in a tidal wave of black leather, studs, and glitter, and nobody showed any interest at all in her opening hours. Quickly recalculating, she fought her way behind the bar and began to dispense Josh's best hooch at a lightning pace. Even when she drew breath to remind her customers about the smoking ban, she couldn't make herself heard. Oh well, she consoled herself, it wasn't tobacco they were smoking anyway so perhaps it didn't count.

Dirk's entourage had adopted the Vicar, and some of his groupies were busy updating his image with purple lightning flash makeup across his cheeks. The Vicar's gentle protests had been steamrollered, and he, with the rest of the group, was on the far side of five or six tots of elderflower hooch. Dirk's reunion with the rest of the band was in full swing when Josh and Russ fought their way

The Blackney Swans

through the crowd to his side. Josh was waving a photocopied pamphlet, whilst Russ carried a couple of boxes containing the stocks. 'Here it is, Dirk.' Josh yelled, 'The schedule of events for the Midsummer Festival! Of course, your set is starring, but the usual programme can't be left out, or they'd never speak to us again! You're on at eight pm but the programme starts at half six with the School Recorder Group, followed by the Young Farmer's Ukelele band. Then we'll have a short break and you come on. For your final number, all the acts will take the stage together for a rendition of your greatest hit ever, Devil Love.' Dirk's mouth was open as he took the schedule from Josh and stared at it. He was speechless. His band gathered to see.

Josh and Russ retreated, intent on their target of flogging the programmes for a pound apiece ahead of opening. The catering, in conjunction with Tom Bullock and Janet, was already set to flog a record breaking number of 'chicken' burgers, and barrels of hooch were already lined up for the night. Not only that, but word had spread afar that the Midsummer Festival at Blackney Forloren would be something special this year. People were already arriving in numbers and they had set up a road block, manned by some of the school kids who were sharing in the profits and charging all non locals a fiver apiece to come into the village. This was looking like the most profitable venture yet.

Dirk and his team had their heads together over the programme. 'What the hell is a Recorder group?' wailed Dirk. His band were quick to comfort him. 'It's not like we haven't had dodgy warm up acts before,' consoled Trasher. 'They'll forget all about it when we get on stage.'

'And exactly how do you suggest we incorporate recorders and ukeleles into a new framing of Devil Love?' Dirk complained bitterly. His greatest hit was familiar to more people than the Bible, famous for a number of attributes, including being the loudest rock song ever performed, and having such evil lyrics that it had been raised in the House of Commons. 'Not a problem,' announced Trasher confidently. 'We'll drown 'em out. Just up the volume a bit.'

The Blackney Swans

As well as Dirk's crew and followers, the crowd was swelled by all and sundry from Bridgwater, even from Westonzoyland and Langport. Then the BBC outside broadcast vans turned up to film flamingoes on the levels and found themselves in the centre of a secret gig by none other than Dirk Thrust and his Pistons.

Someone was heard to mutter, 'they will be telling us Storks and Beavers will be back next.'

'Perhaps we will have a fly past by Concorde or a formation of microlites,' said another.

'I here tell there is a flamingo at Abbotsbury amongst all the swans, should make a nice little end of news piece if we don't catch it here,' said the BBC producer.

The BBC were then directed to the side of the village green to park their vans, where some lads already had a burger van set up and the women from the village shop were doing a good trade in crisps and snacks. The local school children, who for some reason were not in school as term didn't finish till next week, were making a pile of money charging for entry to the village and parking.

Lesley was beside herself, though a little disappointed that Peter Scott was not with the outside broadcast crew. All this because she had found a large pink feather in the churchyard and written to the BBC.

Chapter 15

Half past six had arrived.

'Bloody hell, this is really going well,' Josh said as he handed over another swan burger.

'You can say that again,' Russ replied. 'I've just got the takings from the road block and we're still selling programmes. You and me mate, are rich.'

Just then, there was a cheer from the large crowd now seated on the grass in front of the music stage. A large screen had been erected to the rear of the stage and from behind it the boys and girls of the recorder group trooped out. The Vicar, as was traditional, was the master of ceremonies and he stood at a microphone and introduced the children. A sudden hush fell over the crowd.

The children all looked nervous, not surprisingly with such an audience. In previous years they had been lucky to get more than their parents and a few drunks from the pub. Sally the Vicar's wife who led the group, whispered quiet encouragement and they all put their instruments to their lips.

Josh looked at Russ. 'Are they going to be any better than last year?'

'Not a chance,' Russ replied. 'I suggest you do what I'm about to do and put something in your ears.

Dirk and the band were backstage and out of sight but not of sound when the recorders started. The noise caught them all off guard.

'What the hell is that?' someone shouted over the sound.

'My best bet is 'Greensleeves,' another voice said. 'Bloody hell, how long is this going on for?'

The Blackney Swans

'They've got the stage for half an hour,' Dirk said. There were groans from all around.

Out on stage, the audience was just as bemused and when the first song, which had indeed been Greensleeves, finally came to an end, there was complete silence. Eventually, someone clapped and others fitfully joined in. Taking this as encouragement, the group started again and regaled the audience with several more possibly recognisable tunes. It really was not going well and then it all changed. With the addition of a real rock band for the evening's proceedings, Sally had decided the children should really play something more modern. And she had added a little twist of her own for the finale. An accomplished recorder player herself, she picked up her instrument and started to play. Initially, the audience braced themselves for more ear torture and then they realised this was someone who could actually play and what's more they all knew the tune. Then Morgana appeared on stage with a guitar and started to accompany Sally. Slowly, the children added their input.

From the safety of the burger van, Russ turned to Josh. 'I didn't know Morgana could play the guitar.'

'Bloody hell, nor did I,' Josh said. 'She kept that quiet but she's rather good isn't she? Wonder what the song is?'

Russ looked at Josh. 'Why am I not surprised? It's Stairway to Heaven.'

'Never heard of it. Mind you the audience seem to have. They're all starting to sing along.'

And they were to the extent that although the children were still doing their best to murder the tune, everyone was being carried away by the moment. When they finished, there was another moment of silence but this time followed by thunderous applause with many of the audience getting to their feet.

'I wonder if that applause is for the last song or just relief that it's all over?' Josh said.

'Both I expect,' Russ replied.

Meanwhile, outside Misselania, Daisy and Violet had no need to go out to hear the music. It was perfectly audible from where they were sitting. Anyway, they were busy, gazing in wonder at Georgiana and her kittens, now all snuggled up on an old blanket. There were five kittens, two tabbies like Georgiana, two black ones and, rather surprisingly, a pure white one.

'How clever of you Georgie,' said Daisy stroking her gently. 'Although seeing those two little black ones, I think we now know what that Lucifer from the pub was up to when he was around here. Mind you, I'm not too sure about your taste in males.'

'There does seem to be a lot going on around family relationships at the moment.' She looked at Violet.

Violet was silent for a while, twisting her hands together anxiously. Eventually, she said, 'what do you think will happen now? Zack's gone to watch Dirk and his band. I wonder if they'll ever talk about everything? And supposing...'

'Look,' interrupted Daisy, 'You can't do anything for now, so stop agonising over it. Do you want to shut the stall now and go and watch the band? We might as well, it will be like old times.' She looked down at the cats with a smile. 'They will be OK. There's food and water for Georgie and they're warm and safe inside. Come on, let's go and join in, I could do with a bit of excitement for a change.'

Chapter 16

There was a brief lull while the Young Farmers set themselves up.

Still backstage, Dirk turned to his drummer. 'I have to hand it to them, that last song was actually quite good and it seems to have really created an atmosphere. I wonder what this lot are going to do?'

Pete Sturrock was a little miffed. In previous years, his ukulele band had been the stars of the evening. Now, that last number by the school kids was going to be hard to top. He looked at his chaps and did wonder whether they should have been at the cider quite so much but it was too late to worry now.

When they were all ready and sitting on the straw bales they had dragged onto the stage, he turned to the audience and introduced them all. In previous days this would have been a waste of time as everyone knew everyone else but this crowd was massive. In fact, he was starting to feel a little nervous. He had never had stage fright before, maybe he should have actually had more cider.

They started into their set and all went well, although he distinctly got the impression that the audience were only marking time waiting for the main act. He needed something for their last number. In the gap before the last song, he said to the chaps. 'Remember that Wurzel song we re-arranged a few weeks ago with the different words?'

Grins of agreement met the question followed by nods from everyone. 'Right then, let's do that one to finish.'

When the song ended, there was yet another moment of silence followed yet again by tumultuous applause.

'I knew that song, you will probably be surprised to know,' Josh said to Russ.

'Yeah but I bet you didn't know those lyrics,' Russ said. 'That has got to be the most disgusting yet incredibly funny version of 'I've got a brand new combine harvester' I've ever heard.'

The Blackney Swans

'Yes, the Vicar's wife didn't look amused at all. Mind you, it was clear some of the schoolkids knew what they were on about and hopefully the little ones were oblivious. Right, we've got a fifteen minute break now. Most of the burgers have gone but there's plenty of the so called 'Pink Swan' left and no nosy copper around to cause yet another fuss. By the way, are they all white again?'

'Yes, thank goodness,' Russ replied. 'The new feed seems to have done the trick. Right, get ready here they come.'

As the short interlude started, Janet had reached a conclusion. Whatever ideas she might have harboured about getting Dirk to take on the pub, she realised he would need an incentive. And then she had a brainwave. It was interesting where a bit of flattery could get you. As the Young Farmers' performance came to an end, Janet went up to one of the men standing by with the Pistons' equipment.

'That's a skilled job you've got,' she said, 'handling all that complicated stuff. Well paid, is it?'

'So so.'

'I'm surprised. Can't be all that many people good enough to work with the big stars. He should value your skills.'

'I suppose.' He grinned. 'Not that it's him who pays anyway. It's his manager.'

'Oh. And is he here too?'

'No fear. Not Bernie. He doesn't know anything about this gig.'

'Bernie?'

'Bernie Steinberg. When Dirk took off for his little break, he decided to stay in London till Glastonbury.'

'Oh, that's where he lives, is it?'

'Yeah. Stays at the Dorchester when he's in the UK. He does himself proud, does Bernie.'

'The Dorchester, eh. Nice for some. Well, I won't keep you. You must be busy.'

Armed with this useful information, Janet went back to the Swan and headed straight for the telephone. She didn't know for certain, but she had a strong suspicion that Mr Steinberg had no idea what his clients were up to in his absence.

She made straight for the telephone and dialled Directory Enquiries.

'Could you give me the number for the Dorchester Hotel in London?' she said. 'There's someone staying there I need to speak to.'

Morgana had been thrilled at being on stage earlier, pleasantly surprised at remembering how to play guitar, it had been quite a while and especially playing one loaned to her by one of the Pistons. Now she was even more excited as she was taking part in the 'Devil Love' finale. 'Wow. This is fantastic' she thought to herself. She could see Josh in the audience. He'd applauded wildly when she'd played with the recorder group. Maybe he wasn't so bad, not exactly cool of course, but kind of OK. Perhaps she'd make up with him later, but right now she would be performing with the stars.

While the audience were enjoying the refreshments, the roadies quickly got the amps and drums on stage. They had parked a big generator up by the pond and well clear so its noise wasn't intrusive. They were a practised crew and it was all ready in minutes.

'What setting on the amps Dirk?' one of the roadies asked.

Dirk grinned 'Well we're outdoors and this lot need to hear some real rock and roll. Turn them up well.'

At the stroke of eight o'clock Dirk strode out onto stage. The band were behind him. They all took up position, he put his guitar strap over his shoulder and stood next to the microphone.

He looked out over the sea of expectant faces. God, he loved his job. This was going to be fantastic. In time honoured fashion, he spoke into the microphone, knowing his words would echo over the village.

'HELLO Blackney Foloren.'

'I'm Dirk Thrust and these are my Pistons.'

His arm dropped to the guitar and hit the first chord of the song.

The band played until the sun started to set. It was clear they were going down well with most of the audience, although it was also clear that some people, mainly locals, were not enamoured by

The Blackney Swans

the sound levels. He grinned to himself, they hadn't heard anything yet.

It was time to finish. The recorder band gingerly made their way on stage. Sally had thoughtfully supplied most of them with earplugs. The Young Farmers strode onto the stage, cider was what they had used to manage the sound levels. Morgana tentatively took her place.

Dirk looked around, gave a nod to the sound man, miming turning a knob up to maximum which was acknowledged and then turned to the audience.

'Thank you Blackney and to finish, the Pistons, the Farmers and the School Kids bring you DEVIL LOVE.'

Once again, his arm dropped to the guitar to hit the first chord of the song.

Chapter 17

The moment it took for Dirk's arm to fall was something that was talked about in the village for years to come. It was rather like people saying they remembered where they were when JFK was shot. It was a seminal moment, a timeless moment, a defining moment for all sorts of reasons.

For Lesley, sitting with her back to her favourite tree, it was a beautiful few seconds of peace. She heard birds singing and the rustle of the leaves in the tree as it spoke to her.

For Morgana, it was ripe with anticipation. The song was one she had loved since childhood and now she was going to actually play in it live.

For the girls from the shop, it was a moment's peace. Although for Violet it was also a reminder of her innocent times as a young girl in love with the young Dirk.

For PC Cridge, who had decided to come late and in civvies it was the time he was waiting for. If anyone was misbehaving this would be the time to catch them. He stood up from his place next to the pond and started to study the crowd.

For Russ and Josh it was a moment to look up from the money they were counting and grin at each other.

For the majority of the crowd, it just increased the air of anticipation to fever pitch.

For Dinsdale the swan it was the moment he finally managed to get free from the chapel, and with a fully healed wing, he found the take off run he needed to take to the air and fly to freedom.

Dirk's hand hit the guitar strings and the famous opening chord of Devil Love smote the ears of the assembled throng. It was loud, it was very loud and it did not just smite the humans it also smote the ground. The peaty and quite soft ground, the ground that had been

The Blackney Swans

putting up with large, noisy pressure waves for quite some time. If a straw could actually bring a camel to its knees then the sound pressure brought the peat to a new state. Instead of being relatively solid, it decided to turn relatively liquid instead. The effect was immediate and the results spectacular, if somewhat slow to be realised.

The first person to realise was Cridge. The surrounds of the duckpond had been reinforced many times over the years but the ground below was still just peat so when it decided it wanted to change state, it completely undermined the pond's edges. Cridge had been in the pond several times. However, this time the pond came to him as a small tidal wave of water, mud and pond weed swept him off his feet and into the ditch behind him.

The next thing the water hit was the generator which immediately stuttered to a halt and the music stopped. Luckily, the water then decided to keep following Newton's laws of gravity and headed off down the road away from the crowd.

By this time, the audience had realised that they were now sitting on what was quickly turning into a soft slimy mess. Panic ensued, not helped by the fact that the ground nearest the stage was getting softest first. Mud splattered people ended up climbing over those behind them who were still not sure what the hell was going on. Luckily, the process was progressive and quite slow to spread. Within minutes, everyone was on higher ground around the pub. They were all various shades of muddy brown but no one seemed to notice as they turned back to watch the stage to see what was happening there.

What they saw was very strange. The stage was sinking slowly. The Young Farmers were doing a sterling job of grabbing the school children. They were managing to ferry them off to one side where the ground seemed a little firmer.

They saw the whole village green turn to mud, the bale stage sank slowly into the muddy liquid, roadies pulled plugs, people ran in all directions, many away from the village centre some towards it to save those sinking, the chaos was unbelievable. The BBC producer was ecstatic, this would make his career. Of course, it would be a tragedy if anyone was hurt but he could dine out on this event for years.

Weirdly, the band seemed to be playing on. What most people didn't know was that after years of high decibel music, the band were all quite deaf. To retain what little hearing they had left, they all wore very small but very effective noise cancelling hearing aids. These days they knew their music so well they really didn't need to hear it and Dirk really didn't need to hear his singing. They had all realised something was going on but in true 'keep playing while the Titanic sinks' style they played on not realising that they were making very little noise at all.

But by now even Dirk had realised something very strange was happening. Being at the front of the stage, he could see the audience better than his band behind him. What the hell were they doing? Nobody ran away from Devil Love. The normal reaction was for everyone to get up and start dancing. He kept singing but turned to look around and realised the kids and farmers had gone. Then he looked up.

That stopped him from singing. As he stared open mouthed at the sky, the Pistols had finally also realised something was very wrong. Being good friends of many years, having stuck together through thick and thin in many strange places, they independently decided to look after themselves. They quickly followed the farmers and got the hell off the sinking stage.

That left Dirk alone and open mouthed, staring at the sky. The sun was setting behind him in a ball of pink and orange fire. Its rays were lighting up the sky and thin clouds in a spectacular show. The sky was full of fantastic steaks of pink and flying sedately through it and over Dirk's head was a large, majestic and very pink Swan.

Dirk pointed up transfixed and yelled at the top of his voice that was heard by everyone despite the lack of electric amplification.

'I BLOODY TOLD YOU SO!!!!!'

Epilogue

'Well that went well,' Russ said the next day over a hair of the dog at the pub.

'Went well?' Josh asked aghast. 'The bloody pond is empty and needs major restoration work.'

'True but Dirk said he would pay for it.'

'And the village green is a mess, we're going to need tons of hardcore to fix it.'

'True but Dirk said he would pay for it.'

'And we were on the morning BBC news.'

'Yeah but that was good publicity. Especially as they filmed the acoustic session that the band played outside the pub afterwards. That was really great and even better, no one asked for their money back.'

'Good point. And so we made a ton of money.'

'That we did.'

'That young lad Zack did a brave thing,' Josh said.

'Yes he did,' Russ replied. 'How he got back on the stage and managed to rescue Dirk was quite a sight to see.'

'The girls from the shop seemed to have something to do with it judging from their reaction afterwards. There's more there than meets the eye.'

'Oh come on work it out,' Russ said. 'Did you see Zack and Dirk standing next to each other? Didn't you see the resemblance?'

'Ah yes, I take your point. I'm sure it will all come out in the wash. Trying to keep a secret in this village is pretty damned pointless.'

'Sure is. And there's something more we don't yet know about Dirk and Janet but I'm sure we'll find out what quite soon.'

'Then that fat bald bloke turned up and had a blazing row with Dirk. Not sure what it was about but Dirk seemed to get the better of it.'

'That was his agent,' Russ said. 'Apparently they are parting ways after Glastonbury and don't be surprised to see Dirk back here afterwards.'

'Hmm, somehow that doesn't surprise me he seems to really like the place.'

'One bit of bad news, Dinsdale's finally buggered off for good,' Josh said. 'I went over and checked first thing this morning. I suspect that was who Dirk saw when he was alone on stage, as he flew over in the setting sun. Mind you, I don't suppose he'll ever be convinced that pink swans don't exist after that.'

'Oh but we know that they do, don't we? Russ said with a grin.

The Gold Swan

The 'Gold Swan' means everything to the residents of Blackney Foloren.

Chapter 1

Despite all the excitement, Russ and Josh were in a mellow mood. The sun was setting and it was sampling time. The latest brew was ready. Summer was drawing to a close and the mellow fruitfulness of autumn was getting up its head of steam. It had been a hot summer and the hedgerows were overloaded with fruit.

'Blackberry and Sloe,' Russ said as he took an appreciative sip. 'You mate, are an artist when it comes to flavouring the hooch.'

Josh took the praise by simply raising his glass and taking another swig.

'And it's nice that things have gotten back to normal,' Russ continued. 'The pond is back where it should be and the Green is no longer a swamp.'

'True but it was a shame to see Janet leave. Mind you I don't think her heart was ever really into running the pub and the new landlord seems very much up for it. We must make sure we acquaint him with village traditions before next Mayday.'

'Good point, but I'm sure he'll see it as an important event of the year in the village. My only real worry,' Russ said, 'is that word gets out that our global celebrity is now running a small pub in the

The Blackney Swans

back of beyond. The last thing we need is to be overrun with groupies and tourists.'

Josh shuddered at the thought. 'He says he's kept it all very low key and is not intending to do any advertising, so fingers crossed.'

Just then, the sound of footsteps was heard. The two men exchanged glances, but before they could react, a well-known head appeared around the corner of the old shed where they kept the still.

'Oh, good evening Vicar, nice to see you again,' Josh said. 'Can we help?'

'Well, a small sample of the latest brew would be a good start. I think I need it after our discovery today,' the Vicar said with a knowing grin.

Russ poured him a glass which was tasted with relish. 'So, is there something more you need from us today?' Russ asked. 'Apart from wanting to see what the latest brew tastes like.'

'To be honest not really, although I thought you would be amused to hear that Dirk is really getting into his historical research. Arthurian legends and our fixation with swans for a start.'

'As long as it keeps him busy, we don't want him getting bored with the pub or the village,' Josh said.

'Yes, on that point,' Russ said. 'Saint Cygnus and the church and the whole swanny thing. We've all heard the vague story about the good saint but do you know the real story? I think it's important we know now.'

'Ah,' the Vicar said, holding out his surprisingly empty glass for a refill. 'Now that's something I've researched over the years. Let me tell you the tale. Back in the years after the Romans left, there was a village called Foloren. The residents lived out on the levels, probably because it kept them away from the Romans. However, in those days the water levels were much higher and prone to floods. The story goes that there was a young girl called Megan who was the village swanherd.'

'What, like a swineherd but with swans?' Josh asked.

'Exactly,' the Vicar answered. 'In those days swans were a valuable source of food, things were very different to nowadays.'

He didn't notice the two men exchanging looks as he continued. 'One winter, it seems that the floods became very bad and the villagers were in despair. In those days, no one really went more than about five miles away from where they lived and so they had no

The Blackney Swans

idea where to go to save themselves. Then one very foggy night, Megan claimed to have seen a ghostly swan. It glowed with a saintly golden light apparently and somehow she convinced the rest of the village that it would lead them to safety. So, with her in the lead, the whole lot of them set off into the swamps following a young girl and a ghostly swan. I'm sure there's a grain of truth in the story. Maybe they did follow a swan which was returning to its mate. Who knows? Anyway, after a night plodding through the mire and managing to keep to enough solid ground under them not to drown, the villagers found higher ground. It was declared a miracle and the village of Blackney Foloren was founded. The term 'ney' in the name means little island, by the way. Megan was declared a Saint and in honour of her accomplishment, she was named Saint Cygnus. There's a star constellation called Cygnus the Swan, which is easily visible from here and I do wonder if that was part of the inspiration for her name. Of course, over the years the story was embellished. A chapel was built but abandoned later on. Apparently, there was some sort of plague and half the village ended up in the ground there. Most people don't even know it exists.'

The two men exchanged yet another look.

'One thing that does relate all the way back is the church's golden swan. The story goes that the villagers were so grateful to their rescuer that they commissioned the statue. Some years back, the gold was assayed, and it was discovered to be almost certainly Roman in origin. So maybe the villagers at the time dug up a Roman cache and used it to make the figure.'

'Ooh, does that mean that there may be more treasure buried around here?' Russ asked with his eyes alight.

'Who knows?' the Vicar replied. 'Although there is little evidence that the Romans were ever actually here. It's more likely the gold was found elsewhere.'

Russ nodded, slightly disappointed, but secretly decided it might be worth investing in a metal detector.

'So that's why Lesley and her crowd of loony ladies worship the swans as well? Josh asked.

'Very much so,' the Vicar replied. 'Back in those days, there was still a great pagan tradition. They revered the birds probably more than the Christians and the two belief systems have run side by side ever since.'

'And it's a great excuse to run around naked in the woods.' Russ said with a grin. 'You don't get to do that in your church Vicar.'

He smiled, 'No, not one of our teachings but what one gets up to in the privacy of one's own home is another matter of course.'

Russ and Josh exchanged yet another look but both decided not to take that one any further.

Just then, another set of footsteps was heard and Morgana appeared, looking out of breath and rather flustered.

'Oh there you are, I thought you two would be here but it's the Vicar I need.' And before Josh could object, she took his glass and downed the contents in one, then handed it back to him.

'Good brew, Josh,' she said, coughing only slightly. 'Vicar, we are in trouble. I mean the whole village is or will be when they find out. And we won't be able to keep it secret for very long. You know how tongues wag round here.' She grabbed Josh's glass, which he had just refilled, and tossed down the lot in another spectacular gulp while looking at the Vicar expectantly.

'Perhaps you'd better tell us all exactly what on earth you are talking about, my dear?'

'Oh yes, goodness. Well, you know that little statue of a swan that has pride of place in your church? You know the one on the shelf above the altar.'

'Yes, my dear. What about it?'

'It's not there anymore. I popped into the church this afternoon as I do most days. And I saw it. Gone. I searched high and low but it isn't anywhere. So all I can conclude is that someone has pinched it.'

To Morgana's total surprise, the men didn't look at all alarmed.

'Ah, yes my dear. I'm afraid we already knew that,' the Vicar said.

Chapter 2

Earlier that day

It was one of those lovely October afternoons, when the morning mists have lifted and the falling sun touches the damp edges of the leaves so that they softly glow with gold. The Vicar of St Cygnus, walked beneath the chestnut trees, scuffing the fallen leaves with his shoes and bending to collect the mahogany coloured conkers before stuffing his pockets with them like hamsters' pouches. Once fully loaded, he strolled to the church and carefully opened the heavy oak door.

'It's only me, Mrs Thing,' he called out. He'd been accused in the past of creeping up on her, to expedite her entry into the next world.

'Is that you, Vicar?' she called back.

'Yes, only me, I can see you have been using plenty of elbow grease, and the polish smells wonderful, freshens the old lady up.'

'Do I need freshening up, Vicar?'

'No, no, Mrs Thing, I was referring to the church, I always think of ships and churches as female. You know, Mother Church and all that.'

'I'm not finished cleaning yet. Have you come to lock up, Vicar?'

'No, I've come to empty my pockets of nature's bounty,' he said, as he heaped handfuls of rich glowing chestnuts onto a side table. 'I'm preparing for the annual conker competition.'

'You've got some beauties there Vicar,' remarked Thingy. 'I hope it doesn't end in tears like last year.'

'No, this year no knuckles will be wilfully bruised, and to avoid intimidation, we will string each of these chestnuts to the rung of a ladder balanced across the aisle. Participants will wield their own conkers and the least damaged surviving one will be the winner. It might even be one of mine.' The Vicar beamed.

'Ooh, if you're bringing in a ladder, can I use it first? The poor old swan has all but disappeared behind the dust and cobwebs, and the case needs a good clean. I used to have a long handled feather duster, but it died the death a couple of years ago and we couldn't find one to replace it.'

'I will fetch the ladder now, Mrs Thing, and go up myself whilst you are here. We don't want any accidents or either of us spending hours on the floor injured with no one to sound the alarm.'

The Vicar left to go to his garage and Mrs Thing nipped out of the side door and around the back for a quick smoke. The Vicar wasn't very long but he did have to carefully brush any cobwebs and bat poo from the ladder. He didn't relish having his ears chewed off for traipsing dirt into the church.

'Here we are, Thingy,' he called, but there was no answer. He set the ladder up and went in search of the lady in question. He found her around the back having a chat and cigarette with Russ and Josh.

'Ah, I'm just going up the ladder to clean the swan case, would one of you hold it for me as you are here?' he asked.

'Oh don't worry Vicar, we'll do it,' exclaimed Josh. They all trooped in behind him. Russ held the ladder as Josh went up with the duster, which Mrs Thing had handed to him. He began to dust and then paused.

'Erm Vicar, I hate to tell you, but well, the glass case is sort of missing. It's not there, just a piece of paper stuffed in its place.'

'What?' the others all cried. 'Are you sure?'

Josh descended the ladder and handed the paper to the Vicar, who unrolled it and read it out aloud.

'You leave me dusty and unloved
Above eyesight and lost from view
But I see and I have judged
It's time you cared and showed it too.'

'Well I never,' cried Mrs Thing. 'You mean they have stolen it because my feather duster died?'

'So it would seem,' sighed the Vicar.

'Oh shute, we'll have Cridge round poking his nose into everywhere,' moaned Josh.

'There'll be no peace from him,' grumbled Russ.

'Please keep this to yourselves. We don't want Cridge or any outsiders involved,' the Vicar said. 'I will see if we can solve this by Sunday, and if not, I will announce it at the service. So you must all be there. But this rhyme looks like the sort of clue you get on a treasure hunt. It's not the sort of thing a thief would leave.'

'You mean a treasure hunt for the statue, like the Golden Hare one,' Russ enthused.

'What Golden Hare one?' asked Josh. 'Hares are brown anyway.'

Russ explained. 'This artist, Kit I think his name was, buried a hare sculpture made of gold and then wrote a book with lots of clues in words and pictures, puzzle type of things. The thing is, the winner didn't follow all the clues but found the Hare anyway.'

'But who said they could borrow our swan without asking?' steamed Mrs Thing.

'No one knows they have taken it, Mrs T,' the Vicar said. 'We don't know when it was taken but I will try to find out. So keep it quiet and I'll tell the congregation when I can watch everyone's faces from the pulpit. I suppose whoever it is has a point. We have neglected it, to our shame, but we will make sure it is in a prominent but safe place in future.

'Well I never, Morgana will love this story,' grinned Russ. 'And the hunt for the swan, if that is what this is.'

'Don't tell her,' the Vicar said. 'The fewer who know about this for the moment, the better. So remember, it's a secret until Sunday. But make sure she and as many others as possible come to the service. Nothing we can do about it for the moment though.' He rubbed his hands together. 'So let's set up for the conker competition. Put the ladder over the aisle at the back, and we can use some hassocks to protect the pew ends. Then you can string these beauties, longish strings mind, and we'll tie one to each rung for the competitors to attack in turn.'

Josh and Russ set to work moving the ladder. Mrs T followed them, sweeping. She shooed them outside to pierce and thread the conkers.

The Blackney Swans

Before long, the Vicar said, 'Let's finish up and I'll stand you a pint for your help. Port and lemon Mrs Thing?'

'Well, that's very kind of you Vicar,' said Mrs T as her eyes lit up. 'I don't mind if I do.'

The following Sunday for his sermon the Vicar chose to talk about truth, honesty and respecting the property of others before announcing the disappearance of the golden swan. He scanned the faces before him but couldn't discern any discomfort or guilt. He noted who was missing, too. No one was squirming, except a few small children and old grandpa Thurrock, who often had to pop out halfway through the service. So he told them about the missing swan and then read out the verse from the piece of paper, about it being neglected.

A few looked uncomfortable but most clearly hadn't thought much about the statue, apart from it belonging to the parish, and were indignant that someone had pinched it. The Vicar went on to explain that he didn't think it had been stolen by thieves and there was a good chance that it might be found.

Eyes brightened, ears pricked up. A treasure hunt! Excitement spread amongst the congregation, perhaps a little avarice showing here and there. He bade them all to keep the information within the parish and to make sure that a certain long arm of the law did not find out about it, before announcing the last hymn, 'Onward Christian Soldiers'.

Following his closing words, he blessed their efforts in finding the missing symbol of the church's patron saint. After leaving the church, the parishioners, half scandalised, clustered outside in tight groups, arranging to meet in the Back Swan to decide on tactics and trains of enquiries. Already, factions were forming, furtive glances towards other groups were cast and noticed.

'Oh dear, human nature,' sighed the Vicar, 'Usually it's dashing home for the roast and Yorkshire pudding.' Which reminded him how hungry he was.

Chapter 3

That afternoon in a very busy pub

'Please, Dirk, please.'

Pete could hear a whiny note edging into his voice, and he didn't like himself for it. But the man was being impossible. True, since he'd taken over from Janet, the pub had become a lot more congenial. The average age of the clientele had fallen by about thirty years. There were many more women and girls around the place. And there was a juke box, finally. Apart from the traditional events, Janet had stood out firmly against any kind of music in the bar except for old Reg Scott doing requests on his squeezebox at the Saturday night singalong. Mind you, the juke box was no great shakes. The choice was confined to 1960s pop because it reminded Dirk of his youth.

'At least consider it.'

'OK, I'll consider it. But don't get your hopes up.'

Was it really so much to ask? Just the odd performance from the great man. But Dirk had continued to be adamant.

'Look,' he kept saying. 'I've never been happier than I am here. I reckon Blackney is the paradise I always dreamed of retiring to. Peace and quiet. No fans. No screaming crowds. No agent hauling me in and out of rehab and no press poking their noses into my business. I reckon what happened at the Midsummer Festival was an omen. Finding yourself disappearing into a giant puddle is not something you forget in a hurry. And it's changed me. I've enough money now. That part of my life is over. I've got better things to think about than strutting up and down in front of the crowds. More important things. The Vicar thinks he might have found another connection between the Thrusts and the Round Table. Imagine.'

Pete couldn't understand it himself, that fascination with the past and wanting to prove your family was special. There'd been

The Blackney Swans

Sturrocks around this part of Somerset for centuries. Farming quietly, getting on with their lives, sending lads off to wars from time to time, and just because they never made the history books didn't mean they were inferior. Perhaps it was something in the air around Blackney that got to people. Tradition was all very well, but the whole swan business seemed to have sent some of them right over the edge. All that stuff with feathers and dressing up and chanting and what-not. At least Russ and Josh had their heads screwed on straight about swans and what they were good for, though they weren't as keen as he was on getting Dirk on stage again.

'We've got a nice little business going now with the meat and the hooch,' they told Pete. 'We don't need hordes of strangers turning up and disturbing the set up. And if we start getting the crowds here, that'll just give Cridge an excuse to come cycling over and poking his nose in where it's not wanted.' Which was true enough, Pete had to agree.

It was going to be interesting to see what happened at Halloween, though. It might be a while away yet, but at Blackney festivals people came from miles around expecting the old traditional ways to be continued, and once they knew who was in control of the pub these days they'd be hoping for something special this year. In fact, Pete had more or less promised at the last Young Farmers meeting that it'd be worth the journey this year. What could he do to make sure it was?

Then, just as he was sipping his pint and thinking, the door flew open. Standing there, breathing heavily as if she'd been running was the Vicar's wife.

'Anyone seen my husband?' she asked and she waved a large piece of paper that she was clutching in one hand.

A chorus of 'Nos' greeted her question, along with some other remarks she chose to ignore.

'What you got there then, Sally?' Dirk asked as he gave her a large glass of her usual sherry.

While she took a gulp, Dirk looked at what Sally had brought in. It looked like old parchment and the writing was in red. His brow creased as he studied the words.

'Come on Dirk, whatsit say?' someone asked.

'Not really sure,' he said and so he read it out loud.

> ***'The Golden Swan has gone from here***
> ***The reason why may not be clear***
> ***But look for clues and you will find***
> ***You truly need to use your Mind'***

'It was on the church door,' Sally said to the room. 'Someone had nailed it there. It must be the clue my husband referred to in his sermon about the Golden Swan.'

Total silence greeted her words.

Dirk hadn't gone to church that morning and didn't understand the look of surprise and anticipation on people's faces. 'Er, what Golden Swan?'

He was inundated with replies but soon got the message that the swan statue meant a great deal to the villagers and it had been nicked. He didn't think he had seen his clientele so animated before.

Before anything more could be said, the Vicar, Russ, Josh and Morgana came in together. The Vicar saw his wife. 'What's going on?' he asked.

She took the piece of paper from Dirk and handed it to him. He read it with a frown on his face, then handed it to Josh, who read it and passed it to Russ.

Josh said. 'That must be some sort of riddle or clue.'

Cries of 'No shit, Sherlock,' and other rude remarks greeted that pronouncement.

A general discussion broke out. Everyone had an opinion, nobody had the slightest idea what the words meant.

Then the Vicar spotted Jane, the lady of the manor who lived in the large Manor House with her seldom seen and reclusive husband. The two of them started talking. It didn't take long for everyone to work out that they might have an idea what the clue was about.

'It's at the Manor house,' someone shouted. 'I just heard the Vicar say so.'

Immediately, chaos broke out as everyone tried to get to the door at the same time.

Chapter 4

As Daisy was busy retrieving a kitten from the curtains, where it hung like a rather cute bat, she heard a bit of a commotion going on outside. Looking through the window, she said to Violet, who was snuggled into her usual armchair, 'What on earth are those idiots up to now? There's a whole herd of them coming out of the pub, pushing and shoving each other but trying to pretend they aren't. It looks like the start of a badly organised race.'

This was followed by 'Ouch' as the kitten sank its needle-like teeth into her hand.

'Oh, who cares?' said Violet. 'It's probably just another of their stupid games.'

Meanwhile, with a lot of jostling, but as Daisy had observed from her vantage point, trying to look as if they weren't, the crowd from the Black Swan were following the Vicar and chattering excitedly. By the time they arrived outside the Manor House, they had almost broken into a brisk trot, with some of them breathing heavily.

When the Vicar stopped, rather abruptly, at the large porch over the front door, there were a few collisions and exchanged words, not all of them apologies.

'Now,' proclaimed the Vicar, waving his arms around, 'You see that inscription over the door?' He pointed up into the gloom where there was indeed some kind of intricate carving in dark wood shadowed by the porch. Words could just be made out, although it was difficult to see.

There were mutters of 'What?' 'Where?' 'Can't see a thing.' Also, 'Get off my foot'.

'You see,' the Vicar continued, getting into speech-making mode, 'I happen to know that it is a quote from Juvenal, the Roman poet, from around the first century AD.' This led to more muttering and some groaning from the crowd, including someone saying indignantly. 'Who's he calling juvenile?'

'It says,' the Vicar persevered. 'Mens sana in corpore sano, which, translated from the Latin, means 'a healthy mind in a healthy body.' Mind, you see, use your mind, as the poem says. I think the next clue is somewhere up there,' he said, indicating the carvings.

'I just remembered the inscription and its meaning,' Jane said. 'It's supposed to be the family motto, although rarely used these days. Most people don't even know it's there and I hadn't thought about it for years.'

The Vicar nodded and said, 'What we really need is a torch.'

Jane dashed into the house and quickly returned with one. The crowd, less restless now, quite hushed with excitement, peered upwards, trying to be the first to spot something. There was a greater chance of this when Jane shone her large torch on the inscription and carvings.

After several minutes of diligent looking, helped by another torch being produced by someone, nothing was found. The leaves and flowers around the inscription were quite deeply carved and rather dusty, so it was hard to see if anything had been hidden there. People began to look disappointed and to wonder if it was the wrong place.

'A step ladder, that would help,' said Morgana. 'I bet it's up there but we're too low to see it.'

Jane disappeared into the garage around the side of the house and came back carrying one. Josh hurried to help her with it and there was then a scramble as several people tried to get on it at the same time.

'This is my house, my ladder and I'll be the one to use it, thank you,' said Jane firmly, pushing her way through and climbing up. Torches were shone and, under Jane's direction, moved methodically over the carvings. She reached out and carefully swept her hand lightly over them, dislodging clouds of dust.

'It's rather dusty...' She stopped. 'Hang on, I think I can feel something papery, but...' She sneezed violently, wobbled precariously, and reluctantly came down the ladder. 'I can't quite reach it.'

The Blackney Swans

'I'll go up, I'm much taller than you,' interrupted Pete Sturrock, and before anyone could argue, he almost ran up the ladder and stretched out to where Jane had been trying to reach.

'There is something! It feels like ... yes it's a tightly rolled piece of paper.'

He came down with it and bedlam broke out as the entire crowd began pushing and shoving, trying to see it.

'Right, everyone stop, or you'll damage it!' the Vicar said, in a surprisingly powerful voice. 'I will read it out so everyone can hear it at the same time and we'll make copies for those who want them, so no need to fight over it.'

He unrolled it carefully, shone a torch on it and read it out.

> **'*You found the clue, so you're doing quite Well,***
> ** *But it's time to think of St Cygnus now***
> ** *And the story of sacred swans we tell.***
> ** *Never forget they're our why and how.***
>
> ** *Now look for something that doesn't belong***
> ** *In a special place where magic is strong.***
> ** *It may be low, or it could be high***
> ** *But hope will Spring if you really try.'***

Silence. Puzzled looks, heads being shaken.

'Who the hell is doing this anyway?' said Pete.

'And why?' wondered Jane.

'Oh come on,' someone said loudly. 'It's bloody obvious where it is. It's the well.'

There were shouts of agreement, and within seconds everyone was stampeding back across the village green towards the woods at the back of the village.

The Vicar wasn't going to charge along with the herd and took up the rear with Morgana and Jane.

'Not going to rush then?' Morgana asked.

'Sometimes when things are that obvious, maybe there's more to it,' he replied.

The Blackney Swans

Even so, it wasn't long before everyone had arrived at the well. It was still strewn with the decorations from earlier in the year. But by the time the vicar arrived, much of those had been grabbed and examined.

'Oh dear,' the Vicar said and then called out loudly, 'Leave that all alone, you vandals. Let's think about this sensibly. Some of you here helped decorate the well in the spring. Have you seen anything that doesn't belong, something out of place?'

Silence greeted his question, and then Russ spotted something almost hidden at the back of the well. It was an item of clothing that for some reason, no one had made any effort to touch.

'Er, I'm pretty sure that wasn't put there in May,' he said, pointing to it.

'Oh yuck,' Morgana said. 'Is that what I think it is?'

Surprised, Josh turned toward her. 'How on earth would you even know to ask that question?'

'Because many years ago I had a boyfriend who used them and he put them in the washing machine with my washing when he thought I wasn't looking. Now someone is going to have to look in it, aren't they, Josh?' she said, giving him a stare that brooked no disagreement.

Everyone made space as a reluctant Josh went over to the back of the well and prodded the offending item with a piece of stick he had picked up.

'There's something inside,' he announced. He reached in and very carefully, with two fingers, extracted a slip of paper. He studied it for a second and then read it out to the assembled throng.

> **'There are many places that water loves**
> **The village will hold the truth**
> **Search high and low**
> **To find your way'**

'Oh bloody hell, what does that mean?' Pete Sturrock asked.

'My guess,' the Vicar said, 'is that there is another well or water source hidden in the village and we will need to search for it. But, look everyone, it's getting late, it will be dark soon. We can search tomorrow. I don't know about you lot but I'm going home.'

The Blackney Swans

The crowd broke up and went their own ways, but all with one purpose for the next day. Russ, Josh and Morgana decided to go back to the pub, along with many others.

'You've got to hand it to whoever is doing this, 'Russ said. 'They had to pick something that would be left alone, something no one would want to touch. What could have been better than a Rugby player's old and worn jock strap?'

Chapter 5

Russ and Pete Sturrock had spent most of the evening in the pub in deep conversation. The two men knew the village quite intimately but neither could think of the location of another well. Mind you, just about the whole clientele in the pub were having the same conversation.

'There is something else,' Pete said.

'Oh go on then.'

'Well that Swan is made of quite a chunk of gold. Everyone seems hell bent on following the clues but I bet no one has thought beyond that.'

'Sorry, what's your point?' Russ asked.

'Simple really. I'm guessing that the end game is to get it back and replace it in the church, but if it was never found, the village would have to live with that. And if some enterprising chaps did manage to stumble across it first, then maybe it could make them a rather nice chunk of cash. Melted down that is.'

Russ sat back and considered the idea. 'We would be in deep, deep shit if anyone ever found out. But there again, it would be worth quite a lot of dosh. I tell you what. If we do get it first and we are sure no one else works it out then let's go for it. But just you and me. Josh is under Morgana's thumb and she would go bananas at the idea.'

'Agreed.'

The next day, they met up outside Russ's house and started the search. They had decided to start with a general walk around looking at the known water courses. Pete had got hold of a detailed Ordnance Survey map and they were using it to work out a route. The only problem was that they were not the only ones with similar ideas. Everywhere you looked there were small groups of people furtively walking around studying the various houses and poking their noses into areas where they were clearly not wanted. That was if the shouts of annoyance from the various householders was anything to go by. At one point, they met Josh and Morgana clearly also out for an 'early morning walk'. They exchanged pleasantries but nothing more.

'The whole place has gone barking mad,' Pete said at one point

'Yes, but let's not forget the prize,' Russ said. 'Now let's go back to the well and follow the stream from there.'

By lunchtime, success had eluded them, as it clearly had everyone else and they retired to the pub to contemplate what to do next.

That morning, Police Constable Charles Cridge was on patrol. He had avoided Blackney ever since the fiasco at the summer music festival. However, the trauma of being swept away by the water from the collapsing duck pond had diminished. He was determined to re-establish his credentials and authority over that den of miscreants. All his working life, he'd just known that the inhabitants of the village were up to no good, but not once had he been able to prove anything. The moment there was the slightest hint of interference from outside, they all closed ranks. He was not going to let this stop him, though. They would make a mistake eventually and he would be there.

Today was turning out to be very unusual. Everybody was being nice to him. That had never happened before and immediately roused his suspicions. As he pedalled on his repaired official police bicycle into the village, several people gave him a friendly wave. But something was definitely going on. Every now and then, he would see small groups of villages hurrying out of sight. It was almost as if they were looking for something, but for the life of him, he couldn't work out what or why.

He dismounted by the village shop and the two silly women who ran the place greeted him with a friendly 'good day' and chatted to him, asking how he was after his mishap in the summer. One even offered him a kitten as they seemed to have acquired some extras. Completely taken off guard, he even found himself replying pleasantly, although he made his dislike of pussycats clear. Well, if everyone was being nice to him, he decided to try the pub. That hotbed of gossip would no doubt give him a better idea of what was really going on.

The new landlord, the famous rock star, greeted him like a long lost friend and offered him a drink on the house. As he looked around the bar, he got several friendly nods of acknowledgement from some of the locals, who were all sitting in odd little groups. What the hell was going on? The one thing he definitely was not going to do was let them pull the wool over his eyes. The whole damned village was up to something, that was very clear. The problem was that he could hardly accuse them of malfeasance when everybody was being so pleasant.

As he pedalled away later that afternoon, he vowed he would find out what was really going on even if it meant he had to be more clandestine in his approach. Going undercover was what was needed. He wouldn't tell his Sergeant what he intended until he had made arrests. Then he would get the recognition he knew he deserved.

After Cridge had left, a small group of witches led by a man in black robes made their way wearily back to the road from hours of tramping along the streams. They were all well wrapped up. At this end of October no one had fancied going sky-clad.

A few had dangled something feathery but their hearts hadn't been in the hunt without Lesley. And then there was that Gilbert standing up when they'd first assembled around lunchtime to hunt for the missing statue and spouting a load of stuff about how he had specific instructions from Lesley to lead them in her absence.

'Greetings,' he'd said. 'I am studying the true way and I have a message for you all from our great mind, who wishes henceforth to be known as Celeste. She has gone to seek enlightenment on Dartmoor till next Friday and wishes you to know that she will be channelling her desires through me while she's away. So, as I'm in charge today, I say we go out the far side of the chapel and look there.'

They seemed to do a lot of walking to no purpose, and when they reassembled, Gilbert just said, 'No luck this time, then,' and walked away.

'So much for 'our great mind',' said one to another as they set off for home and lunch. 'How come Lesley's decided to change everything without consulting us? And now we can't even get hold of her for a week. Celeste, I ask you.'

'I know,' said her friend. 'She's taking liberties. As it happens, she did tell me about the Celeste thing. She wanted my advice. And I did say I didn't think anyone would mind if she wanted to stop being Lesley. After all, it's not very witchy, is it? But that's just one thing. I joined her in the first place because we were all women and that's what I was after. A place to get away from blokes and the kids, and be a bit silly if I felt like it. Dress up or go starkers. Let go. It was bad enough Lesley giving Gilbert a part at the Beltane ritual, whatever he was supposed to be with that thing stuck on his face, but at least she apologised afterwards, said she'd got carried away by her search for the male principle in all creation. But she'd never talk about channelling her desires, that's not her kind of language. I reckon he's lying.'

'So, are you going to carry on with the hunt for the statue?'

'I reckon I will. What did that clue say? In a special place where magic is strong. I don't know about that, but I'll tell you something for nothing. Pete Sturrock is up to no good with Russ. I saw them talking around the back of the pub and they looked shifty. I shouldn't be surprised if they've pulled some kind of stunt and know exactly where the golden statue is. Forget Gilbert, we'll follow them.'

Chapter 6

Josh and Morgana had wandered around fruitlessly, even calling in at Misselania, to talk to Daisy and Violet. As Josh said, although they didn't seem to be taking an interest in the search, they had lived in the village for years and probably knew a lot about local history and might have some ideas about locations of springs and wells.

The conversation had proved useless and rather annoying, seeming to keep coming back to cats. There were a number of kittens in the shop, hurtling around and climbing on objects and people. As they left, Josh had to detach one from his trouser leg, where it hung on as if by Velcro.

'Well, I can see why it wants to escape,' he said grumpily, examining the scratches on his hand. 'I find those two irritating after about five minutes, and they were no help at all.'

'It was worth a try.' Morgana sighed and began, 'Where shall we search...'

At which point, a large red-faced woman, who lived in one of the more expensive village houses came striding up to them. They didn't really know her, as she rarely got involved in village life and was one of a few incomers known to have a low opinion of the locals.

'How dare you?' she shouted at Morgana. 'I know they're yours, it's your responsibility to look after them and I will be expecting compensation for the damage they've done. My garden is ruined.'

'Just a minute,' interrupted Josh. 'Who are you talking about? And what gives you the right to shout at Morgana like that?'

Morgana had a horrible feeling she knew who 'they' might be. 'Are you talking about my goats? Because if you are, they were safely shut in their field when I left them earlier.'

Josh groaned, muttered something about 'déjà vu' and trudged after the indignant woman, who had stormed off, gesturing at them to follow her. Morgana trotted behind him, also muttering to herself.

When they reached the scene of the crime, they saw Gertie relaxing nonchalantly on a garden table with what appeared to be a sock draped over one of her horns. Sybill was strolling around the lawn with a length of pink fabric hanging out of her mouth, which she was chewing on happily.

Morgana and Josh rounded up the miscreants, and Morgana retrieved the object from Sybill's mouth. It was very slimy and appeared to be a very large pair of ladies' knickers. Trying to keep a straight face, she held them out at arm's length.

'Yours presumably?' Mrs Red Face by now looked positively purple and seeming beyond speech, merely nodded. She snatched the unpleasant object and held it behind her back.

Morgana reluctantly apologised for the damage but insisted that Sybill and Gertie must have been released by someone. Admittedly, the garden was rather a mess, some haphazard 'pruning' of late roses had taken place, lots of plants were trampled and washing had been pulled off the line and was stencilled with neat little hoof prints.

Back at the goats' paddock, it was obvious that some of the treasure hunters had been there. The gate was wide open and there were footprints all over the place, especially in the corner, which was always wet and muddy.

'Someone must have thought this was a spring or the site of an old well,' said Josh. 'I don't think it is, it's just a bit boggy. Nothing magical.'

'Idiots!' Morgana was furious. 'Just wait till I get my hands on them. They'll need a bit of magic, especially if I end up having to pay for that garden to be sorted out.

'If anyone owns up of course,' said Josh. 'We may never know.' Just then they heard some very loud excited voices coming from somewhere over the other side of the village.

'Sounds like something's happening, come on!' said Josh, never one to ignore the obvious. He grabbed Morgana's hand and they dashed in the direction of the voices.

The Blackney Swans

That afternoon, Sally, bearing dowsing rods and yellow Marigold gloves had set off with the Vicar and Mrs Thingleton. Once outside, they were agreeably surprised to be joined by Dirk, who had locked up the pub and, after rootling around in his outbuildings, had found what appeared to be a grave digger's spade. Or it might have been a peat cutter. It was tall and narrow with a slight curve. Sally shook her head and decided not to digress down that rabbit hole and focus on finding clues in wet places. They all sported wellington boots with thick socks turned over the tops, so they didn't chafe.

Mrs Thing had come in for elevenses earlier and they had poured over old maps and ordnance ones, making a plan to check out the field belonging to the butcher, who was out on his rounds and Mrs B was manning the shop, so they couldn't join in the hunt. They said it was OK for the vicar to do so, as long as they told them if anything was found. The field had little clumps of reeds growing in it, just like on the old maps, as it had in the past been designated a water meadow.

Russ and Pete had been out on the levels and circled almost completely round the top of the village. There was plenty of water but no wells and no springs. As they got near the back of Russ and Josh's two terraced cottages, Russ spotted movement at the rear. He pointed it out to Pete.

'That's where you keep your little enterprise isn't it?' Pete asked. 'And that looks like Tolly and Constance. What are they up to?'

'No idea but it looks as if they've just come out of the still. Josh must have forgotten to lock up again. We'd better see what they've been doing, although from the way they are walking I can guess.'

As the two men approached, they could hear the two young girls. 'Yup. they've been at the hooch,' Russ said. 'We'd better intercept them. If their parents find out they've been drinking our moonshine there could be real trouble.'

Then one of the girls said something that stopped them in their tracks.

'The whole village is looking in the wrong place.' Tolly said to her friend in a rather slurred voice.

'Yes,' Constance said, giggling. 'And we've worked it out. Shall we go there now?'

'Yes, why not? It's a nice day and we can see what the next clue is. Maybe we can solve the whole thing.'

'Or maybe we can finish this off first,' Constance said, holding up a half empty bottle. 'It's really nice stuff, don't know why mum says it's bad for you.' Both girls started giggling again.

Pete and Russ looked at each other. 'They haven't seen us yet. Let's keep clear and follow them, who knows they might even be right.'

No sooner had Sally Dirk and the vicar set off than they heard a commotion. They all stood with their mouths agape at the sight of Constance and Tolly, both weaving about and giggling, one of them clutching a bottle at an alarming level of near emptiness. Sally immediately decided a motherly approach might succeed, removed her Marigolds and slapped them, together with the divining rods, into the chest of the vicar, who snapped out of his mesmer in surprise with the impact and automatically clutched them to himself.

However, a group of the local witches then appeared with a determined look on their faces and managed to get in everyone's way, the result being that everyone failed to capture the girls, who seemed completely oblivious They all followed them, the crowd growing by the minute to the field behind Russ and Josh's house which, conveniently, had been their planned search area anyway. The girls were clearly heading towards the two ancient standing stones at the end of the field.

People were watching each other, little groups semi-merging, keen to be in on the search but keeping their allegiances despite all going in the same direction. The girls were being quite loud and impolite about how silly all the searchers were and how they knew the source of the other spring.

The Blackney Swans

The Vicar, sensing trouble, donated the Marigolds and rods to Mrs Thing and ran with Sally and Dirk close behind to the group now gathering at the standing stones.

'What have you got there?' someone called.

''S a clue innit?' Tolly said, holding an empty bottle unlike the other one that Constance was taking a swig from. She looked around in mild surprise at the crowd now starting to surround them. 'You silly sods were all looking for a well or a great spring of water. But we come down here quite often and remembered it's all wet.'

'Yeah,' Constance said between hiccups. 'That's where the little pond in the corner gets its water.'

'Yeah and it's the lowest part of the village and the stones have always seemed a bit odd you know,' Tolly said, still clutching the bottle she had found. 'It was in the soggy ground just there and look there's a bit of paper inside.'

Tolly raised the liquid-free, muddy bottle containing the rolled up piece of paper for all to see. Samantha, Tolly's mother, demanded she hand it over. Pete Sturrock made an attempt to grab it but was trumped by Dirk with his superior height, who reached in and relieved Tolly of her prize containing the clue. He handed it straight to the Vicar, who after much difficulty, helpful advice and some verbal abuse, eventually with the help of one of the dowsing rods managed to coax the paper out of the bottle and read aloud the clue to the now silent crowd.

> *'You've been searching since sunrise*
> *found clues and empty nests*
> *Seek an Arthurian surprise*
> *As an Antipodean rests'*

There was a collective groan and muttering started with all sorts of theories being bandied around and more than one person asking what the hell 'Antipodean' meant. The general consensus was more thought was needed and the best place to do that was in the pub.

'Stop,' called Dirk as he got to the pub door and held aloft the door key. 'Let's get the girls sorted out and some black coffee into them first. I'll open up for everyone after.'

The Blackney Swans

Tolly's mother was very cross but knew she couldn't manage to steer the girls home on her own and that everyone else would want to follow the clue. She reluctantly let them be helped to the pub. When Dirk opened the door, he let the Vicar, Sally, Mrs T, the now looking not very well girls and Samantha in. They sat the girls down and Mrs T headed behind the bar to make strong coffee. As soon as things were settled, Dirk opened up and what seemed like the rest of the village poured in.

Chapter 7

Cridge chuckled to himself. No one had recognised him. Why hadn't he thought of this before? Mind you, his Sergeant wouldn't be best pleased, but there again he would never know. His morning visit had raised all sorts of suspicions. Now he was going to find out. He had chosen his disguise carefully. He was even finding it strangely arousing. Dressing as a woman would be the last thing the locals would expect. His only worry was that his wife would discover he had borrowed some of her clothes. He had been careful, knowing that many of her dresses and shoes rarely saw the light of day, so hopefully they would not be missed for a few hours. The wig was the hardest thing to source. In the end, he had to nip into Bridgwater and had found a hairdresser that sold them. It wasn't cheap but he felt it was worth every penny. He had even practised in front of the mirror and was confident that he had everything, including the walk, well-rehearsed.

His first stop at the shop had gone well, so he completely missed the action down at the field. The girls didn't react when he went in and bought some sandwiches, explaining that he was lost and asking for directions. His next stop had been the church, but there was no one there so he realised he was going to have to risk the pub. When he entered, the place was packed but no one even turned to look. He gave the same story to Dirk at the bar, explaining that he had taken a wrong turn and discovered the village by accident. So he ordered some food. Taking his ploughman's and a drink, he sat himself in a corner and started to listen. The place seemed strangely animated with all sorts of talk about some bloke called Arthur.

Unfortunately for Cridge and what he didn't know was that he had been spotted long before arriving at the village. Pete Sturrock's dad had recognised Cridge's car from the seat of his tractor as he had been working one his fields next to the road. What he didn't recognise was the woman driving it. He knew exactly what Carrie

Cridge looked like as he had been 'visiting' her for some time when her husband was out. The woman at the wheel definitely was not her. He had jumped off his tractor and managed to follow the car as it was only a few hundred yards from the village. The person who got out looked awkward and seemed to spend quite some time fiddling with her clothing and bra before setting off on foot. He was able to sneak up quite close and observe without being seen. He very quickly realised who it really was. The person was wearing one of Carrie's dresses which didn't fit too well and had a blonde wig that might have been in fashion twenty years past. Taking a short cut, Pete's dad had gone through the strangely quiet village and headed for the pub.

Cridge was getting frustrated. All the conversation he could hear was banal rubbish about some silly rhyme and talk of missing swans. There was no mention of what was clearly going on. Luckily, that young farmer, Sturrock, and his dad, along with that crook Russ were within earshot. Maybe he would get some intelligence at last. He settled down to listen.

'You been busy, Dad?' Pete asked.

'Not really,' his dad replied. 'It's been quiet lately. It'd be nice to have something actually happen for a change.'

'Yes,' Russ said. 'Even that busybody Cridge would get bored. Haven't seen him for a while. I wonder what he's up to.'

'Damned busybody,' Pete said. 'Didn't he get half drowned during the music festival when the pond burst its banks?'

'Sure did,' Russ said. 'Only been seen once since then, this morning. Hopefully, he's got the hint that the pond has it in for him.'

'Well, he always seems to end up in it anyway,' Pete said and they all laughed. 'Probably been fired by now, otherwise we would have seen him snooping around a lot more.'

'Yeah, he's a real pain in the arse,' Pete's dad said. 'But I have it on good authority that he's still working. Shame really, as his wife is rather cute.'

Cridge had been hearing all this and getting more and more angry. Was this how they spoke about him behind his back? Where was the respect for the law? The final remark about Cassie caused him to nearly choke on a pickled onion.

At the noise, all three men turned to look at him as did everyone else in the pub. Suddenly it was very quiet.

The Blackney Swans

'Sorry Miss, is there a problem?' Russ asked.

'No, of course not,' Cridge said in his high pitched voice keeping his eyes lowered. 'Just a piece of pickle going down the wrong way.'

The three men walked over and sat at Cridge's table. 'You didn't really think that disguise would fool anyone did you, Cridge? Pete asked. 'Dad saw you park up and walk in and we know the car and that wig is bloody awful.'

Cridge knew when his cover was blown. 'Right, I know something is going on in the village and I'm bloody well going to find out what.' He stood to leave.

'Oh no you bloody well don't,' Pete said. 'But we'll help you out, don't you worry about that.'

Pete and Russ grabbed him by both arms as Josh who knew what was coming next opened the door. The four men went out, the door closed and a hush descended over the pub. A few seconds later there was a distant cry and the sound of a large splash. A cheer went up as three men came back in.

Laughing again at Cridge's latest ignominious swim in the pond, Dirk was clearing up after everyone had at last gone home. He hummed one of his old songs as he worked and suddenly realised, with surprise, that he felt happy. How had that happened? Shaking his head he began wiping tables and pondered on this latest clue. It was all quite good entertainment and although the clues were terrible poetry and not really difficult, this last one had got them all thinking. An Arthurian surprise and something about an Antipodean?

Still letting his mind wander he thought that he'd never imagined that he'd end up running a pub, but there was something about the Black Swan. He'd liked it as soon as he walked in. He stopped abruptly, cleaning cloth in hand. Black Swan – Antipodean! Of course, black swans were from Australia, so they were Antipodean. The clue must be somewhere right here!

He knew there were stories about Arthur in these parts, as he had been researching them for some time, but he needed to find something in the pub. He looked around quickly; no suits of armour

The Blackney Swans

he'd never noticed before. Despite his investigations, his knowledge of the Arthur stories was still a bit sketchy and largely based on American movies filmed in a very inaccurate mock medieval setting. No chalices or strange looking goblets, so what was there?

Dirk slowed down and started to look more methodically, working around the room. Nothing. Feeling deflated, he sat down with a sigh in front of the dying fire, looking up at the assortment of old photos, small paintings and odd bits and pieces on the wall above the fireplace, many of them darkened with soot. Amongst them was a plaque of some kind, quite small and very grubby. It looked very old and rather battered. Examining it more closely, he realised it was shaped like a shield. He took it down and carefully wiped the surface. Emerging from the grime he saw colours and patterns, red and blue, three golden crowns and maybe a bird of some kind. It definitely looked like a heraldic device of some sort.

The back felt rough and turning it over, he saw, with growing excitement, a small piece of card stuck firmly to the wood. There was tiny writing on it. Dirk rushed off to find his glasses, cursing that his eyesight wasn't so good now. He still couldn't read it. He really needed a magnifier, which was frustrating. Then, with sudden inspiration, he fetched a clean heavy bottomed glass from the bar, placed it over the card and began to read.

He'd found it! When no-one else had! He quickly looked at his watch. It was a bit late but what the hell, he really needed to tell the Vicar. He picked up the phone and dialled, so excited he was actually shaking.

'Sorry to disturb you so late, Vicar, but this is urgent. I have found the last clue and you need to hear it before tomorrow!'

The next day, word had gone around the village to be in the pub at lunchtime. No one knew why but speculation was high. Dirk and the Vicar were standing by the bar as the place filled up. At one o'clock, Dirk tapped a beer glass with a pair of ice tongs and immediately the place went quiet.

'Ladies and gentlemen,' he boomed out. 'Last night I solved the last riddle. The antipodean reference was this pub, as black swans originated in Australia. Above the bar, I found a small heraldic crest. On the back of it, someone had stuck another clue.'

A collective groan went around the room.

'Yes, yes, I know. I think it's safe to say we are all getting rather fed up with this now. Anyway, let me read it out.

'Gather to commemorate
Those at their final rest
And your Cygnus re-dedicate
From the hands of dear Celeste'

Speculative muttering immediately started up. Comments like 'Celeste, who the bloody hell is Celeste?' and 'Has someone died then?' were heard, but before everyone got carried away, the Vicar called for quiet.

'I can see some of you have already worked it out,' he said. 'But for those who haven't, you might remember seeing the posters around the village and at the church for the All Hallows Eve service tonight. Otherwise known as Halloween. So if we want to find out what this has all been about, the service starts at eight tonight. I expect I will be seeing more of you in church than I have for a long time.

Chapter 8

Lesley, no dammit Celeste, she reminded herself yet again, was ready. It hadn't been easy to sneak into the church, what with the preparation for the All Hallows service and the whole village knowing something was going to happen, but she knew the church intimately. Now that she was ensconced in the little minstrel's gallery by the organ, she was safe from view and could wait in safety. It was really quite high up but it also meant she would be visible to everyone once she stood up for her great revelation. Her one worry had been that the villagers would be too damned thick to work out the clues over the last few days. She needn't have worried though, even if the solution of one of the clues had relied on the intelligence of two young girls who had been at Russ's hooch. She had had contingency plans, which is why she had recruited her cousin Gilbert. From what she had seen from a distance, that hadn't been such a good idea, as all the girls had apparently given him a stiff ignoring. Luckily, she hadn't needed to use him. In fact, her biggest problem had been to remain out of sight, but once again her intimate knowledge of the village had helped, along with dressing up as an old man.

So now she was going to wake everyone up to their responsibilities and remind them of the origin of Blackney Foloren and the debt they all owed to Cygnus and the swans. In some ways, it was a shame that she had needed to use the church to get everyone together but it was one of the only two places most of the village could be tempted into. The alternative would have been the pub and there had been enough disasters and fights in there over the years to make that a very poor choice. Her religion and that of the Vicar had rubbed together alongside each other for all the years and she felt sure he would support her underlying premise if not her actual tactics.

The Blackney Swans

She heard the main doors open and the chatter of people coming in. Looking at her watch she saw it was coming up to eight o'clock. Not long now. She made a final check of her preparations. The Gold Swan was in its case which gleamed from a thorough cleaning and polish. Inside was the little torch which she could reach down from the open top and turn on at the right moment. The much bigger torch was taped to the railing behind her and should illuminate her nicely. Finally, she checked over her clothing. The white dress, made almost entirely of swan's feathers was clinging to her nicely. It was a simple white summer dress which she had painstakingly glued the feathers onto one by one. On her back were her wings. Each one was a simple frame made of wire connected to a harness around her shoulders. The wires were covered with more feather-covered cloth. Getting the design right had taken a lot of time but she was sure they would look spectacular. When she stood with the gold swan in her hands and the light from behind, it would be a breathtaking sight. No one in the congregation would be in doubt of her intent and their shame.

The volume of conversation from below was increasing. She looked at her watch. It was just about eight, when everything suddenly went quiet except for the sounds of several pairs of feet slowly walking. They were presumably heading up to the altar, which was just off to one side and below her hiding position.

With trepidation mounting, she reached down and turned on the little torch in the golden swan case and then, while holding it under one arm, she turned on her main light, stood and started to speak in her loud voice. Her first words were meant to be, 'dwellers in the ancient village of Blackney'. What she actually said was 'Aaaargh!!!'

The minstrel's gallery was old, in fact as old as the church itself. The wooden trusses that went into the wall were also that old. They had been sitting in damp stonework for centuries and had lost most of their strength. As no one in recent years had ever used the gallery, it hadn't really been an issue. Celeste had noticed the wood groaning slightly as she crept up but had far more important things on her mind to worry about.

As she stood to make her spectacular appearance, the extra load of the sudden movement made the wood cry out and the section she was standing on simply gave way. The balustrade around the edge was made of sterner material, otherwise she and her swan would have plunged fifteen feet onto a very hard stone floor. She was lucky, part of her swan costume saved her. Her wonderful wings caught on the balustrade, which had only partially broken, and arrested her fall.

For the congregation and the Vicar, it all came as a bit of a surprise to say the least. Everyone had been expecting something but not a strangled cry from above, followed by the cracking and creaking of timbers and a massive cloud of white feathers flying in all directions. All as a strong white light from above illuminated everything in a shimmering cascade.

There was a stunned silence as the feathers fluttered down and over everyone. Then they were able to see what had happened. There was Lesley, the well-known local witch, hanging at a very odd angle from a wooden beam. She was wearing a simple dress, most of which had caught on the beam and therefore gave the whole village an understanding of her underwear preferences. Years later, they would become known as Bridget Jones Granny Pants and to no one's surprise, they were decorated with rather cute little pink birds. As a topic of debate in the pub, it dominated the conversation for months. There was much speculation about whether they were in fact really cygnets or ducks. She was hanging from some sort of harness by what looked like a pair of wings.

However, Celeste was made of stern stuff. As soon as she realised she was not falling and that she still held the golden swan, she started to speak.

'Residents of Blackney, you have forgotten your roots. You have forgotten the strength and beauty of the swan and what it means to all of us. I have here our neglected Golden Swan now restored to its beauty.'

There was another ominous creak from above.

'Oh bloody hell,' followed by, in a less strident tone, 'come on you sods, someone get me down from here!'

Russ and Pete exchanged a rueful grin and along with several others, including the Vicar leapt to the rescue.

Epilogue

'Well that went well,' Russ said.
'What bit was that, then?' Josh asked.
'Oh, you know, the swan being back where it should be.'
'Suppose so, but there was quite a lot of damage to the woodwork in the church.'
'True, but Lesley, sorry Celeste, did offer to pay for it.'
'Yes and you and Pete Sturrock didn't manage to nab the swan first and melt it down.'
'How the hell did you know we planned to do that?'
'I didn't until you admitted it just then, and anyway I've known you for a long time.'
'Bugger. Fair enough but if we had, no one would have ever known.'
'Not that you idiot, you never invited me to be in on it.'
'Oh, yes, well you were with Morgana and she would have gone ballistic.'
'True and I wouldn't have wanted that.'
The two men sat sipping the latest brew.
Then Russ broke the silence. 'Cygnets.'
'Ducks.'

The White Swan

A white swan symbolises the history and spirit of the village.

Chapter 1

An air of autumnal calm had descended on Blakney Foloren. In the church, a gleaming gold swan was displayed prominently above the altar. Morgana was happy feeding her two goats and looking carefully around to see where their latest escape attempt was being planned. Violet and Daisy were happy playing with their five little kittens and plotting who would get one, whether they wanted one or not. The Vicar was happy, attendance at the church was on the up. Celeste and her coterie were all happy that they had re-established their position in the village and were planning their next rituals. Dirk was happy planning more improvements to the pub. Russ and Josh were happy working in the shed, perfecting the latest brew. All was well.

'It's been quite a year so far,' Russ said.

'It certainly has, only two months to go,' Josh replied. 'Still, not a lot can happen before Christmas.'

Russ looked up. 'Did you just say what I thought you said?'

Josh looked back and grinned.

The Vicar and Dirk had been through all the relevant documents in the Vicarage about the Thrust family ancestors.

'I think we need to widen our search Dirk, we could ask at the Manor House to look through their archives.'

'Good idea,' Dirk said.

So the Vicar rang Jane and asked if they could call.

'Yes, you can come now if you like,' she offered so they both hot footed across the village green to the Manor.

They knew that they only had part time staff now at the 'Big House' so were not surprised when Jane answered the door herself.

'Come in, come in.' She urged them and showed them straight into the study where her husband was watching the horse racing on a small television. He immediately offered them both a drink.

The Vicar explained they were investigating the historical documents, tracing local families and events. His Lordship extended an invitation for them to check the storage boxes in the attic, as he only kept their own family papers in the study. Dirk was soon talking horses with his Lordship so Jane took the Vicar to the attics, which were quite chilly and dusty. The room she showed him to was shelved all around and full of boxes, and even had towers of boxes on the floor.

'Gosh, it's going to take me ages to check through all this, is there a system to the filing?' he asked Jane.

'No idea, just work your way through, though the wiring has gone up here, so take a box at a time to the Vicarage to search, then swap it for another when you are ready. Make sure you don't mislay anything.'

'That is very kind of you and I will be very careful. Now my guess is the oldest will be behind the door on the bottom shelf, so I will start there and work my way around the room, how does that sound?'

'Splendid.' Jane said. And they both went back downstairs to join the 'boys' in the study, who were having another drink and a small each way bet on the current race.

A few minutes later, the Vicar excused himself and left them all to it with the racing and briskly retraced his steps to the Vicarage, unable to contain his excitement at the age of some of the documents he had spotted. He just couldn't wait to study them.

The Blackney Swans

It took Zack a long time to process all the discoveries of the Summer Solstice at Blackney. He'd known he was adopted for years. Mum and Dad had explained as soon as they thought he could take it in.

'We love you very much,' they'd said. 'We chose you specially. When we saw you in your little cot, we just knew you were the one.'

'So you're not my real parents.'

'Well, yes and no,' Dad had said. 'Mum didn't grow you inside her. But your birth mother wasn't able to look after you properly, so she decided to let someone else do that.'

All through his childhood, he'd wondered occasionally about those shadowy figures, his birth parents and once he'd hit his teens, he enjoyed flirting with the idea that he was actually the son of someone famous or rich or, better still, both. It'd be like the movies. A millionaire tracking him down and offering him a whole new life. No more driving the crummy delivery van. He'd have his own Lamborghini. And no more hanging around on the streets of Glastonbury and Taunton, he'd be living the high life on a yacht in the Caribbean. His mother was a more shadowy figure. He couldn't imagine why anyone wouldn't have been able to look after their own baby properly. Perhaps she'd died having him. Perhaps she was only young. There'd been that girl at school who left to have a baby and she was only fifteen.

Admittedly odd people had been pointing out over the last year or so that he had the same chin as some ageing rock star called Dick or Dork or whatever but he'd never paid much attention. He wasn't bothered. Just because you had a dimple didn't mean anything. There was that old Hollywood star, whatsisname, the guy who said, 'I'm Spartacus.' He had one too. So what?

And then there'd been Festival Day and everything changed.

He hadn't said anything to Mum and Dad. He didn't want to hurt their feelings and for some reason he couldn't quite put his finger on, he thought Mum especially would be upset if he told them about the scene in the shop.

The Blackney Swans

Violet Coombes, for heaven's sakes. She'd always been so wet ever since he'd started going there. If one of the twins had to be his real mother, then he'd have preferred it to be Daisy. Only there was something about Violet that day he'd never seen before. She was really alive, not just lurking in the background but proud and loud, and part of him hated that he hadn't felt able to ring that evening like he said he would. On top of that everyone called him a hero after he managed to drag that old git off the stage and to safety. He really had no idea why he had done it and was soon fed up with everyone talking about it.

But as the summer passed into autumn and autumn into winter, he stayed away from the village.

Then one night in November, he ran into Pete Sturrock in Bridgwater. Pete had had a few and he stopped when he saw Zack and greeted him like a long lost friend, though they'd never hung out together.

'Ah, Dirk Junior,' he'd said, 'long time no see. Where have you been keeping yourself? You missed all the excitement in Blackney last week.'

'What excitement?'

'Treasure hunts and gold statues and naked ladies in the church.'

'What? The place looks half asleep most of the time.'

'Sure. But every now and then they have one of their festivals and all sorts goes on. Swan this and swan that. I guess that sort of thing's becoming NFB.'

'NFB.'

'Normal for Blackney. They're all weird out there, and the people who move in are the worst. Take the Vicar. He's got a real bee in his bonnet about King Arthur and the knights and chivalry. And he's got Dirk eating out of his hand.'

'What do you mean?'

'He keeps coming up with these scrolls saying Dirk comes from a noble family and Dirk loves it. He struts about the place. Most of the village are getting fed up with it. Russ and Josh think he's lost it entirely. And he's stopped buying their hooch. Not very chivalrous if you ask me.'

'How are Russ and Josh?'

The Blackney Swans

'Oh, you know. Up to this and that. They've got this poultry thing going…'

But Zack wasn't really listening. It was the word 'chivalry' that had got him thinking. Suppose, just suppose Dirk was his real dad and Violet his mum. She must have been a fair bit younger than him when they met. He was already making a name for himself. And when she'd found she was pregnant what had he done about it? Nothing. And now he wanted everyone to look up to him when he was just a rat. Well, he wasn't going to get away with it any longer.

'Listen,' he said, interrupting Pete in mid flow. 'I've a few things I'd like to say to Mr Thrust. Fancy a trip to Blackney tomorrow?'

Chapter 2

It was well after dark by the time Pete and Zack reached the outskirts of Blackney, but as they passed the 30 mph sign, Zack ducked down so his head was below the dashboard.

'What are you doing?' Pete said.

'I don't want anyone to spot me. They might…'

'Might what?'

'Tell that man I'm coming. Warn him.'

'And what if they do? You're not planning anything drastic, are you? You said you just wanted to say a few things. I haven't brought you out here to get violent.'

'That depends on him.'

'Oh come on, Zack. If he is your real father, and it does seem extremely likely, you don't want to go punching each other. For a start, he's a lot bigger than you.'

'OK. But he might have a go at me.'

'I doubt it. From what I hear, he's so grand these days he'd be more likely to hurl some high-falutin insult at you and stalk off.'

Zack sat up in the passenger seat again. 'Sorry. I'm just a bit nervous.'

Pete parked his car and as they walked towards the pub, he said, 'you may spot a few changes since the summer. Starting with that.'

He pointed to the Black Swan sign. No longer the slightly dingy depiction of a swimming bird it had been in the Grinters' day, it now showed a resplendent animal, wings outstretched and boasting a gold crown set back on its head.

'I see what you mean,' Zack said. 'I suppose he's been tarting up the whole place.'

'Just a bit.'

As they pushed through the door, Zack looked around in amazement. The walls had been painted a vibrant yellow and were covered in heraldic shields, individually lit. The place was heaving with customers. The barmaid pulling pints was dressed in a tightly corseted Tudor costume which left little to the imagination.

At the far end, near the door to the skittle alley, a dais had been installed with a round table in the centre of it. And at the table sat

The Blackney Swans

Dirk, also in Tudor costume and now boasting a full beard. The effect of grandeur was, however, somewhat undermined by the small tabby kitten sharpening its claws with gusto on his left boot, a cat that seemed familiar to Zack but maybe too small. What was it doing here?

He nudged Pete. 'That's thingy,' he muttered, 'the moggy from the shop.'

'One of her kittens. I believe his majesty bought her off Daisy Coombes.'

A thousand ideas raced through Zack's head. What had been happening here since the summer? The memory of his last visit was suddenly vivid in his mind. Not just the revelations from Violet and Daisy, but the chaos when the stage began collapsing. That split second when he'd looked at Dirk floundering, panic in his eyes. He'd seen himself, he had... he'd known... Violet and this man were his parents... they had to be. And yes, the pub had had a makeover, but what else had changed? Were the sisters still in the village? Oh, why hadn't he rung that night like he said he would?

'Bought her?' he said. 'Why?'

But before Pete could respond, Dirk had spotted them. He'd removed the cat from his boot and put it under his arm before rising to his feet to bellow, 'Evening Pete, And welcome, um, Zack, isn't it? I'm told I owe you my life.'

The Blackney Swans

It was one of those cold crisp early November mornings. Morgana was out walking, following another of the maze of footpaths near Blackney. She had realised two things as she walked. The first was that there was still a lot of the area which she had never explored but actually wanted to, coupled with a growing appreciation of the natural world around her, a new experience for a former 'townie'. The second was also quite unfamiliar; she actually felt content, even happy!

The footpath she had chosen interested her because although at first glance it was quite overgrown, as she started down it she could see it showed signs of regular use. It headed towards a wooded area and as she drew closer, she could just see what looked like the top of some kind of building. Even more intriguing were the sounds she could now hear, the honking of birds of some kind of geese maybe? And also, someone whistling very off-key, which sounded vaguely familiar.

Morgana crept forward between the trees and saw a small pond surrounded by a grassy area with a roughly made chain-link fence around it. In the enclosure were some geese, a few ducks and several swans. They all looked rather muddy and miserable and she noticed that two of the swans were limping. She could now see the building, which looked like an old half-ruined stone chapel. The whistling was coming from inside. Morgana quietly tip-toed round to the side where there was a window and standing on some blocks of fallen stone, peered inside. There were pens and cages containing more swans and feeding them was the whistling man. It was Josh.

The shock of seeing him made Morgana recoil, fall off her stone perch, land in some brambles and let out a cry of pain, plus a few choice swear words. Suddenly, the natural world didn't seem so charming. 'I knew I recognised that awful whistling,' she muttered to herself, trying to disentangle herself from the brambles. As she struggled to her feet and examined her injuries, Josh came rushing out of the chapel and round the corner, sliding to a halt when he saw who it was.

The Blackney Swans

There was a brief but extremely meaningful silence as they looked at each other, Josh shocked and Morgana agitated.

Then Josh pulled himself together and said indignantly, 'what the hell are you doing here?'

'Never mind what I'm doing, what the bloody hell is going on here? How could you do this? Those poor swans! Now I know what's 'special' about your so called Swan Burgers. I thought when you changed the name in the summer it was just for marketing not that you were actually killing swans to make them.' She paused and glared at him. 'You disgust me and I never want to see you again,' and she stormed off, half sobbing with anger and outrage.

During this diatribe, Josh had just stood there, stunned, open-mouthed. As she turned away, he finally found his voice and began to say, 'wait, let me explain, it's not.....' the words died away. Morgana didn't even look back. Josh put his head in his hands and groaned. He made to follow her, then realised he would have to finish feeding and watering the birds and, very importantly, lock up and do a better job of concealing the path.

When Josh had eventually finished his chores, he headed back to the village to find Morgana. He felt very worried, not only because of her anger with him but also wondering if she had already told anybody what she had found. During the rest of the day, he looked everywhere for her and that evening, although there was a light on in her cottage, she wouldn't open the door. He spent an anxious and miserable night, dreading the fact that he would have to tell Russ, who would probably also be angry with him. Most of all, he was in despair at probably losing Morgana. He hadn't realised how much he wanted to be with her.

Morgana also had a sleepless night, crying, angry with herself at once again being deceived by a man she felt something for. Her mind was flooded with memories of her former life and the unhappy, humiliating experiences which had led to her escaping to Blackney Forloren and starting a new life. The next morning, now cold and angry with Josh, she was determined that no man would ever get emotionally close enough to hurt her again.

Later that morning, after again searching, Josh gravitated towards the pub and decided to have a drink to give him courage before going to see Russ. Sitting at the bar, deep in conversation with Dirk, was Morgana. When Josh entered, she downed the rest of

The Blackney Swans

her drink, said to Dirk 'See you later' and very pointedly, left. Josh immediately followed her, wrestling with the feeling of jealousy which seemed to have overtaken him. He caught up with her but she wouldn't listen. She went into her cottage and slammed the door in his face.

He decided he'd better let her cool down a bit. She could be quite scary when angry. It would appear to be true about people with red hair, in Morgana's case anyway. Then that reminded him how much he loved her red hair and another wave of misery washed over him. He decided that things couldn't get worse, so he went to see Russ to own up.

Things could get worse.

Russ was livid, called him an idiot, amongst other things, for not covering the path up properly and a coward for not making Morgana listen to him. Russ insisted that he go and sort it out with her now and not take no for an answer.

Dragging his feet like a reluctant schoolboy, he returned to Morgana's, took a deep breath and then hammered on the door. Silence from inside.

He called out, 'look, I know you're there and I know you're angry with me but please will you at least let me explain. If you give me a chance, I can make things right.....' He banged on the door again, then leaned against it despondently. At that point Morgana relented and opened the door, Josh falling through and landing at her feet.

'That's about where you belong,' she gazed down at him sternly.

'Yeah, you're probably right. But can we at least talk, and will you please just listen?'

They went and sat down. Josh talked. Morgana listened.

Much later that day, Josh went to see Russ again.

'I spoke to Morgana, explained things and she understands now and has promised not to say a word to anyone.'

'Can you trust her?'

'Oh yes, we're back together again, although apparently it's a probationary situation and I've got to be on best behaviour and to prove myself worthy of her.' Josh gave a sheepish smile.

The Blackney Swans

'Oh dear,' said Russ, laughing. 'What you need is a miracle then. In the meantime, please at least try to make her happy enough to keep her promise about secrecy.'

They clinked glasses of their latest brew to celebrate a lucky escape and the return of romance into Josh's life.

PC Cridge pulled up in his car on the outer edges of the village, with a feeling of de ja vous. He remembered the last time he had come to the village and was seen by a nosy farmer. Unfortunately, he was undercover and dressed in his wife's' clothes, the locals chucked him in that bloody duck pond again, they really enjoyed that. Well, today he was in uniform and on police business so they had better behave themselves. He decided to investigate the top of the village, an area hadn't really had an opportunity to study before. He made his way past the pub and up the little bridleway towards the trees. All was quiet and as he got to the top, he saw a faint opening on the edge of the woods and decided to follow it. It wasn't a heavily worn path, only light footfall, some snapped branches and flattened grass but clearly someone walked here. The path was uneven and a little muddy in places making it difficult to keep his eyes open for signs of life while watching where he was going. At that moment, he heard someone whistling, albeit out of tune, and hid behind a large bush. It was Josh or Russ, whichever one he was, he could never remember which one was which. When the young man had walked far enough away, he decided to walk in the direction from where he came, he was probably up to no good.

After walking another five minutes, he came to an abandoned building. It looked a little like an old chapel. The noises echoed coming from within its walls, and sounded like birds of some sort. Scanning the outside, looking to make sure the young man's troublesome friend wasn't there, he opened the gate. He looked through the broken window and could see swans, geese, and ducks. 'What the.....?' he muttered under his breath. What were they doing

The Blackney Swans

up here? Then he remembered they had been selling 'special swan burgers' on occasions. They really were made of swan then, he thought. There must be something illegal about all of this.

Cridge's mind was turning over and over. He looked up and realised that it was starting to get dark, the path was treacherous enough when you could see. Leaving everything as he left it, he started walking back to his car. His mind still going over all the laws they must be breaking when he lost his footing, ending up on his knees, 'those damned boys. It's all their fault. When he got to his car, he checked to see how much mud he had on him, he didn't want to drag too much into the car.

Driving back out of the village, his mind turned over all he had seen. He pulled up at home not remembering any of the journey. Sitting in his kitchen, he took out his notebook, writing everything down. The list of what he needed to check was short but it looked like he was right, it was more than enough to make some arrests. Taking another look, he decided he might need some additional help to secure the locals, from previous experience, they got feisty. But then he changed his mind, this would be his arrest and no one else was going to get any credit. There must be a law against eating swans or keeping them hostage, he was going to have to consult the law books at the station and make a few phone calls to some environmental experts. 'This time I've got them,' he thought with mounting glee. Did they really think they could get away with any of this?

Chapter 3

Morgana was cross with her goats. They refused to go out of the old stable where they were housed so she had had to lug extra hay and feed in for them. The reason for this inconvenient behaviour was that the November chill had turned to freezing cold for a few days now. Everything was frozen solid, trees covered in ice crystals like living chandeliers and grass white-edged and crunchy.

Sibyll and Gertie were unimpressed with these beautiful sights and seemed to take all inclement weather, anything other than warm and dry, as a personal affront. At least it was relatively warm when Morgana was milking them, although she thought vengefully, her hands were definitely not.

Finishing her chores with a sigh of relief and dreaming of a cup of hot chocolate, she carefully fastened the paddock gate and headed home. Then she heard an odd noise. She stopped and listened. It was a loud rustling like a large cloth being flapped, accompanied by a kind of grunting and hissing. She walked on and realised it was coming from the pond.

The pond had been mostly frozen over apart from the deepest part in the middle, but last night the temperature had dropped even further and that had frozen too. Sitting on the ice was a swan. As Morgana approached the edge of the pond, it flapped its wings and made the sounds she had heard. At first, she wondered why it was doing that, but then she realised that the poor creature was trapped. As water birds do, it must have slept on the pond, safe from predators last night and the remaining free water had frozen around its feet. It flapped and hissed again, then subsided, its neck drooping, its distress evident.

'Oh, you poor thing!' She looked around frantically for help, but of course no one else was out at this time on a freezing morning. There was only one place to go, one person to ask. Morgana headed briskly to Josh's cottage, trying not to slip over on the icy path. Her feelings towards him were still a bit icy too. She had agreed to keep the secret he had with Russ but she was hurt and angry that he hadn't trusted her enough to include her. However, she thought as she banged loudly on his door, she would put all of that aside for now and see if he could do something for the swan.

Josh emerged, still half asleep and wearing an enormous and rather ancient woolly jumper over his pyjamas. Morgana sighed. He currently seemed to live in that horrible jumper and she hadn't known that he even owned pyjamas. She rapidly explained the emergency.

'Right, Ok,' Josh thought for a moment. 'Come in while I get some clothes on and get some kit together.' He dashed upstairs, reappearing rapidly still wearing the jumper but with jeans and thick socks. He immediately flung open the door to the under-stairs cupboard, disappeared inside and began throwing an assortment of objects out: an ancient tennis racket, a bag of assorted old clothes, a box of tins of paint, a football, and eventually with a cry of 'Aha' a roll of bright pink plastic. This was followed by a small cardboard box and a sleeping bag. Leaving the chaos, Josh grabbed the last three items, gave them to Morgana and said 'Right, bring those, I'll get the tools,' and left.

Morgana followed, Josh reappeared from the shed, toolkit in hand. When they reached the pond, the swan looked more droopy and distressed than ever. Josh quickly unrolled the pink plastic, which was patterned with seahorses, starfish and other marine creatures. He took a small pump from the cardboard box, attached it to the plastic object and began pumping as quickly as he could, as Morgana watched, slightly bemused.

'You have a Lilo? A pink Lilo?'

'Yeah,' Josh sounded a little embarrassed. 'Don't ask.'

'Well, no secrets, remember? So, I'll need the full story one day but Ok maybe now isn't the time. So, what's the plan?'

'OK, so I know the ice is probably pretty strong near the edge but further out where the water's deep it might not be safe to walk on. Give me a hand and I'll show you.'

Josh took the now inflated Lilo and slid it out onto the ice as far as he could reach, then with Morgana's help, laid the sleeping bag onto the ice nearer the edge. He took a hammer and chisel from his toolbox, then lay down carefully on the sleeping bag, wriggling

The Blackney Swans

forward and pushing the Lilo closer to the swan, which watched with interest.

Also watching were a few villagers, who had come out, disturbed by the noises. Among them were Violet and Daisy, then Dirk came and joined them. Glancing round, Morgana couldn't help noticing that Dirk had put a protective arm around Violet, who was shivering rather dramatically. Morgana sniffed and turned back to watch Josh. He had reached the swan which was now hissing and pecking at him, as he cautiously chipped away at the ice trapping it. Morgana realised she was holding her breath and worrying about Josh's safety.

'Ouch, ungrateful thing.' Josh muttered but he kept going. One foot was free and the swan was now lifting its head and weakly flapping its wings. Then suddenly, the other foot was free and Josh flung himself flat as the swan pulled itself out onto the ice and half ran, half flapped trying to get enough lift to fly. It was exhausted but somehow, in spite of that and the short take off, it managed to get off the ground and flew away low over Morgana's cottage towards the Levels.

A cheer went up from the onlookers as Josh wriggled back to dry land, pulling the Lilo with him. Laughing, he took a bow and then nearly fell over as Morgana rushed up to him and flung her arms around him. She hugged him for a long time.

'I think I can forgive you now,' and she looked at him with tears in her eyes. 'That was amazing. No wonder I love you.' She stopped, gasped and put her hand over her mouth. 'Oh, hell, I said that out loud, didn't I?'

'That's OK, I don't mind at all, cos I love you too.' Josh paused and took a deep breath. 'In fact, I think we should get married. I've been thinking about it for ages and carrying this around, hoping I could give it to you. It was my grandmother's. He rummaged in his jeans pocket and took out a small blue velvet bag. He opened it and carefully shook out on to the palm of his hand a ring, a round moonstone surrounded by tiny diamonds. He held it out to her silently, his expression serious for once.

One of the watching villagers, who were enjoying a thoroughly entertaining morning, said 'Mind you don't drop that...'

'Don't worry, I won't' Josh and Morgana spoke together.

'Does that mean yes then?' Josh looked at Morgana anxiously.

'Yes,' she said and to another round of cheers, she took the ring and put it on her finger.

The day after the excitement of Josh and Morgana's decision to marry, Daisy and Violet were on a mission. They had discussed their plan fully and agreed that it was a good idea, so were now standing outside Cobweb Cottage, Violet holding a cardboard box. The box moved from time to time and little noises came from it.

Daisy knocked on the door and after quite a long pause it was opened by Josh, looking rather dishevelled.

With a smirk, Daisy said, 'morning Josh, having a lie-in?' Josh began to reply but was rescued by an equally dishevelled Morgana appearing from behind him.

'We have something for you,' said Daisy. 'A kind of early wedding present,' chipped in Violet, holding out the box. Josh took it and Morgana opened it and peered inside. As she did so a small fluffy black head popped up and emitted a high pitched mew.

'One of Georgiana's kittens!' exclaimed Morgana, lifting the little scrap out of the box and clutching it to her tenderly.

'It's a male, and we thought maybe a black cat would kind of suit you, but you've got to look after him, both of you.' Daisy gazed sternly at them.

'Oh we will, we will,' promised Morgana. Josh nodded vigorously and reached out and stroked the kitten gently, with an especially daft grin on his face.

'His name will be Vincent,' said Morgana decidedly. They all looked at her, questions visibly forming in their minds. 'After Vincent Price, Prince of Darkness, you know, the actor in the horror films. Because his father is Lucifer, and he's jet black and is going to be a super-star'.

Daisy laughed happily and to everyone's surprise, including herself, Violet hugged Morgana and then Josh. Vincent purred loudly.

Chapter 4

Morgana couldn't wait to tell her sister Samantha and niece Tolly about her engagement. She rang their doorbell and looked around their garden as she waited for the door to be answered. There were almost no flowers now, she supposed they would have to order some from the florists at Langport. Despite the reward she and Sam had shared for the capture of the crooks, money was not plentiful and they would have to improvise.

Tolly answered the door. 'Hello Aunty Mo,' Tolly greeted Morgana enthusiastically. 'Coming in for a coffee and a chat?' She held the door open for Morgana. 'Mum will be down in a minute.'

Morgana stepped into the hall and caught a wiff of bacon. 'Mm that smells good, bacon sarnies.'

'Yes, I'm just making them, would you like one? I can put more bacon on.'

'Ooh yes please.' Morgana closed her eyes and inhaled again. 'I can't think of anything nicer on a cold morning and tea please, a match made in heaven.' Morgana started to giggle and was smiling from ear to ear.

'Well, I know you like your food but you are showing an extraordinary delight in the idea of a bacon sarnie and a mug of tea this morning.'

'That's because I have some news for you and your Mum. But I will wait to tell you both together.'

'That sounds interesting,' said Tolly as she lifted the bacon from the frying pan and put some slices of bread in to soak up the flavour and fat.

'Have you got a lot of college work on before Christmas Tolly? Or are you reasonably free to do things?' asked Morgana.

'I'm Free,' chirruped Tolly in the style of John Inman's catchphrase.

'Good, because I'm going to need a lot of help from you and your Mum.'

'Help with what?' Asked Sam as she came into the kitchen.

Tolly placed a plate of bacon sandwiches onto the table and then added more bacon to the frying pan to make one for herself.

Sam picked a triangle of deliciousness up but it stayed in midair as Morgana blurted out, 'we are getting married, Josh asked me and I said yes.'

Morgana expected congratulations and hugs but Tolly quipped. 'Going to make an honest woman of you is he?' And laughed.

'Well, I'm pleased for you of course,' Samantha said. 'But are you sure you want to settle down here? Not a lot of security in a shared burger van and an illegal still.'

'I think we can make it work, they are starting to do Saturday Markets in some villages and if we use an acre for growing fruits and vegetables, I have been reading about this Permaculture thing how growing fruit trees, currant bushes and veg all together, it's surprising how you can grow an awful lot in a small space and the goat muck will be free fertilizer.'

'Ha, if the goats don't eat the crops first,' scoffed Tolly.

'Well I'm going to marry him at the winter solstice and I need both of you to help me with a dress and flowers and the Church, make it a really pretty, happy occasion.'

'If it's what you really want Mo then yes, of course we will help you won't we Toll?'

'Love to Aunty Mo, are you having a white dress?'

'Yes, long too and I think some feathers to make it swanny and hopefully warmer as it's mid-winter.'

'Where will we get the feathers?' asked Tolly.

'Oh, the boys say they can provide them. Some of the down ones would be fluffy. How do we wash them though?' Morgana pondered.

'Well, you swish them gently then steam them to kill any bugs. I was using some pheasant ones for a college project and that's what they told me to do. You can use a hairdryer to make them fluffy again.'

'I see a feather boa coming on at least,' mused Sam. 'I expect it depends on how many they have.'

'I think we should ask Sally Fairweather to help as well,' suggested Tolly. 'She has lots of good ideas, and a sewing machine and will know where to buy nice materials and a pattern, this is exciting. And maybe college can help, we can sometimes buy stuff from the college art shop.'

'That sounds as though it would be my sort of price,' Morgana said. 'I don't want to spend too much but I don't want to look cheap or tacky.'

'Why don't we ask Sally over for tea?' Sam suggested. 'Then we can have a chat with her and start to make a plan. You start making notes about what you would like and then we will all put our heads together.'

That afternoon, Sam had made scones and Tolly called in at Misselania on her way back from issuing the invitation to Sally at the Vicarage. She bought clotted cream which surprisingly, was still in date, thank goodness. Sally had agreed to come at four pm with ideas and a notebook. She was very good at organising things and Tolly had briefed her about the dress and not spending a lot.

When Morgana and Josh met at his cottage that evening, she was so bubbly and full of how well the plans were progressing. She asked him about the feathers but would not tell him exactly what they were for, this would be revealed on the 'big day'.

'I'm so pleased we have no real secrets anymore,' Josh said.

'Yes, me too,' said Morgana. 'It's nice having someone you can tell everything to.'

Team Morgana had a few excursions to look in posh bridal shops, even as far as Weston super Mare for ideas about dresses and tiaras. Morgana asked Tolly to be her bridesmaid, she didn't want little ones as they could be as unruly as the goats.

Sally, Tollemina and Mrs Thing would see to the flowers. Sally had suggested winter box and Daphne as they were both evergreen and would probably be flowering at the solstice and would make the church smell nice. With Lisianthus from the supermarket as they last well and don't droop quickly. Tolly volunteered to go in search of pussy willow and Ivy with Constance's help but Conny could only help a little as she was looking after all her brothers and sisters because her mum was embarrassingly having another baby.

She vowed to Tolly she would march her mum to see the nurse after this one was born. Enough was enough.

They did the dressmaking and feather dressing at the vicarage, as it had more room and Sally put sheets on the floor to keep the fabric clean.

Meanwhile, the Vicar amused himself by tying a little clutch of feathers together on the end of some string for the new kitten to play with while he and Dirk poured over some of the old documents they had liberated from the manor.

The vicarage had acquired the kitten due to the Vicar being waylaid at Misselania whilst enquiring about fuse wire for the ancient Victorian fuses in the vicarage. Daisy knew exactly where it was but prevaricated whilst allowing the kittens to mob the Vicar, she had the feeling he would be susceptible to an angelic little bundle of fur and of course, she was quite right.

'I know it's here somewhere Vicar. Oh! Are the kittens escaping? Could you keep them in the basket while I look please?'

'Yes of course Daisy , they really are quite charming but they do have sharp little claws. Oh goodness, the white one is climbing up my trousers ow, Ow.'

'Just lift it off by the scruff like its mother would and give it a cuddle, it won't take me much longer to find your fuse wire.'

'It really is a delightful creature, is this one a boy or a girl Daisy?'

Daisy glanced to see which kitten he had hold of. 'The white one is a boy we think Vicar,' she hid her smile whilst rummaging in another drawer. 'He would love a home you know.'

'I think I'll have a chat with Sally, we could do with a good mouser.'

'That's exactly what her ladyship said they needed at the manor. They've put their name on one of the tabbies. Of course, you will have to take it for its injections and things,' she added.

'Yes, of course, we would want to look after the little fellow well.'

Daisy decided that enough time had elapsed for the Vicar to become smitten with the little white bundle of fur and suddenly produced the card of wire like a magician. It wouldn't be long before the kitten was moving to the other side of the village green 'job well done,' she said to herself.

And so it was that Gabriel, the white little angel son of Lucifer one time resident of the Black Swan, would now live a happy life at the vicarage with lots of fuss, feathers and little furry things to run after.

It was with all these comings and goings at the Vicarage that the idea of Dirk giving Morgana away was mooted. She was going to ask her sister Samantha but they were all still a bit old fashioned at heart and thought a man was more suited to the role. As Sam's husband was still awaiting Her Majesty's pleasure, a replacement was needed.

Mrs Thing polished the church till it shone and smelled of beeswax and cedar polish, a good backnote to the flowers.

Sam made a lovely wedding cake with three tiers from sandwich cakes and iced it in buttercream, she put two little people on the top holding little goats and swans with ribbon leads. It was quite pretty she thought, for all it was her own efforts and Morgana loved it. Half the village had been making and baking for what seemed like days, quiches and sausage rolls, sandwiches with the crusts cut off and quartered into triangles. After great discussion, it had been decided to have the reception in the Black Swan as the sports hall would be cold and austere and the school hall too institutional. Dirk promised a roaring fire, Arctic roll and Vienetta for puddings and spiced cider when they came in from the church to warm everyone up.

Russ and Josh would of course provide 'Swan' burgers and booze. To give the boys the day off, the Bullocks had offered to cook the burgers. It was lovely that half the village were joining in, contributing food, lending china, cutlery, tablecloths and time. Morgana and Josh were very touched by how kind everyone was being.

The day before, Sally, Tollemina, Sam and Mrs Thing made two huge flower arrangements for the entrance to the aisle and some lovely ones for near the altar. Tolly made little Ivy circlets with ribbon bows for the pew ends and Dirk asked her to make

The Blackney Swans

buttonholes for the men, nothing too fussy, so out went the winter box and pussy willow, instead an ivy leaf with a carnation. He also asked her to make two bouquets, one for Morgana and one for the top table at the Black Swan, similar but different, which she thought was very thoughtful of him. Tolly wired up feathers into the bouquets and thought it was a pity the swans couldn't be there.

Chapter 5

To an outsider, it would have looked as if Blackney Foloren was fast asleep. It was a beautiful winter's day. Cold, clear and not a breath of wind. The village was white under a blanket of snow that reflected the golden sunshine. There was no one about.

Today was the twenty second of December. This was the day stolen by the Romans and completely buggered up by the ensuing centuries from claiming its right to be the first day of the New Year. The previous night had been the Winter Solstice and this was the first day that would start to have daylight hours getting longer until mid Summer. So, if it could actually be asked its opinion, it would politely point out that any logical person would be calling it New Year's Day.

It had actually been chosen by Morgana for its ancient significance but the inhabitants of the village couldn't give a toss about ancient cockups with the calendar. No, today was a village event. It was an event that many didn't expect to happen. An event that many had lost bets on actually happening. An event that many couldn't care less about except that there would be a hell of a party afterwards.

Today would mark the wedding of Josh and Morgana and just about everyone had managed to crush into the church.

The Vicar stood at the front by the altar. He was quite staggered that quite so many had crammed themselves inside and even more surprised that Josh was standing expectantly with his friend Russ off to one side of the altar. Both were looking smarter than anyone had ever seen them before in dark suits with a flower in their lapels. Another book had been started in the pub the previous night. It had been giving good odds that Josh would somehow mysteriously

The Blackney Swans

disappear before the critical moment. The Vicar had done rather well with that one and with so many in the church, there was no way Josh would be able to make a bolt for it now. His winnings were secure.

The inside of the church looked lovely. The village ladies had excelled themselves with the flowers and decorations.

He was just about to make a start when he noticed the large floral display at the rear of the nave start to tremble and then shake. A munching sound could then be heard. For a second, he was flummoxed and then he caught sight of a small brown tail and knew exactly what was going on.

'Is Pete Sturrock here?' he called as he scanned the crowd. A hand at the rear went up.

'Ah, there you are Pete, you're a young farmer. We seem to have some uninvited guests, or should that be goats? Would you please do the honours and get the bride's two little monsters out of here and securely shut up at home.'

There ensued what looked like a small rugby scrum, accompanied by annoyed bleating and more than a little cursing. The doors then opened and shut again. Peace resumed.

'Right, anyone else want to eat the decorations, jump off the gallery holding a swan or cause any other upset?' he asked acerbically.

Silence.

'Good,' he nodded to Mrs Thing at the organ and she struck up the wedding march. The doors opened and in walked Morgana on the arm of Dirk.

As befitting a bride, she was dressed totally in white but that's where convention ended. In keeping with local tradition, there was a strong swan connection. She looked over at Lesley/Celeste and her crowd as she walked past, giving them a quick, triumphant smile. The number of times they had mocked and given her the cold shoulder were not forgotten. Today she was Blackney Foloren's white swan with her white dress and the fascinator on her hair resembling the head of the village's favourite bird. The witches could just get totally stuffed.

Josh looked round at her and did a double take which he quickly managed to conceal. Not so Russ, who just stared in fascinated awe.

The not so blushing bride, reached the two men and Dirk gave her hand a gentle squeeze before sitting down next to Violet and Zack in the front pew.

The Vicar looked at his two candidates and kept a very straight face as he launched into his welcoming speech which included the usual 'dearly beloved' and other platitudes. He then got onto the bit he always half dreaded and half anticipated. He sternly asked if anyone present knew of a just impediment as to why Josh and Morgana should not be joined in holy wedlock. Knowing this lot and how long many had already been in the pub already, he was mildly surprised when all there was were a few silly grins and nudges but no one actually spoke.

'Good then let us proceed.......'

He didn't get a chance to say anything more. The doors at the end of the nave flew open with a blast of cold air.

Immediately people started shouting 'shut the bloody door its freezing enough as it is' and 'what idiot did that?' Comments that quickly turned to groans as people recognised who was there, 'Oh not that moron again.' 'Chuck him in the bloody pond.' 'Why can't he stay buggered off.'

Indeed, standing in the door, in his best uniform, looking stern and official, was Police Constable Charles Cridge.

'Stop the wedding,' he called in a loud and authoritative voice. 'Russell Cooper and Josh Summers you are under arrest.'

More muttering broke out as Cridge strode forward towards the two men, none of it was complimentary. All of it was ignored. He was clothed in the armour of righteousness. This was his moment. This was when he would show these villagers just what authority he had under the law. And to be honest, this was revenge for the number of times he had ended up in the bloody duckpond.

The Vicar was incensed. 'PC Cridge, this is not the time and place. Please leave.'

'Sorry Vicar,' Cridge replied. 'The law takes precedence.'

Russ could see that Cridge was pretty sure of his ground. The big question was what had he found out? Had he finally found the still? If so, they could be in real trouble.

'On what grounds? You fat, little, self important man?' Russ asked, trying to burst Cridge's bubble of smugness.

The Blackney Swans

'The illegal raising and killing of birds, namely swans, in contravention of The Countryside act of 1981.'

His triumph was immediately marred by the ripple of laughter that swept the congregation. It also confused Russ and Josh but Russ replied.

'What the hell are you on about Cridge?' We're not raising and killing swans.'

'Oh yes you are,' Cridge replied. 'I found your swan farm out at the old chapel in the woods. You've been raising them and then selling swan burgers through Bullocks the butcher, and I'll be talking to him as well,' he said, looking around.

'Cridge you idiot, we're not farming swans, we're rescuing them, especially cygnets that lose their parents to foxes and accidents but also wounded adults.'

There was a chorus of confirmation from the congregation. It was an object lesson to Russ and Josh about how utterly impossible it was to keep a secret in the village.

'Hah, what about the Swan burgers then? Explain that.'

'In all your snooping, did you not happen to notice that we also have geese and chickens in the same place?' Russ said, looking angry for all sorts of reasons now. 'We discovered that a special blend of goose and chicken makes a very tasty burger. We just called them 'Swan burgers,' as a sort of trademark. The Bullocks have loads in their freezer, you are more than welcome to take one for testing.'

Cridge's confidence was disappearing fast.

'Yeah, we've been doing it all year after we accidentally shot that one in the spring,' Josh said and then received a sharp kick to his shin from Russ, 'Oi why did you do that?' and then the penny dropped. 'Oh bugger.'

'Ah, so you admit to killing a swan, do you?' Cridge said with his confidence back on the up. 'Then, by your own admission, I am putting you two under arrest. You do not need to say anything but anything you…

'Shut up Cridge,' the Vicar said.

'What? Sorry Vicar I need to read these two their rights.'

'No, you bloody well don't. You've interrupted this wedding and once again gone off more than half cocked. Wait there, I will be back in a few seconds.'

The Blackney Swans

Within the minute, the Vicar returned holding an ancient looking piece of paper. He held it up to be seen.

'Some weeks ago, I discovered this in an archive in the manor. Many years ago, this village was visited by King Henry the Eighth. Goodness knows why, he was probably lost but visit he did.'

'This has nothing to do with my arrest,' Cridge blustered.

'SHUT UP Cridge,' nearly every villager shouted at once. This sounded really interesting, they wanted to hear more.

He subsided in angry silence.

'As I was saying,' the Vicar continued. 'The good King seemed to have enjoyed himself rather well. Apparently quite a few red haired babies appeared in the surrounding countryside over the next year. As a parting gift, Henry gave this charter to the village. As you may know there are some organisations that to this day have rights over swans, like the lot down at Abbotsbury, the Queen and two Worshipful Company of Vintners in London whatever they are. I've just had this document verified as legally binding even now. Let me read the pertinent bit and I apologise in advance if I get my 'Ss' and 'Fs' mixed up, Tudor spelling and use of letters was seemingly random. Here we go.'

He held the parchment up and began to read. 'Beloved refidentf, sorry residents of the demesne of Blackney Foloren. In af, as, much as I have been royally content in my vifit, visit, to your dwellings, be it known that now and forever I grant all occupiers the right and tenure of all fwans, dammit swans, to you within a circle of twenty leaguef.'

Cridge was looking a bit sick but refused to give in. 'You're telling me that anyone who lives in the village can kill swans legally because of an old piece of paper? Come on, this another of your bloody tricks.'

'Are you calling me a liar Cridge?' the Vicar said. 'I can show you the correspondence between myself and a London firm of lawyers who specialise in historical issues like this.'

Cridge realised that it was clear, even to him, that the bloody village had won yet again. He deflated like a popped balloon, turned and walked dejectedly back down the nave. The last words anyone heard him say as he left were. 'Don't worry, I'll throw myself in.'

The Blackney Swans

The Vicar looked hard around him. 'Right, can we now get on with this wedding?'

To his horror, he saw Dirk raise his hand.

'Dirk, what is it? Please don't tell me you know that one of these two is already married?' he asked, looking at the potential bride and groom.

'Absolutely not Vicar,' Dirk said as he stood up and partly faced the congregation. 'Some of you may have already noticed that Violet and I have been getting together a little bit.'

A titter ran around the church.

'Alright, I know you lot probably know it all and have been making various bets as well.'

A sea of innocent faces greeted the remark.

'Anyway, last week she agreed to be my bride and we were going to go to the Bridgwater registry office next week but we already have our licence. And anyway, what is the point of trying to do things on the quiet in this village? So, Vicar how about two for the price one? If you agree, all drinks in the pub tonight will be on the house.'

The roar of approval could probably have been heard in Bridgwater.

Epilogue

'Well that went well,' Josh said.

'Hang on, that's my line,' Russ replied 'I always say that when things go well or maybe not quite so well.'

'Tough, it's my turn and anyway it did go properly well just for once.'

'What, the booze up in the pub after the wedding? In that case, I have to agree. Best party the village has had for years and that's saying something.'

'And who would have thought that little shrinking Violet would come out of her shell like that?'

'Getting married to Dirk and hoovering a large amount of hooch certainly showed us another side. I'd never in a million years imagined seeing her dancing with the Vicar quite like that.'

'The Vicar seemed to enjoy it.'

'Yes but you should have seen the look Sally gave him.' They both stopped with grins on their faces for a second as they contemplated the scene.

Josh then reached down and prised off a little ball of fur and claws that was climbing his leg. 'Yours, I believe,' he said, handing the kitten back to his new owner.

'Ah yes, that's little Al. Something else to blame on Violet. I was so surprised when I was in the shop the other day and she actually talked to me, in fact she didn't actually stop. In the end, I agreed to anything just to escape.'

'Al?'

'Surname Capone, seemed appropriate. Now, changing the subject, the honeymoon. You still haven't told me where you went you know.'

'Oh that's right, well we went abroad.'

'Really?'

'Yup, went on a proper ferry over the water and everything.'
'How long did that take?'
'Oh almost an hour.'
'Was the weather nice? Better than here?'
'Bout the same really?'
'And the beer.'
'Bout the same really.'
'And the language, did they all talk oddly?'
'No, bout the same really.'
'Josh, did you go to the Isle of Wight?'
'Yes, that was it, couldn't remember the name for a minute.'

Russ decided it really wasn't worth saying any more and so changed the subject again. 'Have you heard about how Cridge is getting on?'

'Broken leg and concussion but on the mend now. You know, most people would check before throwing themselves into a duck pond, to make sure it wasn't frozen completely solid.'

The Blackney Swans

Some notes about swans and the Levels

The British monarch has the right to claim ownership of all unmarked mute swans in open waters, but this right is limited in practice. Other organizations, including the Worshipful Company of Vintners, Worshipful Company of Dyers and the Abbotsbury Swannery also own swans.

> The Crown has held this right since the 12th century.
>
> The Crown has granted ownership rights to the other organizations in the 14th century (apparently including Blackney Foloren)
>
> The Crown usually only exercises its right from Sunbury-on-Thames to Abingdon in Oxfordshire.
>
> The Worshipful Company of Vintners and the Worshipful Company of Dyers share equally with the Crown in the number of swans in the Thames.
>
> The Crown holds the title of "Seigneur of the Swans".
>
> Swans are a protected species and are no longer eaten.
>
> Killing swans was outlawed in the 1980s.
>
> The Crown's right of ownership exists by Royal prerogative. The tradition of royal swan ownership continues today, and King Charles III inherited his claim to some of the country's swans.

The Somerset levels cover a large area of south Somerset and were flooded for many years until drainage recovered much of the land. Many villages in the area have place names that end in 'Zoy' or 'Ney'. These terms mean 'little island'. This is a clue to anyone wishing to buy a house in the area. The levels are still prone to flooding in winter. It seems that quite a few people don't know this!!

Printed in Great Britain
by Amazon